DILLINGER'S DECEPTION

Ronald K. Myers

DILLINGER'S DECEPTION

DOUBLE DRAGON

PROLOGUE

In the darkness, Ralph squinted toward the low hanging branches of full leaved maple trees. They seemed to be a black impenetrable wall. He hoped no one was hiding there. A ways from the wall, two roads triangulated the land he was standing on and led to the machine-gun-turret protected Jungle Inn Casino. It was 1934. In the center of the land, a man, the world thought was in prison, stood below a black and white street sign perched on top of a steel pole. Although the sign read, 'PETROLEUM', no streets ran alongside the sign.

Standing in grass up to his knees and making sure they weren't being watched, Ralph surveyed the area. Then he looked up at the sign. "Is this it, Snorky?"

Snorky placed his hand on Ralph's back. "Well, Mister Ralph Alsman, can you think of a better place to keep your money out of the FBI's hands?"

Ralph took a moment to consider the question. As he watched dim moonlight beam down on the grass and brush-filled patch of land, he answered. I can't think of anyplace better, but I'm still not used to being called Ralph."

Snorky adjusted the white fedora on his head. "For a million dollars and freedom for the rest of your life, I think you'll get used to it pretty quick."

As if getting to do some serious work, Ralph freed the top button on his white shirt and loosened his tie. His dark vest fit perfectly, and he seemed to be comfortable. He smiled a faint smile. "Where do we dig?"

"We don't."

Snorky bent over, placed a weird brass key in the base of the steel pole supporting the Petroleum sign, and pushed. The pole tilted to a forty-five degree angle. He inserted another brass key at the base of the pole and pushed the pole back to an upright position. The ground rumbled. Right before Ralph's feet, a steel plate slid back revealing a hole with a set of wooden steps. Snorky flicked a flashlight on and stepped into the hole. "Let's get your first half of the million."

When Ralph followed Snorky into the hole, he descended into one of the many abandoned coal mines of the area. But a lot of work had been done to this mine. Before them, at the other side of a concrete floor, a long brass vault, as big as a coffin, lay on a stone pedestal.

Snorky stepped to the vault and opened it. Except for a brown envelope and a piece of folded brown paper sewn shut like the string on the top of a dog food bag, it was empty.

Ralph grabbed the cleft in his chin and gasped. "That folded paper's not big enough to hold a half million dollars. Did somebody take the money?"

"Looks like it, doesn't it?" Snorky gestured to the brown envelope. "If I'm not here, and if by some unforeseen chance your money's not here, put an IOU in the vault. That way, I'll know you've been here before I had a chance to drop the money." He pointed to the sewn-shut, folded brown paper. "That's for the man who took my place in prison. It should be gone when you come back.

Sliding his hand along the smooth brass surface of the vault, Ralph said, "It seems such a waste to use a big brass vault just for two little pieces of paper and an IOU."

Snorky closed the vault and patted it. "Don't judge a vault by its cover. If someone finds your IOU in the vault, they'll think you took all the money out."

He reached under the pedestal and pulled out a stone the size of three bricks. Then, he reached into the opening and pulled out a long metal box. "Here's the real vault." He opened the box. It was filled with a long line of banded bills.

Exhaling a measured breath, Ralph reached over and ran his hand across the money. Snorky closed the box and handed it to Ralph. Then he bent over and placed the stone back in the opening below the pedestal.

Pointing to the stone, Ralph asked, "Is that where the other half will be, too?"

Snorky stood up and brushed his hands together. "Just as soon as you're officially dead, the money will be there."

Gripping the box, Ralph nodded. "Anna's going to rat me out. My official date of death will be July 22, 1934."

Smiling, Snorky patted Ralph on the back. "Okay, Ralph Alsman, after you're dead, your picture's going to be all over the front pages of the newspapers. We don't want to take a chance on anyone seeing you after you're supposed to be dead. Come directly here and pick up your money."

Even though his picture and the news of his death were everywhere, on July 23rd, accompanied by a beautiful girl, Ralph drove a black 1933 Hudson Terraplane Eight to the mine, but someone was already there. A 1932 Chevy Phaeton with full white-wall tires and flashing spoke wheels sat alongside of the road. Although it was dark, Ralph admired the car's light-blue body and dark blue fenders that ran the length of the running boards.

The last time Ralph had seen Snorky, the lapels on his tailor-made suit were hand-stitched. A silk tie had stood out on his white-on-white shirt, and a gold tie clasp showed the man didn't go for cheap crap. After today, Ralph would be able to wear tailor-made suits and wear gold tie clasps for the rest of his life. He figured the Phaeton was something Snorky would buy. He proceeded to the mine to see Snorky.

When he got there, a thin man with a mustache was crawling up the steps. As he held his side, blood flowed from between his fingers. With a pleading look, the man reached up with his other hand. "Get me out of here."

In an effort to help the bleeding man out of the mine, Ralph took the man's hand and pulled. Grimacing in pain, the man struggled out of the hole and stood up. With labored breaths, he managed the strength to speak. "Thanks, Ralph."

No one was supposed to know Ralph was still alive. He wanted to know who the man was. He looked into the man's face. "Who are you?"

Wincing, the bleeding man collapsed to the ground. With his arms outstretched and his hands clawing at the ground, the man's breath caused blood bubbles to form on his wounded side. Then the man's hands quit clawing. His body became motionless. He was dead.

Another man, with blood trickling from one of the open gashes on his face, walked up the blood-soaked steps, grabbed the pole, and hung on.

Before Ralph could help the man, a uniformed cop appeared out of the darkness and shouted, "Hey, jackass, where do you think you're going?"

The man holding onto the steel pole looked as if he were about to pass out. Apparently not wanting more injuries, the man cowered next to the pole. The cop reared back and lifted his huge foot to kick the man from the pole.

Ralph yelled, "Leave him alone! This wasn't part of the deal."

Instead of kicking the man, the cop dropped his foot to the ground and lifted his hand. "Where you're going, you won't have to worry about any deal." In his hand, he held a police officer issue 38 Colt. He laughed once and fired right into Ralph's chest. Ralph grimaced, but didn't fall over. The cop's old 1927 police-issued Colt didn't have enough velocity to penetrate the bulletproof vest Ralph had stolen from the police station. Once again, the vest had saved his life.

As if there were something wrong with it, the cop looked at his Colt.

In pain, Ralph groaned. "What did you do that for?"

Surprised, the cop could only gape.

Ignoring the pain, Ralph turned in fury, pulled his own 38 Colt Super, and emptied it into the cop. The man hanging on the pole grabbed his side and collapsed. Ralph made sure the cop was dead and went over and checked the man's pulse. He was still alive. Ralph ripped a length of cloth from the dead cop's shirt and placed it on the man's bleeding side. Holding the cloth on the man's wound, he looked over his shoulder and shouted toward the beautiful girl sitting in his Terraplane, "Billie, come here!"

Billie's lovely legs swished through the tall grass until she stopped at the man's feet. Ralph took her hand and placed it on the cloth covering the man's wound. "Hold this here. I have to make the withdrawal."

After Ralph made his way into the mine, he reached under the pedestal, pulled out the secret stone and pulled out another long metal box. It felt light. When he opened it, it was empty. Snorky had not made the drop. He put the box back.

For a moment, Ralph studied the big brass vault and wondered why such a worthless object was secretly entombed in the mine. But he didn't have time to worry about it. He hoped Snorky would come back, find out he had been there, and put the other half of the million in the box. He lifted the vault's lid and placed in his IOU.

Back up top, Ralph closed the mine and dragged the cop and the other dead man into the Chevy Phaeton. Then, Billie and he gently placed the wounded man from the pole into the Terraplane.

Standing next to the Terraplane, Billie asked, "What do we do now?"

"Jump in the Terraplane and follow me." Ralph pointed to the Phaeton. "After I get rid of that, you can pick me up."

Billie tilted her cute head toward the man in the back seat. "What about him?"

"We'll drop him off at the hospital."

With Billie following in the Terraplane, Ralph drove the Phaeton to a place called Patagonia and stopped at the top of Myers Hill. He placed the car in neutral and gave it a big push. The Phaeton and the two dead men sailed down the hill and slid into the deep dark waters of the Shenango River.

Even though the river raged, churned, and twisted around rocks and eroded stony banks, the Phaeton would stay on the bottom until the spring floods. Then, the powerful force of tons of water would sweep the Phaeton and anything in its way downriver.

With his new identity, a half a million dollars, and the FBI no longer after him, Ralph got married and moved to Oregon.

The vault remained in the mine.

CHAPTER 1

Thirty years later, outside the shantytown of Patagonia, Pennsylvania, Freddy Crane walked around a barrel-sized trashcan overflowing with cardboard containers and rotting food. As if sweating under the punishing evening sun weren't enough agony, roaring amplified by the whining tires came up from behind him. A hurricane of dust from the slipstream of a huge truck hit him like a hot gale. The suction wasn't far from pulling him off his feet. Staring at the wavy glare of the heat waves that stretched down the tar and gravel road, he sauntered around the corner.

Before he got to the hamburger stand affectingly called 'the Burp' he knew the people would be falling over one another to be a part of Neal McCord's humbuggery action.

With the sun making its late afternoon roll toward the horizon, a pony-tailed girl with a figure good enough to be on Playboy walked away from a 1950 Ford; and with a sensual sway, she showboated her way toward the gathered crowd. A teenage boy beamed an affectionate smile and waved her over.

The crowd was so thick Freddy couldn't see what they were watching. The teenage boy turned sideways to talk to the girl. Then, Freddy knew what everyone was watching. And there he was: In the center of the blacktopped parking lot. Black hair slicked back, wearing his familiar black T-shirt, hunched over on his bongo board, rocking side to side on a cylinder of wood. With his feet spayed and his hips moving to and fro above his bandy-legged stance, he swayed with the rhythm of the up-beat little tune he had made up. "Dit-a, dit-a, plonk-oh. Dit-a, dit-a, dit-a plonk-oh!"

Neal McCord's very existence was something apart from the known properties of a normal human being. Even though the crazy times of the '60s overflowed with understanding and open minds, Neal was a person Freddy could not understand. At times Neal was half-boy, half-man. He could become a delusion, a phantom, or a mirage. At other times, he was welcomed as a savior of a boring situation. With one hand in his pocket and the other hand waving in the air, Neal looked like a bull rider; but instead of waving a cowboy hat in his hand, he clutched a wad of money.

"Watch this." He flashed his famous Neal McCord smile in the direction of the crowd. "It's so easy a pet monkey can do it." With a single sway of his hips, he rolled the bongo board on the cylinder until it was at its very end. Bending one leg and holding the other straight, he stopped the board. Balancing in this unnatural pose, he threw his arms straight out from his sides and held them there. "See. Nothing to it." He grinned. "All you got to do is stabilize yourself by distributing your weight on each side of the vertical axis."

A teenager with a cast on his arm and a big scab on his elbow stayed perched at the end of the parking lot curb. "Yeah, that's what you told me, and look what happened." He held up his arm. A thick white cast coated his forearm.

Still keeping one leg bent and the other one straight, Neal dropped his arms, held the money in both hands, and thrust it toward the kid.

13

"You could've had half of this." He shook the money at the broken-armed kid. "All you had to do was stay on for ten seconds." He straightened one leg and bent the other until the board rolled over the cylinder and stopped on the board's center. "You want to try it again?"

The kid lowered his broken arm. "I'm not crazy. You make it look too easy."

Neal fanned the money out and offered it to the fifteen teenagers standing around him. "Here you go," he said in a loud, colorful sales spiel. "Get in on the humbuggery action at the hamburger stand. It's easy money."

The pony-tailed girl turned her cute head toward a kid about five and a half feet tall with jet black hair styled like Elvis.

"Come on, Markey," she cooed. "You can do it."

Markey cringed for a moment, but his expression changed to one of a person with a casual lack of concern. He lifted his hands and held them limply in front of his chest. "Now, what would I want to do that for?"

Neal had a rhythm to life that gave him an advantage when he wanted to push people off the ragged edge of their little universe of common sense. With the confidence of a salesman who had already closed the deal, he lowered his head and lifted his arms in a what-more-do-you-want-from-me gesture, and looked to Markey. "For no particular reason." He flicked his hands down. "That's why."

With all eyes on him, Markey exhaled a defeated stream of air. "No reason's a good enough reason." He reached for his wallet. "Here's five

14

bucks says I can stay balanced on that thing for five seconds."

In one motion, Neal swept the money from Markey's hand. Jerking a wisp of hair away from his forehead, he winked at the girl. "Hey, everybody likes to be included." He tromped on the end of the board. It flew up. He caught it in one hand and handed it to Markey. Then with the toe of his shoe, he nudged the cylinder toward Markey. "You're on."

Markey put the bongo board on the cylinder, scrunched down, and placed one foot on the end of the board. With a quick hop, he slapped his other foot on the other end of the board. Zing! The board flew out from under his feet. Whap! It hit the blacktop. Markey staggered sideways, but caught his balance.

The girl covered her mouth and muffled a laugh.

With a big ear-to-ear smile on his face, Neal hooked his thumbs into his wide belt and leaned back. "How many seconds was that?"

A big groan came from Markey. "Very funny."

As Neal put the five dollar bill in his back pocket, the kid with the cast walked up to him and stopped. "Come on, man, you know we'll never stay on your crazy board. Why don't we bet on a car race?"

Neal cocked his head to the side, arched his brow, and waved his hand down. "Naw, naw, naw, racing cars is out. That's old stuff."

The kid with the cast made a helpless gesture. "We can't just stay here and let you take all our money. You have to do something we can bet on and win."

A look of hurt streamed from Neal's baby blue eyes. "You wanted to play. It's not my fault you don't want to win."

A kid wearing a polo shirt waved his skinny arms. "Is betting on a bongo board all a garbage man can do?"

For a moment, Neal stood perfectly still and stared at the kid.

Freddy felt a wave of shame crawl over his body. Before he met Neal, he had a low desire to live. Although Neal and he made pretty good money hauling garbage, being a garbage man on the bottom of the success chain wasn't what he wanted to do all his life. But it didn't bother Neal. Without missing a beat, he waved his hand in the air. "It's only a temporary thing, you see. There's always bigger and better things on down the road."

"Yeah, we know," the kid with the polo shirt said. "Come on, you guys. Let's quit playing penny ante and do something we can bet some real money on."

Leaning against the bulbous fender of a 1948 maroon Plymouth, Neal held his head aloft; and as if he were searching for an answer, he looked around the parking lot of the burger stand and sat on the fender. As if on cue, the rusty springs squealed. He raised his money-filled fist.

"I'll bet this wad of money." He thrust his money-filled fist toward the clown-faced clock under the peak of the burger stand. "All of it." He paused for effect. "I'll bet all of it that we can drive from the Burp to Canada, get a cup of coffee and a souvenir, and come back in twelve hours or less."

16

"That's three hundred thirty miles one way," a kid with a broken tooth and thick glasses said. He tapped his finger in the air as if he were using an adding machine. "You'll be lucky to go fifty in that old clunker." He quit tapping. "And with no stops at fifty miles an hour, it'll take you thirteen point two hours."

"Even if you pull it off," the kid with his arm in the cast said. "How will we know you even went there?"

As if he were ready to go, Freddy ran to the Plymouth and jumped into the passenger side. Neal opened the driver's side door, sat behind the steering wheel, turned back to the crowd, and rested his feet on the running board. "I'll bring back a Canadian flag and the paid bill for the coffee."

A skinny kid with red hair combed into a flip, stepped out from under the green awning of the burger stand and stood next to a 1956 Fireflight Desoto that had a hideous, two-tone paint job.

"That's not so great," he said. "Last week I drove to Cleveland just to get a cup of coffee."

"So, what's the big deal?" a kid with a flattop haircut asked. "Anybody with enough money could do that."

Neal stepped out of the Plymouth. Placing each foot just so, quiet and careful, he moved easy as if he knew just what he had to do. Freddy knew he wasn't going to jerk or get wild eyed like a little kid making up a new lie. He was about to come up with something new.

"You may have a point there," Neal said. "But I've heard that everybody is always going somewhere. And when they come back they always

17

brag about how great it was. But the thing is—" He tilted his head toward the kid. "I've been told by reliable sources that in Canada they got the best beer in the world, and all the bars stay open all night, and you don't have to worry about drinking too much and getting into a wreck, cause they have taxi cabs that run somewhere all the time, and they don't have half-witted cab drivers that get you lost and drive you around in circles just to get a bigger fare."

The kid with the flat-top shrugged. "It doesn't matter, anybody could still do it."

Neal hunched over. Using exaggerated strides, he walked around the Plymouth and stopped at the driver's side. He held his hand up in a stopping motion. "All right, gentlemen. If anybody with money can do it, then I'll do something nobody has ever done before." He swiveled his head around and looked at Freddy. "With no money, we'll drive to Canada and be back in twelve hours or less."

Freddy didn't know if such a feat was possible, but if he were going to share in any money there was to be made, he had to go along with whatever Neal said.

"That's right," Freddy said, and pointed to the road. "Canada and back in twelve hours or less."

Reaching into their pockets, a few onlookers stepped closer.

"I'll take a piece of that action," one kid said, and pulled out a ten dollar bill."

Bets were made. Bull, the stocky kid with huge arms, collected the money. The skinny kid with red hair gave Bull a twenty dollar bill. Then, in great haste, the skinny kid gave Neal a thumb's up, jumped into his '56 two-tone Desoto, and drove away.

Being in his usual hurry, Neal jumped into the Plymouth and sat behind the steering wheel. "Okay, we're set to go." He held his hand out, palm up. "Anymore takers?"

Markey reached into his pocket, but shook his head. "I'd bet more, but I'm on empty."

Neal turned away from the steering wheel, lifted his arm above the roof, and waved his hand in a come here gesture. Just as the pink and green neon lights buzzed on around the top of the white burger stand, a 1940 Ford coupe appeared around the far corner of the building and coasted into the lot. Neal and Freddy's buddy, Rafferty, opened the door and stepped out.

Usually, when Rafferty's green eyes peered from under his wave in his carrot-orange hair, he was looking for humor in a situation. When he found it, his contagious smile would beam across his freckled face; and his skinny body would shudder with quiet laughter. But this time, his face had a look of seriousness. He propped his knuckles under his chin, and Freddy could tell Rafferty was trying not to smile. But he couldn't do it. As if a light bulb were glowing over him, his eyes crinkled and a smile spread across his face.

Freddy looked at the faces of the kids who had bet. Their strained, stunned faces showed the realization that Neal may have tricked them again. As if they were paralyzed, they stood with their attention fixed on the Ford.

Oohing and aahing, the non-betting kids gathered around the Ford.

"What's it got under the hood?" one kid asked, and then the questions and commentary of the others flowed.

"Does it have overdrive?"

"Check out those new tires."

"Stick shift, no waiting for an automatic transmission to shift."

"How fast can it go?"

"It didn't make any noise when it pulled in; probably got a six cylinder under the hood."

"Yeah, probably can't do over sixty."

"How come it has Ohio license plates when Neal lives in Pennsylvania?"

In a sliver of shade, Rafferty leaned against the front fender, placed his hands behind his head, and leaned back. The pony-tailed girl peeked into the side window and pointed to the radio. "Does that thing get WLS out of Chicago?"

Rafferty smiled an engaging smile. "It'll get any station you want, sweetie."

In a show of jealousy Markey stepped between Rafferty and the girl. Before tempers flared, Neal stepped out of the Plymouth, sauntered toward the Ford, and opened the driver's side door. "Okay, Rafferty, let's get in."

Markey and the girl stepped back. While Rafferty stepped into the driver's side and slid to the passenger side, Freddy ran around and the car and placed his hand on the door handle.

Bull held up his hand in a halting gesture. "Wait."

Neal held out his hand. "You got more to bet?"

"No, but we thought you were going to drive the Plymouth."

"Well, ah, ahem," Neal said, and gave a negligent wave of his hand. "Sorry, gentleman, but I didn't actually say that I was going to drive a Plymouth." He looked toward the gathered crowd. "Did anybody here hear me say I was going to drive a Plymouth?"

Markey looked to Rafferty. "Hey, Rafferty, didn't you tell me to call on you if I had a problem?"

A mischievous grin spread across Rafferty's face. "What about it?"

"I have a problem with you guys switching cars at the last minute. What are you going to do about it?"

Shaking his head like a simpleton, Rafferty replied, "I told you to call on me, but I didn't say I would do anything about it."

Shaking his head in astonishment, Markey leaned forward in a helpless heap and began cursing under this breath. As if fooling the kid was an everyday occurrence, Neal continued, "The bet is that I drive from the Burp to Canada and be back in twelve hours or less."

Freddy stepped into the picture. "We never welshed on a deal yet."

Neal put his hands on his hips. "You want to cancel the bets?"

As if he had been defeated in a game of one-upmanship, Bull's face turned sullen, but the kid with the thick glasses stepped up and put his hand on Bull's shoulder.

"Don't cancel anything," he said. "Even if that Ford can do sixty miles an hour, he'll have to keep it on those winding roads and not slow down, and

21

he'll have to stop for gas that he doesn't have any money for, and he'll have to stop to get the coffee and a bill of sale, that he doesn't have any money for, and after he stops at the border, he'll have to buy a Canadian flag that he doesn't have any money for. Even if he had the fastest car in the world he would never make it in twelve hours."

The kid with the cast on his arm bent over and looked into the grill on the front of the Ford. As if he were straining to see inside, he leaned close to the horizontal bars. "It still has the stock radiator." He straightened up and grinned. "If this thing had a new engine in it, they would have had to change the radiator."

Freddy knew this wasn't true, but he wasn't going to say anything to spoil their chances of winning the bet.

Bull stared at the kid with the thick glasses. "Are you sure they can't make it in twelve hours?"

"If he pushes those six cylinders, he'll burn up the engine before he makes it to the border."

Neal's bubbly smile sunk. "I don't know about all those numbers," he said, and smiled again. "But we'll still make it in twelve hours."

"Okay," Bull said, with a sly grin. "Just to keep things on the up and up, empty your pockets, and let me check your wallets."

Neal reached into his black pants pockets, pulled out his wad of money and some change, and slapped it on the front fender of the Plymouth. Then he took out his wallet, opened it, and turned it upside down. "Okay, we're ready."

"Not so fast." Bull held out his hand and jerked it toward Freddy. "You, too."

Freddy didn't have a wallet, but he walked around the car, turned out his pockets, and put thirty-five cents on the fender.

Bull turned toward Rafferty. "You're next." With his usual smile on his freckled face, Rafferty handed Bull his wallet, shrugged, and plunked a few bills and two nickels down onto the front fender of the Plymouth. Bull scooped up the money and looked up at the clown clock on the peak or the burger stand. The minute hand that was the clown's arm, rotated around with its white-gloved finger pointing to the seconds,"

"It's two minutes to nine." Bull said and jerked his head toward the clock. "Twelve hours from now is nine in the morning, and you're not going to make it."

Rafferty made a brusque gesture with his left hand. "What do you mean we're not going to make it? What do you think we're going to do, stop and play marbles on every street corner?"

Bull smiled. "You might as well." He shook the bet money in front of Neal's face. "Take a good look at it. It's the last time you'll see it." He let out a deep belly laugh and jammed the money into his pocket.

With the evening bugs just beginning to crash into the buzzing green and pink neon lights of the burger stand, and girls without dates, wishing someone would take them to the drive-in movie, watching, Neal jumped behind the wheel of the Ford. Freddy and Rafferty piled in and waited for him to start the powerful V-8 engine, rack the pipes off, and impress the girls. But he didn't.

23

Scarcely giving the hungry engine the gas, he hit the starter. The engine caught and begged for more fuel. To keep what was under the hood a secret, Neal tried to pull out of the lot as quiet and as slow as possible, but the powerful engine growled with awesome power. The kid with thick glasses tilted his head, and scratched his neck with his index finger. "It sounds like they got a big engine in that thing. We might lose the bets."

As the Ford rumbled out of the parking lot, Bull lifted his palms and pushed away from his body. "No problem. We got it covered."

Beyond the neon pink triangle peak of the burger stand with the clown's arm on the clock sweeping away the seconds, the sun's last rays peeked through the blowing tree branches and skittered shut. Without a cent in their pockets and bobbing their heads to Neal's stupid 'dit-a, dit-a, plonk-oh!'tune, Neal, Freddy, Rafferty, and the bongo board were leaving the gloom of Patagonia's grassless backyards spattered with tin cans and dirty-white chickens scratching under clotheslines where blue work clothes of mill workers flapped under a sullied sky. They were on their way to Canada.

Ten miles down the road, a huge white sign with black letters read 'Road Closed Ahead'. Neal slowed. On the other side of the sign, a bridge stretched across a wide river. A detour sign, with an arrow pointed to the road that led to the left.

Rafferty shook his head. "That's all we need. The other bridge is miles away. It's going to be a long detour."

Neal turned left and tromped on the gas. "We can still make it."

The Ford rounded a few bends and another detour sign popped up, pointing left again. Neal rolled around the corner and continued driving at a rapid pace. A half-mile later, another detour sign pointed left. Neal followed that for a few miles and stopped at an intersection and looked up. Another detour sign pointed left. No traffic zoomed past. The road was dark and empty. Rafferty leaned over and looked at the gas gauge. "Are we running out of gas?"

"No, but I think we're going around in circles." Neal turned off the lights. "I just saw a flash of light. If he's doing what I think he's doing, he'll come back and see if we took the bait."

Freddy couldn't understand what Neal was talking about. But before he could ask Neal about it, headlights flashed in the distance and headed in their direction. As it neared, the car slowed, but it was too late. Just before it came to the intersection, Neal flicked the headlights on and swung his hand down. "Gotch ya!"

The '56 Desoto that had left the Burp before them approached from the left. Its unmistakable light blue and dark blue two-tone paint job looked dull and disgusting. As it passed in front of them, Neal stuck his hand out the window and waved. As if he were trying to conceal his identity, the driver turned his head to the side and kept on driving. But the red hair betrayed the skinny kid. The Desoto's red taillights faded down the road and Neal laughed with satisfaction.

"That kid's old man works for the highway," he said. "He put up phony detour sighs to throw us off. We could've been driving in circles all night long."

He turned right and wound out the gears. In no time the Ford's headlights were shining on the back of the lumbering Desoto. Under the end of the rounded tail fins, three taillights looked like short glasses turned on their sides. They were arranged vertically: one white in the center; and two red: one on top and one on the bottom. In the center of the almost square trunk, the raised chrome letters 'Desoto' spread across a short section above a big shiny chrome V.

With the horn blaring, Neal frantically waved his hand out the window and passed the heavy car.

At the bridge, Neal hit the brakes and skidded to a stop. He jumped out and kicked the 'Road Closed Ahead' sign down. After dragging the sign to the bridge, he bent over, picked up the sign, and threw it into the river. Brushing his hands together, he jumped back into the Ford. They were on their way to Canada, again.

On the dark road, Freddy figured he had to be crazy to be riding with Neal in another one of his mad, unfathomable schemes that would hurl him into the unknown. He wondered if there was a chance that Neal could actually make it to Canada and back in twelve hours, and he wondered how they were going to get gas with no money. Before he could ask, Neal shut the motor off, coasted into a dimly lit gas station, and stopped in front of the first pump.

Rafferty turned to Neal. "You got some money hid?"

26

Neal put his finger to his lips and pointed to the plate-glass window on the front of the building. Inside, partially hidden behind a pyramid of green and white cans of oil, the attendant was fast asleep. Neal got out, carefully lifted the gas nozzle from the side of the red hand-painted pump, and filled the Ford's tank. Just as he eased the gas pump's nozzle back into the slot, a white Pontiac pulled in. Neal opened the door to the Ford to get back behind the wheel, but paused. He looked into the station window. The attendant was still asleep. On top of the towel box a paper garrison hat sat. Neal grabbed it and placed it on his head. Then he walked to the Pontiac and looked into the driver's side window. "Fill 'er up, and check the oil, sir?"

"The oil's okay," the driver said. "Just fill it up."

Keeping a wary eye on the sleeping attendant, Neal filled the Pontiac and collected the money. When he went to get back into the Ford, another car pulled in, then another. He waited on those cars, too, and collected the money. The cars pulled away; and just as he put the paper hat back on the towel box the attendant woke up, rushed out the building's door, and stood in front of Neal. It seemed as if Neal was going to jump in the car and speed away, but he smiled at the attendant.

"Good evening," he said, but there was no tension in his voice. That was Neal: Cool under any circumstances. He flapped the ends of the money in the attendant's face. "I was just coming in to pay for the gas."

27

The attendant looked at the dials on the gas pump and then looked back at Neal. "Yeah, I watched you fill it up."

Freddy figured they were caught. If the attendant had watched Neal fill the Ford, then he surely watched him fill the other three cars and collect the money. And on top of that, to keep from having to get a Pennsylvania state inspection sticker and pay to have it glued on the corner of the front windshield, Neal had stolen Ohio plates and put them on the Ford. They weren't even out of Pennsylvania and they would be going to jail.

But Neal was one step ahead of the attendant. He held the money in both hands ready to count off the bills. "How much do I owe you?"

The attendant rubbed his sleepy eyes. "Whatever the pump says."

Neal paid him and turned to go.

Stifling a yawn, the tired attendant leaned on the pump and crossed his legs. "Thanks, for being honest." He stared at the dials on the pump. "I might have my eyes closed, but I can see right through my eyelids. No one has ever stolen anything on my shift."

Neal jumped in the Ford. Sitting behind the steering wheel, he touched his forefinger to his forehead and gave the kid a lazy imitation of a salute. "Thanks, for the gas, buddy, and keep up the good work." He drove off into the velvet night babbling about how he used to think that it was wrong to steal anything.

"What do you mean?" Freddy interrupted. "It's still stealing."

28

"I don't worry about it anymore," Neal said. "Besides, I know this guy from before. He's an arrogant son of a bitch who shorted me on change when I was a little kid." His eyes glared. "What makes me feel bad is that the guy's not going to pay for it. The rich ass oil company's gonna pay. And I don't feel guilty one bit. We're only taking money from oil companies and banks and the assholes that got rich off other people's misfortunes."

Freddy sighed, stared at the open road ahead of them, and thought about how he could convince Neal that no matter how good the reason was for stealing, it was wrong, but Rafferty interrupted his thoughts.

"Okay," Rafferty said. "We got the gas and money for more. But we wasted fifteen minutes back there. How are we going to make it to Canada and be back in twelve hours?"

"Come on, Rafferty." Neal reached up, and pretended to be adjusting imaginary glasses. "It's easier than balancing on a bongo board. I thought you'd have figured that out by now."

"What are you trying to say?"

"Back at the Burp, four-eyes said it was three hundred thirty miles to Canada."

"It is," Rafferty said, and cocked his orange eyebrows. "Unless you fly."

"Old Coke-bottle-bottom-glasses thinks we're going to cross at Niagara Falls." A confident grin spread across Neal's face. "But we're going to cross in Buffalo. That cuts off forty miles, seventy miles an hour into two hundred ninety miles gives under four hours to get there and under four to get back."

Freddy spoke from the back seat. "You said you didn't know anything about numbers."

Neal put the transmission into overdrive. "It's all in the game, Freddy. If we had a straight shot, it would only be about two hundred miles, but it's still all in the game. And with overdrive, this Ford will cruise along at eighty-five with no problem." He smiled at himself in the rearview mirror. "There's hardly any traffic at night. We got twelve hours and can make in under eight."

He reached over and twisted the chrome knob until it clicked on. The tube-style radio lit up. Duane Eddy's *Three-Thirty Blues* flowed from the single speaker.

Freddy snapped his fingers and leaned back. "Now we can go to Canada in style."

With the music blasting into his brain, Freddy felt they might be the only people in the world who were not imprisoned by wanting to do the familiar and safe things. Not being afraid of what it would be like to explore something dangerously different made everything up ahead a brand new raw world of profound mystery. And they were headed right for it.

Neal thrust the shifting lever into high gear and mashed the gas feed down. For a moment the black unknown ahead swallowed them up. They flashed past houses, screeched around an elbow bend, rumbled over a set of railroad tracks, and the radio quit.

CHAPTER 2

With the Ford's V-8 engine running smoothly and the rear end hooked into overdrive, as if it were on an evening drive in the country, the '40 Ford coupe cruised on down the dark highway. As lights from oncoming headlights flitted past at great speeds, Freddy began to unwind. He was glad he wasn't walking. He had a slight limp, but it vanished when he broke into a quick sprint. His big biceps and weightlifter's chest gave the impression that he was muscle-bound, but he was deceivingly fast. Although he was always cut from high school sports, he could outrun anyone on the track team, fake out any football player, swim on top and under water for long distances, and he could walk on his hands as well as he could walk on his feet. For a malnourished kid from the slums of Patagonia, he had complete control of his coordinated body. But it hadn't always been that way.

When he had to wear shoes with holes in the bottoms, and clothes with patches, and didn't have the money to go into a barbershop and get a decent haircut, people looked down on him. So, he used Vaseline to slick back his long black hair to look presentable, but then he was considered a hood, a troublemaker. It gnawed at his heart, and he had been ashamed.

When he met Neal, Freddy had been going from nowhere to nowhere walking down the Patagonia neighborhood street that was littered with trash and illuminated by one naked streetlight. But this brothel of broken dreams and misplaced hope never bothered Neal. When it came to making things happen, Neal didn't hesitate. Right off the bat he took Freddy under his wing, and let him in on his hauling garbage business.

No self-respecting teenager would want to be a garbage man, but Neal had an old dump truck with a garbage route over the border in Hubbard, Ohio, where none of the kids at the Burp would see him. All Freddy had to do was run into yards, pick up the garbage cans, and dump them into the truck. At the dump, Neal would rev the engine, tilt the bed in the air, and let the garbage slide out. And the job was done. The smell of the garbage and the dump was awful, but it was easy money, and lifting heavy cans caused Freddy's body to be clad with muscle. As a sideline, Neal had showed Freddy how to be a shell in one of his many con games, but Freddy felt guilty taking people's money.

Neal usually had an answer for everything, and he had an answer for that, too: Waving his bongo board, he had said, "Those people are starved for something to do. And they're all greedy to make a fast buck. They'll stand in line with open pocketbooks and tongues hanging out to get it." He had placed his hand on Freddy's shoulder. "Face the facts, Freddy. None of this could happen if they didn't want it to. We're like any other business. We provide them an entertainment service. It's a small price they pay for what we do."

With this new attitude that masked his true feelings, and a percentage of the profits, Freddy was able to dress like other teenagers. He wore the blue jeans and white T-shirts with the sleeves rolled up. Behind his back, people still called him troublemaker and put him down. But now that he had money, it didn't matter.

Neal wasn't ashamed of anything, and his presence was contagious. In addition to having a smile that could sell toothpaste, he emanated power. He seemed to be every place at the same time. If he would have stayed in one spot for a few minutes the verbal shards meant to reduce his worth would have had some effect; but attempts to degrade his demeanor zinged past his series of charismatic gestures as if they were well-aimed bullets that couldn't hit the moving target. Neal was incandescent. Just hanging around him brightened anyone's life. Freddy felt better about himself, too. But right now, the excitement overload was too much for him. He was tired.

Not wanting Neal to fall asleep behind the wheel, Freddy leaned forward to see if Neal's eyes were drooping. But his eyes were wide open. He never seemed to tire. As long as the engine purred beneath the steel hood and put power to the wheels, he was in his element.

After they crossed the border into Canada, Freddy had no idea where they were. A sign had read Toronto, but the way Neal was driving Freddy figured he didn't know where they were either. Looking for something familiar, Freddy slumped in the dark of the back seat of the Ford and squinted one eye. A light mist wet the windshield and made it difficult to see.

Zany Rafferty excitedly threw his arm up in front of Neal and blocked his vision. "Look! There's a free souvenir."

33

Neal batted Rafferty's arm down and mashed on the brakes. The Ford slowed. Neal looked up. His eyes flew wide open.

"Ah, yes!" he said. "That little piece of cloth's gonna prove we crossed the border." His head bobbed with laughter. "And we won't have to buy it."

Freddy jerked his chin up off his chest and peered out the window. Enclosed inside an iron picket fence and up on a porch, a Canadian flag waved. The Ford slowed to almost a stop.

Freddy leaned forward and nudged Neal's shoulder. "Don't go slow past the place. They'll know we're looking for something to steal."

Neal nodded. "You got a point there."

He sped down a grimy alley, whizzed around the corner, pulled into a parking lot in front of a shabby four-story red brick apartment building, and stopped. On the side of the building, steps led down from the sidewalk to an alley lined with garbage cans. At the bottom of the steps, a tar-papered section of a rotting roof covered a front stoop, and an alley ran back into the darkness. Overhead, ragged clothes that seemed to have been there for years, flapped on a clothesline that was strung form a window to a wooden pole alongside a fence that separated one building's backyard from the next.

Freddy didn't have to be in the alley to know what it was like. In these types of tenement buildings, it always stank under the stoop and in the alley. The entire structure was in disrepair. Windows were boarded shut and others had dirty broken glass. Flat-black paint on wrought-iron balconies was rust-encrusted, and the bricks were a dull and dirty red. He peered into the darkness of the other side of the building. Barely visible in the darkness of another grimy alleyway, a bum slumped down on his butt and leaned his back against the wall. In front of his outstretched feet, a wine bottle lay on its side. He seemed to be staring at it, trying to decide if it was full or empty.

With the lights out and the motor off, Freddy and his friends waited five minutes. Then they got out of the Ford and started toward the flag.

Neal held up his hand. "Wait. If someone sees us we gotta change the license plates."

Freddy nodded and they went back to the Ford. After Neal replaced the Ohio license plate with a stolen Pennsylvania plate they walked around the corner toward the waiting flag. When they got to the iron fence, it was as if they had stepped on a switch. The last light inside the apartment building went out.

"They must've known we were coming," Rafferty said, released the gate latch, and pulled. The gate opened about a foot and screeched. He stopped pulling.

"That was nice of them to turn the light out for us," Neal whispered.

Making sure no one was watching, he squeezed his lanky frame through the opening and tiptoed up the porch steps. Looking around, he reached up over the porch railing and grabbed the rope that held to the Canadian flag. The porch light flicked on. With its white-fanged teeth flashing, a snarling pit bull came barreling out of the dark.

Freddy figured Neal had the flag and took off running. With Rafferty running right next to him, he slowed for a second and looked back. The flag was

35

still was on the pole, but the pit bull was out of the fenced-in area and right on Neal's heels. The muscles in the dog's thick neck rippled with each stride and it was gaining. They hastened their pace and flew down the alleyway. Huffing and puffing; and with Neal right behind them, Freddy and Rafferty cut around the corner.

From out of the night a voice yelled, "Diesel, leave that cat alone. Come back here." The dog stopped, looked back, and whined one time. "Diesel!" the voice shouted. "Don't make me have to come down there."

The dog looked as if it were about to cry. It turned and ran back to the porch.

Trotting back to the Ford coupe, Freddy flashed Neal a sarcastic grin. "Where's the flag?"

Neal's face scrunched up. "Are you crazy? Did you see the ass clippers on that mutt?"

"No, and I don't want to. Let's get out of here."

Rafferty put his hand on the door handle of the Ford. "So much for that souvenir."

Freddy opened the opposite door and hopped inside. Since they had left the States, just to get a cup of coffee and a Canadian souvenir, another one of Neal's great adventures was disintegrating. A police siren whined in the distance. Alarmed, Neal jumped behind the steering wheel. Like a man winning a trophy he held onto the steering wheel with both hands. "We gotta blow this pop stand before the fuzz comes." He turned the ignition key. The dash lit up. He tapped on the gas gauge. "Hey, this thing says we're outta gas."

Rafferty bent over at the waist and craned his neck to look at the little gauge. "You're crazy. We had a quarter-tank when we went after the flag."

Neal tapped on the gauge again harder. "Look it's below empty."

Looking out the back window, Freddy watched a man in a pinstripe suit and a felt fedora with the brim bent down over his eyes. The man struggled with a red five-gallon gas can, but managed to carry it into the basement entrance of the rundown apartment building. Freddy reached over the front seat and shook Neal's shoulder. "Look, that guy's got a whole can of gas. Maybe he'll give us some."

Shaking his head, Neal added, "Yeah, yeah," and paused. "Hey, wait a minute. That's the guy that stole our gas."

The whine of the siren faded. Freddy leaned forward and lowered his voice. "Maybe those people in the apartment with the flag didn't call. Why don't we call the cops and tell them to get our gas back?"

In one of his know-it-all displays of wit, Neal waved his arm and grazed the cloth ceiling of the car. "You'd have to be some kind of idiot to call the cops. In this kinda neighborhood they ain't like us. When they see a fight or something happens on the street they just stare at it and walk away."

Gazing across the blacktop of the parking lot, Rafferty shook his head. "This is Canada. You don't know that."

"Ah, yes, but," Neal stuttered, and for a moment he followed Rafferty's gaze. "This place ain't no different than back home." He broke into a big triumphant smile. "Cops are the same no matter where they are."

Even when Neal was wrong, he always tried to take control of a situation. When he couldn't think of anything to fit the moment, just to be the center of attention, he would spout meaningless sentences or phrases. Freddy wasn't in any mood to argue about Neal's exaggerated knowledge of this situation. Thinking about what would happen if the Canadian police arrested them, he checked his anger and followed Rafferty's gaze. "But we got enough gas to get away from here."

Neal turned the ignition key off. "There's not an open gas station for miles."

Neal loved to embellish stories and make them even greater glories, and this time would be no exception. Freddy knew Neal was going to make the simple task of getting gas a great adventure. He turned toward Neal. "So, what are we gonna do?"

Neal's face brightened with energy. "We're gonna go in that basement and take our gas back." He flashed a mischievous smile. "And then we'll swing around, get that flag."

Freddy had been awake for two days. He only wanted to get back to Patagonia in under twelve hours, collect the money, and go home.

"I need some rest," he said. "Can't we just buy a flag at a gas station while we're getting gas?"

Neal's baby blue eyes lit up. "We could, but that's no fun."

"Don't you know?" Rafferty leaned toward Freddy. "Neal wasn't born. A crow shit a bunch of uppers on a stump and the sun hatched him. He's never been tired."

The ends of Neal's lips curled up. "Ah, um, ahem, ah, yes." He paused. "But what else are we gonna do with the six hours we got to get back? Yawn and worry our lives away?"

Freddy peered into the darkness of the basement entrance door and tilted his head toward the opened window of the Ford. Somewhere in the distance, the faint sound of dripping water plinked onto a metal surface. As if he were getting ready for the starring role in a movie, Neal looked into the rearview mirror and combed the sides of his black hair back.

Freddy slouched, leaned back into the back seat, and sighed. He would get no rest. They'd be going into the basement to get the gas. While a midnight moon peeked over the top of a line of tall brick buildings, Freddy and his friends quietly opened the Ford's doors and walked to the basement entrance. Except for Neal's black T-shirt, they all wore dark pants and white T-shirts with the sleeves rolled up. Not a proper outfit for stealing something and surely not something anyone would want to wear to a gas heist. A few yards from the building a flash of light caught Freddy's eye. He froze in his tracks.

"Wait," he whispered. "There's somebody there?"

Neal kept right on walking. "Don't be chickening out. All we're gonna do is go in there, take our gas back, and get back on the road."

Freddy ran and caught up to Neal and Rafferty. Neal looked at Freddy and gave him a nod of approval. Being wary of a trap, Freddy slowed.

Rafferty gently pushed him forward. "Don't stop. That's how dumb-asses get caught."

Freddy stepped up his pace and stopped at the top of the three grime-covered cement steps that led to the basement door.

In one motion, Neal hopped down the steps, grabbed the rusty door handle, and pushed down. "It's not locked." He opened the door. The plinking water grew louder, but the five-gallon gas can was setting on the broken tile floor.

Freddy breathed a sigh of relief. "Grab it and let's get outta this dump. We can still be back in under twelve hours."

Neal stepped into the doorway, put his hand on the can's handle, and lifted. "Hey! This thing's empty."

"What could they do with five gallons of gas so fast?" Rafferty asked. "They just got it."

Neal put the can back on the floor. "Maybe they have another can that's full." He jerked his head to the side. "Come on."

Neal walked down the dark hallway toward the sound of plinking water. Freddy wanted to go back to the safety of the car, but he made no effort to protest. Simply nodding his head, he followed. From out of the darkness, a mad dog-like voice barked. "Freddy!"

Freddy turned. That man that had stolen their gas, the man with the pinstriped suit and the fedora covering his eyes, stood right in front of him. A satisfied smile spread across the man's face. "You thought you could get away." He slowly shook his head. "But you all come back."

Neal turned toward Freddy. "Who's your friend?"

Freddy studied the man's face. "Are you my uncle or something?"

"Yeah, right," the man said. "You may have dolled yourself up to look like a teenager, but we know it's you."

"If you know me, then why did you steal our gas?"

The man grinned. "We've been watchin' your friends. We know they tried to steal a stupid ass flag."

Neal butted in. "Ahem, yes, we were going to take it, but only for a joke. You see, we're not really thieves, you know."

The man laughed with malicious defiance. "We'll let Doughnut decide that." He gestured to a door at the end of the hall. "Go in there and wait."

Neal bucked up and gave Freddy that look he gave when he was about to stomp on someone. Freddy stepped aside to give him swinging room.

Neal took one step toward the man. "Look, man. We'd like to stay, but we gotta be someplace in under six hours. You're not tellin' us where to go."

The man reached into his suit coat and held his hand next to his arm. "You want to argue with power?"

Neal held up his hands and backed away. "Don't take that gun out. We'll do anything you say."

Placing his hand on Freddy's back, the man's mouth slanted into a crooked grin. "Look here, Freddy, you're going to have to put on your jacket before you see the boss." He took a few steps and stopped at a line of coats hanging on the wall. He

41

reached up, pulled a suit coat off a hanger, and offered it to Freddy.

Rafferty nudged Freddy in the elbow. "Go ahead take it," he joked. "It's all the fashion. Try it on. Everyone's wearing them here."

Freddy pulled away from the man. "I'll put your suit coat on. But I don't know what you're talking about."

"Yeah," Neal said. "You got him mixed up with somebody else."

The man shook the jacket. "Quit foolin' around, Freddy. Just put it on."

Freddy slipped the suit coat over his muscular body.

The man patted him on the back. "You can't bull shit a bull shitter. This coat's tailor-made. It still fits you to a T. You ain't tellin' me you ain't Freddy."

Rafferty made circles with his thumbs and fingers to resemble glasses and put them to his eyes. "We know he's somebody else. Maybe you need glasses."

The man slapped his shirt pocket. "I don't need glasses. I have 100/100 vision."

Oh, just great, Freddy thought. This guy is so conceited that he's afraid glasses will ruin his looks. And he's so stupid that he thinks that if he says he has 100/100 vision people will believe his eyes are better than the normal vision of 20/20.

Holding back a laugh, Freddy looked toward Neal. Neal looked back with a questioning look. Freddy pointed to his eye and shook his head. Neal nodded. He understood that the man couldn't see very well.

"I'm not knocking your excellent 100/100 vision," Neal said.

As he had done many times in the past to keep the man distracted, and to circumvent anything the man was going to say, Neal talked rapidly. Freddy knew he was setting the man up to do something to him. Without warning, Neal reached up with both hands, grabbed the man's fedora by the brim, and jammed it down over his eyes. Freddy whipped the suit coat off, threw it over the man's head, wrapped the arms around his neck, and tied them in a knot. Frantically trying to grab anything he could and douse their living flame of life, the man's arms windmilled. Before he could get the suit coat off his head and pull his hat up, Freddy and the others took off running. Neal made it out of the door and up the steps first. Then he turned right.

"Make it to the car," he said, with a determined air. "We'll get back to the burger stand before nine in the morning."

The Ford squatted next to a black limousine that was parked so close that the passenger's side of the Ford's door was blocked. Neal ran up to the driver's side door and yanked it open. At the same instant, Rafferty stopped behind him.

Before they could get in, Freddy plunged into the back seat. "Get this thing started, so we can get outta here."

Rafferty slid across the front seat and Neal jumped in behind the wheel. "I can't get the key in," he said. "There's something in the ignition."

Twenty feet from the car, the man, with his rumpled fedora, now pulled up out of his eyes, burst from the cellar, fumbling with his shoulder holster.

Neal didn't hesitate. He reached under the dash and ripped out the ignition wires. Then he took his penknife and cut insulation until three copper wires were bare. Twisting all three together, the starter grunted. The engine caught, but the starter kept running. Neal pulled one wire off. The starter hummed to a stop. Neal caught low gear, revved the engine, and popped the clutch. With the back tires screaming and rolling in circles of blue smoke, he aimed the Ford toward the man.

Before Freddy could see what had happened, he heard a thump. The man was on the roof. Freddy looked out the back window. Sliding off the roof, and still holding onto the gun in his holster, miraculously, the man landed on his feet and stood in a dazed stupor. The Ford skidded to a halt before the cellar door. Neal slung the floor shift up into reverse, backed up, and stopped. Grinding gears, he hooked low, stomped on the gas, and blew through the intersection at the end of the apartment building.

Another man, with a fedora, stood in the middle of the street, but he could not get his weapon out of the holster. Neal accelerated toward him. The man jumped out of the way. Neal blew through the next intersection at forty miles an hour, but it was a narrow one-way street. A car raced toward them. Neal stomped on the brakes and wrenched the wheel to the right.

With its wheels howling, the Ford slid around in a hard U-turn. Neal jumped on the gas and turned at the intersection next to the apartment building. Now, looking in the rearview mirror, he smiled. The Ford was leaving the men and their fedoras in the twinkling of the streetlights. Freddy let out a sigh. Then, the Ford sputtered and stalled.

Neal pounded on the steering wheel. "We're out of gas."

True to his role as team prankster, Rafferty theatrically opened the door, stepped out, and made a gracious half bow. "This way, gentleman."

Neal turned off the headlights, opened his door, and stepped out. "Don't get excited, but we just lost our ride."

Lunging out of the back seat, Freddy looked to Neal for advice. "What do we do now?"

Standing on the brick-paved street, Neal made a rude masturbatory gesture with his hand. "With less than six hours to get back. We can't stand here and play pocket pool."

CHAPTER 3

A sinewy young man with doe eyes and shaggy bleached hair walked into the room in the dingy basement of the apartment building that Freddy, Neal, and Rafferty had escaped from. Being a tall man, the slight bow in the man's back showed signs of a tortured and malnourished childhood, but he didn't let anyone take advantage of this appearance of weakness. On his wrist, Blondie openly wore an expensive gold-link bracelet that begged to be stolen. A mean stare from the steady fire in his opal green eyes caused many a thief to run away.

In this makeshift office of a wanna-be Mafiosi of the Buffalo crime family, Blondie stood next to a fat man who had his head hunched over papers lying on what had once been an expensive hardwood desk. The portly man's fluffy hair horseshoed around his bald head, gave the appearance of a big white powdered doughnut, and resembled a clown's skullcap and wig which Blondie figured fit the man's intellectual level. A brown three-piece suit, that should have been at least two sizes larger, stretched over the man's lard body. As if they were trying to scream out in pain, the buttonholes on his vest stretched taut and choked the threads, and his collar dug into the fat around his sweating red neck.

The door flung open. The man who had been flopped over the Ford walked in holding his rumpled hat. A thrust of air rushed in from the hallway and blew two sheets of paper off the desk. Doughnut rolled his eyes upward and stared.

46

"Sorry, Doughnut," the man said and lowered his head. "They got away."

Blondie looked down. On the papers was some sort of schematic. A feeling of horror rushed into his chest. He hoped it wasn't what he thought it was. Not wanting to seem eager to pick up the papers, he paused as if he didn't want to take the trouble to bend over. When he stooped down, he got a good look at the condition of the desk. Green mold and gray mildew had taken root. Fungus had crawled up the legs and had engulfed the paneled front.

Pretending to be having trouble picking up one of the papers, Blondie examined it closely. He glanced at the other paper. If he could hide it, his hopes for a new life would still be alive. He scrunched the paper into a ball and palmed it. As he handed the other paper to Doughnut, he surreptitiously placed the balled up paper into his coat pocket. He took a deep breath and sensed that he could still use these lowlifes to make one big score and get out of the crime system.

Like a trained dog with no thoughts of its own, Doughnut's goon stood at attention waiting for instructions.

Doughnut straightened up and waved his finger at him. "Nice dodge, Swill. After those kids tried to run your ass over, I thought you'd make air conditioners out of 'em."

Although Swill looked mean enough to be in a zoo and fed meat on the end of a stick, he considered himself a swell guy; and he wanted to be called Swell, but with only a third grade education, he believed the correct way to spell Swell was Swill.

He had a garbage personality, and drank and ate to excess. So everybody called him Swill.

He rolled his hat in his anvil-sized hands and a trace of a grin formed on his saturnine face. "I would have filled them full of holes," he said and sidled nest to Doughnut. "But I know how much we need suckers to take point."

With a tinge of weariness in his voice, Doughnut leaned away from Swill. "Yeah we need some point men bad." He breathed in. His huge stomach ballooned and touched the edge of the desk. Smiling a crooked smile and twisting his handlebar mustache, he grunted. "Where's those dam rent-a-cops? I pay them enough. They should have picked those kids up by now."

Swill stepped off to the side of the desk and leaned his ape-like body against the wall. With the odor of sweat and stale cigarette smoke invading his nostrils, Blondie stared through his sleep-deprived eyes and nodded at Doughnut's mustached-gripping mouth. He knew 'Mustache Petes', who first established the Sicilian Mafia in America, were a thing of the past. The new-breed hated these wannabe mafia men with their phony handlebar mustaches. Doughnut was a bald-headed idiot who didn't know that Mafiosi did not wear mustaches. And he didn't know that he was only considered a half-assed wise guy, a mob hanger-on, living with the delusion that he would someday be made a member of a crime family. Blondie had seen losers like this before. They thought they could control a crime family, but Doughnut couldn't even control his own weight.

Doughnut always said, "It's not my fault that I'm fat. I have Korsakoff's syndrome."

But people with Korsakoff's syndrome had a gross thiamine deficiency. It was also a disorder in skinny prisoners of wars as a result of their diets; but Doughnut would have never gotten through the first day of any military basic training, and he sure wasn't skinny. But he might as well have had the disease. Long-term alcohol abuse could cause him to lose the ability to coordinate his muscular movements. Then it wouldn't be long before he would have visual abnormalities, followed by profound memory disorders. Eventually he would be incapable of learning new information. Blondie didn't care how ignorant Doughnut was of Korsakoff's syndrome or the real Mafia. He would eventually become a vegetable.

Blondie didn't want to fall in the same trap and spend his best years in the ignorance of violence and hustling for what in the end only amounted to nickels and dimes and poor health. He wanted to make enough money to get out of the Chicago mob, and he needed this dummy to get someone even dumber to run ahead of the real deal.

Doughnut drummed his sausage fingers on the desktop, and looked in Blondie's direction. "Well, Blondie, you'll think these apples Freddy brought us will bite?"

Blondie jerked his head. His shaggy blond hair swished out of his doe-eyes and flopped into place. "If we treat them like big shots they should do just what they're told. They'll make perfect decoys."

Doughnut lifted his hands. "Suckers are a dime a dozen, but not here."

49

"These guys are from the States," Blondie said. "After we set them up, no one will trace them to us."

Doughnut lifted his arm and made a sweeping motion. "Chicago Sam might send you over to run interference. Now that Freddy's here, why is he saying that he don't know us?"

"Come on, Doughnut." Blondie smiled. "Have a little faith. Freddy knows what he's doing."

Doughnut held his arm in front of his face. "If you want to work for the Buffalo Arm you only get paid if the job gets done." Admiring the watch on his wrist, he chuckled. "If you want a bonus, or a gold watch, you'll have to steal those someplace else."

Blondie did have a friend named Freddy once. In all their years of friendship, their bond had never weakened. It was a friendship that went all the way back to the time when Blondie was twelve years old. A drunk who had accused him of stealing a greasy cardboard box was beating him. Just before Blondie was about to pass out from the repeated blows, Freddy whapped the drunk in the side of the head with a wine bottle and knocked him flat. Since then, whatever scheme Blondie devised, no matter how insane or ridiculous, Freddy was in favor of it. Growing up in the filthy streets was a battle. They had saved each other's lives so many times that it seemed second nature. They were close.

Even though Blondie's friend, Freddy, was dead, this kid called Freddy had the same muscular build; he could pass for Freddy's younger brother. But the stakes were too high to let Doughnut know this kid wasn't the real Freddy.

Doughnut leaned forward and placed his elbows on the desk. "Do you have a plan?"

"You know the game," Blondie said. "We'll tell them that if they get caught and don't squeal while they're in the can, we'll send a thousand a month to their special post office box."

Doughnut reached into his vest pocket and pulled out a fingernail file. He clinked it against the heavy glass ashtray on his desk. "And don't forget to tell the story that when they get out they'll move up real fast in the Arm."

Just to show disrespect to Doughnut, Blondie sat on the edge of the desk. Doughnut glared at him, but Blondie sloughed it off.

"These kids are young and dumb," he said. "They won't know what the Arm is. Tell them it's the Organization. Then they'll believe they're going to be real gangsters."

Doughnut's face took on a look of caution. "That's a lot of money we'll be sending with them. We've never used kids for something like this before. You think Freddy can get it back?"

"Freddy's run point for the Big Harry before. After they get across the border we'll have the real deal a mile behind them. I'll tip off the New York cops. They'll be so busy with Freddy's suckers that the heroin run will drive right on by."

"That's the problem," Doughnut said, and pulled a chrome flask out of his coat pocket. "We're not running bales of Big Harry this time." He unscrewed the cap and held the flask close to his mouth. "We're delivering something really important to the big fence."

"You sound serious," Blondie said, concealing the fact that he knew what was going to be delivered. "A big fence only handles important stuff."

Doughnut took a long pull from the flask and exhaled. "I don't know what they're delivering. But I know I'm getting paid to deliver it. And I'm not gonna take a chance and let some snot-nosed cop looking for a reputation take it." He took another pull. As if he were searching for a hint of betrayal, he studied at Blondie.

Blondie felt Doughnut's eyes bore right through him, but he didn't flinch. "Freddy had plastic surgery or did something to look the same age as those kids," he said, and nodded. "They trust him."

Screwing the cap back on the flask, Doughnut grunted and uneasiness crept into the office. "Your friend better know what he's doing." With the flask in his hand, he pointed to a shoebox on a shelf. "Do we want that much money layin' around?"

Blondie swept his hand toward it. "We'll tip it over so they can see all the money."

"What for?"

Blondie couldn't believe Doughnut couldn't remember why the shoebox was on the shelf, but he told him anyway. "That money will prove we have more money than we know with to do with. It'll impress them so much they'll want to bow down and worship us."

Doughnut's solemn face turned jovial. "Let's use one of those kids for an Italian rope trick." He let out a chuckle. As his great belly quivered with

52

laughter, he began filing his fingernails. "That'll really impress 'em."

The Italian rope trick was nothing new to Blondie. When he was ten, he had gotten stuck in a blinding Chicago snowstorm. To keep from freezing to death, he felt his way down an alley, snuck into the back room of a butcher shop, and hid in the closet. Through the slit in the door he had watched. A man they had called a 'buckwheat' was tied to a chair. A rope with a single knot had been wrapped around his neck. Two ugly men pulled both ends of the rope tighter and tighter. From time to time, they stopped, took the end of a gun barrel, and bashed the man's nose and mouth until he bled. Then they pulled the man's head back and made his mouth full of blood run down his throat. When he gurgled away on his own blood, they laughed and said he was out of tune. Then they pulled the rope again. In between pulls, one of the men on the end of the rope read the comics in the paper. When they had finally strangled him to death, the man had a puddle of blood around his feet.

One man patted the dead man on the back and joked, "Sorry we had to take so long, pal. But you had a suspended sentence."

Later on, Blondie learned that 'buckwheat' killings were only ordered by the big bosses, and the victim had to have committed an unpardonable act: squealing to the cops, skimming from the gang, or sleeping with the boss's girlfriend. In buckwheat killings, to send a powerful message to others, the executioners prolonged the victim's pain, and the victim was usually glad to accept the much less painless fate of death.

Apparently memory disorders were already affecting Doughnut. He didn't know or couldn't remember that the rope trick had to be ordered by the big boss, but Blondie didn't want to tell him and possibly blow his chance to get the big score. The rope trick scene and the awful coppery smell of the man's blood had given him nightmares for years. For a while he had tried to drink away the nightmares, but after seeing what drinking had done to a lot of the underlings in Chicago's mob, he quit. He wasn't ready to start drinking again, and he never wanted to face those nightmares again.

He shook his head and stood away from the desk. "If we strangle one of Freddy's friends to try and make the other one do what we want, we'll have a big mess to clean up. They're just kids. We can bullshit 'em."

As if he hadn't heard a word Blondie had said, Doughnut looked up from filing his nails. "Where's that rent-a-cop?"

54

CHAPTER 4

Searching for a place to hide before any more mean men wearing fedoras tromped down the sidewalk, Freddy, Neal, and Rafferty stood on the sidewalk a few blocks down from the apartment building they had escaped from. Off to their right, a small flat-roofed building at the edge of the sidewalk met their eyes. Red brush-painted 'Keep Out' signs haphazardly enhanced the ugliness of the structure, but its two hinged wooden-planked doors hung wide open.

"Hey," Freddy said. "Let's push the car in that old garage and close the doors."

Neal jumped behind the steering wheel and closed the door. Frantically waving his arm out the window, he motioned for Freddy and Rafferty to push. They pushed, but the Ford wouldn't move.

Rafferty ran to the window and punched Neal in the arm.

Neal turned to Rafferty. "What?"

Rafferty smiled a big ear-to-ear smile. "Take it out of gear."

A quick shine of embarrassment flashed from Neal's face. He reached over and put the transmission into neutral. Rafferty went to the back of the car. Grunting with the effort, Freddy and Rafferty pushed the Ford into the narrow opening of the garage until the sergeant-striped brake lights flashed red.

They tried to stand behind the Ford and close the doors, but being a horse and buggy garage the narrow building was just long enough for the car to squeeze in.

Inside, Neal tried to open the driver's side door. It bashed up against the brick wall. There was not enough room for him to open the door. So, he stuck his head out of the window and began squeezing out. But the belt of his pants caught on the rough brick. Each time he tried to pull himself out, his pants pulled down.

Rafferty pointed and laughed at Neal's drooping pants. Suddenly, he quit laughing, hung his head down in disgust, and sat on the car's bumper. "Naturally."

"Naturally what?" Freddy asked.

Rafferty pointed behind Freddy. Two men with fedoras with a police officer between them, stood at his back.

The cop waved his hand in a friendly gesture. "Come on in, boys. The boss's waiting for you in his office."

As if it were coming from a chasm, Neal's voice echoed. "Finally, got outta that sucker."

"Don't break your arm pattin' yourself on the back." Rafferty gestured toward the three men. "We got company."

Splayed flat on the top of the car, Neal looked beyond Rafferty. One of the hatted men wiggled his finger in a come-here gesture. "You too, hot rod."

Neal tensed on the roof of the car and searched for a chance to escape. The cop tapped on the handle of the gun in his leather holster. "Don't get cute."

Neal relaxed, slid down the trunk of the car, and fell in line. The cop and the two men escorted them back inside the basement of the building. Outside Doughnut's office, a gray suit coat hung on a nail. The cop reached up, jerked it off the nail, and shoved it into Freddy's chest. "Here put this on."

Freddy put the suit coat on. It was long in the arms, but the chest and back fit perfectly.

The cop nodded in approval. "Too bad you don't have a tie. But it'll have to do." He opened the door to the so-called boss's office. Neal stepped in as if he owned the place. But like prisoners being let to the execution chamber, as they walked through the door, Rafferty and Freddy dragged their feet.

Inside the room, while Neal stepped toward Doughnut's desk, Rafferty cowered next to Freddy. Doughnut had taken off his brown suit coat and wore a white shirt and a vest. With his tie loosened at the neck and his handlebar moustache being much too thick, he reminded Freddy of a fat walrus with a kid's little white inner tube around its head.

Doughnut looked up from filing his nails. "Why are you boys in such a hurry?" He dropped the file onto the desk. "You almost ran over my friend."

"What did you expect us to do?" Neal threw his hands into the air. "He was trying to pull out a gun."

Blondie tilted his head back in a cocky manner. "Swill doesn't even carry a gun, do you, Swill?"

With a cigarette dangling from his thick lips, Swill nodded.

Blondie pyramided his fingertips and pointed them at Neal. "Did you see a gun?"

Neal turned to Rafferty and Freddy. "Did you guys see a gun?"

Freddy searched his mind. Although he clearly remembered seeing Swill and the other guy with his hand reaching for something under his arm, he couldn't remember seeing a gun. "We didn't see a gun, but he was reaching for one."

"That's right," Rafferty said. "He had his hand under his suit coat."

Blondie sat on the edge of the desk and reached into his vest pocket. Thinking he was reaching for a gun, Freddy stiffened, but Blondie pulled out a manila envelope and tapped it on his knee. "Maybe he was trying to give you something, Freddy."

Neal looked to Freddy then back to Blondie. "Maybe he was. But we weren't going to stick around and find out."

Swill jumped across the room and grabbed Neal by the front of the shirt. "You callin' me a liar? I'll bust you in the guts."

Neal tried to pry Swill's hand from his shirt, but his grip was too strong.

Clunk! Doughnut slammed the thick glass ashtray onto the desk. Swill released his grip and retreated back one step, waiting.

"There is no need to get excited, boys." Doughnut jerked his head toward the left. Swill retreated to the corner, took his rumpled fedora hat off and held it. Shaking his head, Doughnut let out a long stream of breath. "Normally I would let my friend take care of you. But you boys are cocky as hell. I like that."

Grinning in their direction, Swill put his fedora back on his head and bent the brim down in the front. With his dark eyes peering out from under the brim, he crossed his arms across his chest and placed his hand on his shoulder-holstered gun.

"We didn't mean to get you gentleman excited," Neal said, and held up his hands in a defensive position. "But we're in a hurry."

Blondie smiled and threw the envelope on the desk. "We like cocky people that are in a hurry. And seeing that you're friends of Freddy, we're going to let off the hook."

Neal stared at the envelope. "You mean you're not going to keep us here?"

"No one wants to keep you here," Blondie said. "Any friend of Freddy's is free to leave anytime."

Freddy didn't know why they were saying they knew him. He was going to ask, but he figured Neal couldn't resist the temptation to find out what was in that envelope. Freddy didn't care if he got back to Patagonia in less than twelve hours, or if he collected the bet money. Now, all he wanted to do was get back in the car, get away, and get some sleep. He elbowed Neal and jerked his head toward the door.

As if he were trying to decide whether to stay of leave, Neal tapped his fingers next to the envelope. Finally, he sighed and turned to the door. "Okay, we're outta here."

Blondie held up his hand. "Not so fast. We got a proposition."

Neal cast a suspicious stare at Blondie. "Now what?"

Swill pointed to Doughnut.

Doughnut tilted his head to the side and looked up at the shoebox on the shelf. Many denominations of green American money splayed out from the box. "You boys want to make some money?"

Neal wheeled around and leaned over the desk. "What do we gotta do?"

Doughnut looked surprised at Neal's eagerness. Tapping his middle finger on the desk, Doughnut gave him a cautious glare. As if someone may be listening that shouldn't be, he talked slow and low. "Make a minor delivery."

Neal glanced back at the shoebox money, and then his eyes swiveled back to Doughnut. "What kind of delivery?"

Blondie pointed to Freddy. "Freddy knows all about it. You guys in?"

Neal gave Freddy a look.

Freddy shrugged.

Neal leaned back and scratched his belly. "Ah, ahem, ah, yes, of course." He paused. "But we'll have to talk about it." He looked at Freddy and Rafferty. "Won't we?"

Doughnut stared at a heavy glass ashtray on his desk. Then, as if he liked to hear the sound, he clinked the chrome fingernail file on the edge of it.

"Go ahead," he said. "But don't try to leave without giving us an answer."

Neal held up his hands. "Oh, no, we wouldn't do anything like that. After all, who wouldn't want to make few bucks?"

Freddy didn't know what Doughnut was talking about. He had never seen any of these gangsters in his life, and he didn't want Doughnut or his friends to hear what Neal was going to say. "Can we go into the hall?"

Blondie flipped his hand toward the door. "Be my guest."

Neal, Freddy, and Rafferty filed out and were met by a wall of three men and the cop. The cop thrust out the side of his chest where his gold badge was pinned. "Goin' somewhere, boys?"

Doughnut blared from inside the office, "It's all right! Just don't let them leave."

Freddy and his friends walked down the hall into the semi-dark. With a moldy odor creeping into their lungs and the sound of water still plinking somewhere, they formed a huddle. Instead of talking about the proposition, Neal looked at Rafferty. "What time it?"

Rafferty jerked his head back and looked at this watch. "It's five to four."

Neal sighed. "Good, we got five hours to make it back."

Freddy figured they could be shot or beat up at any time. He couldn't believe Neal was more concerned about making it back to the burger stand than getting out of the creepy building. Trying to avoid the moldy odor, he placed his fingers on his nose and pinched his nostrils shut. "I think we better worry about getting out of here."

"Come on, Freddy," Neal said, and cocked his head. "Cough it up. What did you do with these guys before?"

Freddy hunched his shoulders. "Heck if I know. I've never seen those guys before in my life."

Rafferty turned sideways. His green eyes glimmered in a slim ray of weak light. "As long as we can make some money." He shrugged. "Who cares?"

61

"Yeah," Neal said, with excitement in his voice. "Did you see that money? They got a whole shoebox full of it, just sittin' on that shelf."

Freddy dropped his fingers from his nose. "I don't know. It seems too easy."

Neal leaned back. "Easy smeezy." He ran his hand down the sleeve of Freddy's suit coat. "You already got a free set of threads."

Rafferty leaned against the wall. "Maybe they'll give you a vest and a pair of pants to go with it."

Neal laughed. "Once we get that money and a full tank of gas, we can take off. They'll never catch us in that Ford, and we can still make it back in time."

"We might be able to do that," Freddy said. "But they act like I already know what we're supposed to do. What am I going to tell them?"

"Leave it to me," Neal said, flashing his confident smile. "Just go along with what I say. We'll wing it if we have to."

Freddy scanned the exit at the end of the hall. "I still don't know."

Rafferty looked at the cop. "I don't think we really have a choice."

Neal turned to go back into the office. Rafferty tapped him on the shoulder.

Neal turned.

"That Swill guy looks like he belongs in a quarantine cage. He's probably got rabies. If I were you, I'd keep my hands away from his mouth."

When they were ushered back into Doughnut's great office, while Doughnut shifted his eyes back and forth, as if he were watching invisible flies playing prison ping pong, Blondie inched toward the desk. In a lightning-quick move he opened a drawer and pulled out a canvas bank bag. It had a zipper lock and looked to be left over from a bank deposit robbery. He held it for a second and then let it fall. Like lead, it thudded onto the desk. Doughnut leaned back. Under his enormous weight, the wooden chair squeaked. He placed his chubby hands behind his powdered doughnut-shaped hair; and as if the chair were in pain, it groaned.

"Okay, Freddy," Doughnut said. "It'll be the usual deal. Half now and half after the job's done. That still okay with you?"

Neal cut in. "Sure, but Freddy never filled us in on the details."

Blondie patted Freddy on the back. "Trying to cut your partners out, huh, Freddy?"

Freddy didn't want to go along with anything these gangsters were trying to get him to do, and he knew Neal would do just about anything for the thrill of it. He wanted to tell them they had the wrong man, but when he looked up, Swill had his hand on that gun again. Freddy figured he had better go along. He nodded toward Blondie.

"I wasn't planning to cut them out," he said. "I just didn't know if you wanted them in on it. I never welshed on a deal yet."

Neal looked to Doughnut. "Well, are we in or not?"

Doughnut let out a breath of air. "Sure, you're in." He looked to Blondie. "Review the details for Freddy's friends."

63

Blondie plucked the bank bag off the desk and threw it at Neal. Neal reacted and caught the bag with no effort. Blondie smiled at his quickness.

"Nice reflexes," he said. "You could have a future with us." He picked up the manila envelope and handed it to Freddy. "Here's the first half. You know what to do with it."

Freddy didn't know what to do with the envelope, but he took it and nodded as if he did.

Neal shook the bank bag and pulled at the zipper lock. "What's in this thing?"

Doughnut gave Neal a hard stare. "If you open it, you won't need to know what's in it."

As if it were a hot match, Neal jerked his fingers away from the zipper. "No problem. Give us the details, man. We'll get this thing done."

"It's a simple thing to do," Blondie said. "All you have to do is take the bag and what's in it across the border and drop it in Buffalo."

Neal spread his arms wide. "Buffalo's a big place."

"Freddy knows the drill. Wrap it in an old newspaper and throw it in the second waste basket at the red light on the corner of Main and Washington Street."

"What if there's no waste basket?" Neal asked. "Kids like to tip those things over and roll them down the street."

"There's always one there, but if there isn't, an old bum with a straw hat will be standing across from the newsstand. Just drop it. He'll get it."

Neal glanced up at the shoebox on the shelf. "When do we get the other half of the money?"

Blondie sighed and looked at Freddy. "Didn't you tell him anything?"

Freddy shrugged.

Blondie continued. "As usual, the other half of the money will be at the newsstand in the 'New York Times', third paper down."

Neal couldn't have looked in the envelope; Freddy had it in his hand. But Neal had asked about the other half of the money, and he always claimed he could smell money. Freddy wondered if he was right. He opened the envelope and looked inside. Green American bills were stacked like the pages of a thick book. He ran his thumb over the edges. Denominations of twenty dollar bills flashed before his eyes.

"This is a lot of money," he said. "It seems too easy."

"Yeah," Rafferty said. "What's in that bank bag?"

"What do you care?" Blondie said. "You're getting paid to keep your mouth shut. The more you don't know, the more you won't have to forget." He stared at Freddy. "Freddy knows the routine."

Swill let out a burst of laughter. "That's good, Blondie. That's real good."

With a faint glimmer of mischief, Rafferty looked at the bank bag and then at Neal. "What if we just take off with the bag and the money?"

"You can." Blondie gave Freddy a thumbs-up sign. "But before you even think about it, ask Freddy what happened to the last kids we paid to do us a favor."

Rafferty looked to Freddy for an answer. Neal waved his hand in front of Rafferty's face.

"I'm sure Freddy will fill us in, on the way." He looked toward the door. "Hey, man, we gonna do this thing or not?"

Freddy stared at Neal in disbelief. "We're not going anywhere. We're out of gas."

"Details, details," Blondie said. "Your car's all gassed up and ready to go."

Doughnut waved his hand at the two men and the cops who were standing in the doorway. They stepped aside.

Waving his hand in a dismissing gesture, Doughnut grinned manically. "You're free to go."

Now that they were free to go, Freddy exhaled and felt the tension in the room fade. He hoped Neal would let the peace prevail, but when he turned, Neal grabbed onto his shoulder.

Freddy turned.

As if Neal wanted to show Freddy something, he turned and smiled at Swill.

Swill walked from around the desk like a bear walking on its hind legs.

"Hey, Swill," Neal said. "Do you like sex?"

Swill's eyes lit up. "Sure. Who doesn't?"

Neal smiled a big in-your-face smile.

With a tone heavy with cynicism, he blared out, "Good! Go fuck yourself."

Swill lunged for him, but Neal whirled around, jumped through the doorway, and rushed down the hall. By the time Freddy and Rafferty walked through the doorway, Neal was outside laughing.

66

CHAPTER 5

A ways down from the Peace Bridge the Ford rumbled along the Lakeshore Road. Here, Freddy commanded a panoramic view of the Lake Erie shoreline. A chilled mist clung to the dark surface of the water and obscured a lonely light above a boat pier. On the other side of the narrow portion of the lake, darkened waves reflected yellow lights from a waterfront tavern on the shoreline of the United States.

"They won't see us there," Freddy said, and pointed to a turn off near the water.

Neal steered the Ford to where Freddy had pointed and hit the brakes. The tires squealed to a stop. Giving everything a ghostly appearance, a clammy fog clung to the ground and deadened the sounds of everything around them. Neal reached under the front seat, pulled out a stolen Pennsylvania license plate and got out.

"Come on, you guys." Has said and waved his hand. "We gotta change plates and break down a tire."

Curled up on the front seat Rafferty opened one sleepy eye and peered at Neal. "Are we getting a flat?"

"No, but we're going to make it look like we got one."

"What are you talking about?" Freddy asked. "Doughnut won't send the cops after us; we're dropping off the bank bag."

Neal let out a muffled laugh. "What makes you think we can trust a man like Doughnut?"

Freddy shrugged. "I guess we can't."

"It's an old trick," Neal said. "They give us a little money and a little dope. Then they tip off the cops. The cops catch us, and while they're busy handcuffing and putting us in the cruiser, the people with the main shipment of dope go right on past."

Now it was clear why Blondie had given them the money and bank bag. Freddy shook his head at his own ignorance.

While Neal switched license plates, Rafferty stepped out of the Ford and Freddy followed. After Neal threw the Ohio plate into the water and opened the trunk, he looked to Freddy. "Okay, Freddy, get that jack."

Freddy reached into the trunk and put his hand on the jack. A swishing sound caused a chill to run up his back. He looked behind him. The fog opened up and revealed a small glade of knee-high grass. Something swished through the grass and out of the mist. The leather-looking face of a man appeared. As he walked near, he projected the self-assured quality of a man familiar with danger. He had a four-foot steel pipe in his hand he was using for a cane, but he didn't appear to be crippled. The pipe looked like a weapon, but when he smiled, his spaced-apart teeth flashed like the lights in a theater marquee.

He stopped right next to Freddy. "What'cha doin', boys?"

Freddy kept an eye on the pipe. "We thought we were getting a flat, but there must something wrong with the steering."

"Yeah," Neal said, brushing his hands together. "We'd like to stay and chat, but we got to go."

68

"Where do you got to go at this time of night?" the man said with a playful tone to his voice.

Neal closed the trunk. "I don't know, man, but we gotta go." He shrugged. "You know?"

The man reached into his shirt pocket. "I know you're in a big hurry, but before you go, would you like to see a nickel screwin' a dime?"

Neal turned to the man.

The man pulled a small matchbox from his breast pocket, leaned on the pipe, and held out the matchbox.

Keeping an eye on the pipe, Neal stepped close. "Yeah, what the heck? I'll take a look."

The man opened the matchbox. Inside, lined up side-by-side — resembling two eyes with a screw for a nose between them — a nickel, a screw, and a dime stared back at him. Neal burst into laughter. The man offered the matchbox to Freddy and Rafferty. They looked in and there was laughter all around.

Neal patted the man on the back. "Thanks for the laugh, old timer, but we still gotta go."

The smiling leather-faced man nodded.

While Freddy and Rafferty climbed into the Ford, Neal jumped behind the steering wheel. With the old man waving, they pulled away from the pier. Neal downshifted at a dark intersection, and looked down the streets on his right and left. On the right, just a block away, the neighborhood looked abandoned. On the left, the road looked like a glitzy tourist-beaten path.

"Which way do we turn?" Neal asked.

Before anyone could answer, a black and white police car pulled out of a hidden driveway. As if the

69

officer behind the wheel were looking for someone, he slowed, and turned to the left. To keep from attracting the police's attention, Neal gently stepped on the gas and quietly turned right. "I would say, we're going this way."

As a neighborhood loomed close, graffiti-covered telephone poles and houses with weeds and grass-choked yards encased the street from both sides. Empty beer cans and smashed bottles decorated the gutters along the street and winked under the light of a few streetlights that still worked. The place wasn't as bad as where Freddy had grown up, but its pall and apathy reminded him of home. "Looks like Patagonia."

"Yeah," Rafferty said. "Hey, Neal, you sure you didn't find a shortcut across the border?"

"Looks like it, doesn't it?" Neal stopped the Ford under the brightest streetlight. "There's nobody around here." He pointed up. "We can break down that tire under that light."

Once outside, Neal took out the spare tire and threw it under the bumper of the car. Freddy put the bottom of the jack on the edge of the tire, and slid it right next to the edge of the metal rim. Rafferty slipped the jack handle into the jack and jacked away. The car went up, and the bottom of the jack pushed down. The side of the tire sagged, but the seal didn't break. Rafferty put his foot on the side of the tire and pushed. The rubber didn't budge.

Hey," he said. "Don't you think it would be easier if you let the air out?"

With undisguised sudden realization, Neal snapped his head in Rafferty's direction. "I knew that." He reached over, and unscrewed the valve stem. Air gushed out. But the seal didn't break. Neal jumped up on the bumper of the car and bounced. The tire slumped down. The seal broke with a whoosh of old air. Neal knelt next to the tire and looked up at Rafferty. "Make sure no one's looking." While Rafferty scanned the seedy surroundings for anything suspicious, Neal slipped the bank bag into the tire, and told Freddy," Give me that envelope." Freddy did and he put that in the tire, too. "Okay, let her down."

Rafferty let the jack down. Neal picked up the tire and bounced it on the ground until its edges were close to the rim and ready to inflate. Freddy fished the tire pump out of the trunk and screwed the hose on the valve stem. "Okay, start pumping."

When the tire was inflated again, Neal sat on the back bumper and exhaled. "Even if Doughnut's on-the-take-cops stop us, they'll never find it in there."

Rafferty tapped the Pennsylvania license plate. "The cops will be looking for an Ohio plate, so this should keep then off our ass."

Freddy tugged on Neal's arm.

Neal looked up.

Bored teenagers sauntered out from between two houses. As if they were waiting for something to happen or were going to make something happen, they loitered on the broken sidewalk. Neal bent over, picked up the tire, and threw it into the trunk. Before he slammed the trunk lid shut, Freddy and Rafferty were in the Ford.

The teenagers surrounded the car. As if he was unconcerned about the threat and the fact they might want to take the tires and the spare, too, Neal walked to the driver's side, opened the door, and slid behind the wheel. Instead of starting the engine, he stuck his head out the window and talked as if the rowdy teenagers were old friends.

"What's goin' on, gentlemen?"

The tallest one shuffled to the window, tilted his head to one side, and looked down at Neal. "What's it to you, buddy?"

"Ah, ahem, ah, yes." Neal paused. "Of course. Just trying to be friendly, pal."

As the other members of the gang crowded around, two pairs of fists banged on the hood of the Ford. A chubby man with a shaved head whispered something in the leader's ear. Then, to Freddy's horror, the fist-banging men stepped back and stood with menacing looks of satisfaction on their faces. Feeble light, emitting through dirty windows, exposed three more gang members swaggering out of alleyways between graffiti-covered houses. The members wore their pants low, dark hair slicked back, and cigarettes dangled from their mean lips. One had a star tire wrench that would fit any lug nut. The second kid carried a jack handle while the third kid had something slung over his shoulder. At first, what he carried resembled an automatic rifle, but as he came closer it turned out to be a car jack.

The chubby man bent toward the window. "Why are you asking us what's goin' on?"

Neal kept his upbeat attitude. "We heard that if you weren't being thrown in jail here, you could have a pretty good time."

The chubby man began to laugh, but as if he had just been stabbed in the chest and he was looking for revenge, his face turned mean. "What business is it of yours what we're doing?"

This gang was looking for an excuse to start something or take the tires and whatever else they could steal. It would be a challenge Neal would not back down from. Before Neal could make a bad situation worse, Freddy leaned to the window.

"A pickup truck with a bag of stolen money came this way," he said, as if he was excited. "Money was flying out the back. Did you guys see it?"

The rest of the gang closed in around the car. The leader's demeanor changed from one of troublemaker to interested citizen. "What did you say?"

Freddy looked to Neal for an answer. Neal glanced back with a blank look. The chubby man banged his fist against the door. "Answer the question."

Freddy had to make the tale believable. He searched his mind for the right thing to say. "We had a flat tire down the road," he said. And a pickup truck came past. Every few yards, money was flying out all over the road."

One of the gang members looked into the back seat. "Did you get any?"

"We were going to, but a police car came and picked it up a few bills, but they didn't see the money coming out of the back of the truck."

"Yeah," Neal said, taking the lead. "We're pretty sure it turned and went this way. It was going real slow, so we think it stopped somewhere close."

The leader snapped his fingers. Opening his muscular arms wide, he pointed in two directions. "Spread out, and find that thing."

The gang dispersed and ran in different directions, turning and cutting across grass-grown yards and up alleyways to watch for a money-spewing truck that was not coming. The leader stood next to the bald man and jerked his head from right to left, watching both ends of the street.

Just to rub the ruse in, Neal asked, "Do you see it?"

The leader retorted, with a flash of anger in his eyes, "Thanks for the tip, buddy. Now get the hell outta here."

Through the slight opening between the sides of the front seat and the door, Freddy watched Neal place his hand on the door handle. With only two gang members left, he was sure Neal was about to jump out and show the leader and his baldheaded friend that he could go anywhere he pleased, and if he wanted, stay here all night which would bring the entire army of gang members scurrying back. And to make matters worse, if Neal got them mad enough, Freddy was sure they would tip the car over.

Neal's hand lifted up the door handle and he tensed to jump out, but before he pushed the door open, red flashes of light danced in the rearview mirror. That cop car was coming down the road. Neal opened the door and slammed it shut. He hit the starter. The engine fired with a burst of blue exhaust. He hooked low gear and sped away. Flying out of the neighborhood, he cut a tight left turn. With the tires screeching in protest, he turned right and fishtailed around an intersection. Down the street, the Ford wheeled around a corner. Freddy watched in the rearview mirror. The cop car sideswiped a parked Desoto, but kept on going, leaving its owner jumping up and down, yelling and screaming.

"What's going on!" Freddy screamed.

Rafferty dug his fingers into the seat and turned toward the oncoming threat. "I don't know, but they want us really bad."

Shifting smoothly through the gears, Neal accelerated away from the jumping, jack-in-the-box man next to the Desoto; and the cop car faded in the distance. Then Neal steered the Ford through a series of wild twists and turns that caused Freddy to lose his sense of direction. Under the shadows of the dark steel beams of a bridge, Neal slowed. To the right, dirt that had been packed flat with years of use looked withered and old. Beneath the gnarled branches of overhanging trees, teenagers milled around orange flames leaping from out of a rusty burn barrel

Neal jerked his thumb toward the barrel. "You wanna stop and ask these guys where the border is?"

"Don't stop here," Freddy said, but he knew Neal would do just the opposite.

Neal hit the brakes. "Did you say stop here?"

Freddy knew it was useless. "Yeah, that's what I said," he lied. "Stop here."

The car slowed more. Rafferty pounded on Neal's arm. "The cops were right behind us. What are you stopping here for?"

"We didn't break any traffic laws," Neal said as if nothing were wrong. "We're doing the legal speed limit as any good citizen would do." Then he reached his arm out the opened window and stopped the Ford right in front of the barrel.

A skinny teenager with a cigarette dangling from his lips stepped toward the Ford.

"Hey, friend," Neal said and smiled a big friendly smile. "Want to make a few bucks?"

The kid stared at the American dollar bills clutched in Neal's hand. "What do we gotta do, man?"

"The cops are right behind us. When they come around the corner tell them we made a right turn."

The teenager jerked the cigarette from his lips and flicked it into the burn barrel. "No problem, man. Give me the cash."

Neal took a long look at the teenager and told him, "You're lying out your ass." He steered the Ford so that the barrel was right in front of the front bumper. Then, he revved the engine. When it slowed to an angry idle, he yelled. "Tell your asshole buddies to get the hell out of the way."

Kids ran from the barrel.

Neal punched the gas.

The back wheels spun on the packed earth beneath the bridge and the Ford lurched forward. The front bumper plowed into the barrel. The barrel flopped over. Neal backed the Ford up. Flaming sticks of wood rolled out of the barrel. As orange sparks sprayed into the black night, Neal shifted into low gear and tromped the pedal down. The Ford's tires squealed onto the pavement, caught traction, and sent the car and its occupants zooming away.

Flying down the road, Neal stuck his hand out the window and flashed the skinny kid a big middle finger, then hooked second gear, tapped the gas, and hit high gear. The Ford shot forward, but before it could get up to full speed, Neal downshifted and leaned into a left turn. Then he gave it full throttle. Freddy felt the speed push him back into the seat. He leaned forward and shook Neal's shoulder.

"What's the matter with you?" he said with great haste. "Now those kids are going to tell the cops which way we went."

"The main thing is" — Neal flashed Freddy a big smile — "don't get excited."

Freddy jerked his head in disgust. "Maybe we should stop and let the cops catch us. I don't think they'll find that bank bag."

"They can't arrest what they can't catch," Neal said, and they flashed through an intersection. Then Neal turned left again, then left at an intersection, stopped and turned out the lights.

Rafferty gave Neal a puzzled look. "What did you do? Lose your mind?"

Neal stopped the Ford. With the confidence of a man who had bet on a rigged horse race, he leaned back and put his hands behind his head. "Don't get excited, gentleman."

Emergency beacons, splashing red light, led the way of a police car with its siren bawling down the street. As its beacons brightened and its siren grew louder, the car zoomed past the intersection, and the taillights and red flashes dwindled to tiny specks. When it stopped next to the bridge, its bawling siren hummed to quiet

Neal laughed. "Right about now, those pissed off kids at the burn barrel are telling the cops which way we went."

Freddy slumped back into the seat. "Wouldn't it have been easier to just give those kids the money?"

Neal cocked his head back toward Freddy. "Sure, it would have been easier. But the cops wouldn't believe a word those kids said. But now they will."

Once again the siren erupted into the night but faded in the distance. Neal drove to the end of the street and made a right turn. He flicked on the headlights, and they were on their way again. Neal banged his fist onto the steering wheel. "All gassed up, my ass."

Freddy looked at the newly lit road ahead. "Now what?"

"Blondie didn't put much gas in the tank. Look for a gas station."

Freddy and Rafferty nodded simultaneously and searched the dark ahead. The '40 Ford was a three-passenger, five-window deluxe business coupe. When it had been manufactured, for an extra twenty dollars, a rear seat had been put in; and the original V-8 60 engine put out eighty-five horsepower. Right after Neal had bought the Ford, he and Rafferty had hung a block and tackle from a tree branch and snatched a big V-8 engine out of a Cadillac ambulance. When they dropped it into the Ford with the turbo charger, the engine got an extra one hundred horsepower. It was fast on acceleration and even though overdrive took too long to kick in, when they hit an open stretch, the cops would be further behind.

Freddy hoped the episode at the burn barrel would give them enough of a head start to get some gas and get clean away. And Neal didn't disappoint. Already going fast, the Ford sped up. It took a dip in the road so quickly that Freddy felt suspended. When the weird feeling in his stomach stopped, Neal slowed and turned off the highway where they bounced down a yellow dirt road, trailing dust behind them like smoke. When he broke out onto a long street and Neal revved the engine, the big V-8 shrieked and wound out high gear. Freddy looked out the back window. The cops were nowhere to be seen.

"Maybe we lost them for good," Neal said with satisfaction, then frowned.

The gas gauge showed empty.

"Just in time," Rafferty said, and pointed up ahead.

As they neared a corner, a firefly wink became a weak shaft of light pouring from underneath a metal canopy above gas pumps. The hoods of a few broken-down cars, parked alongside the gas station building, caught the dim neon reflection of a single neon sign hanging in the window. The gas station seemed like a life preserver on a rough sea, but the sign glowed 'CLOSED'. The Ford sputtered and the mighty V-8 engine quit. Neal guided the silent car onto the tarmac. When the gas cap on the left rear fender was right in front of a gas pump, he stopped.

"It figures," Rafferty said. "We need gas, and they're not open."

"We'll drain every hose in the place," Neal said, and while laughing demonically he jumped out of the Ford, grabbed the gas pump nozzle and stuck it into the tank.

The gas remaining in the hose drained into the tank. He put the nozzle back on the pump and they pushed the Ford to the next pump. He drained that hose, too. After they had pushed the Ford to all the pumps and drained all the hoses, Neal tried to start the V-8 motor.

"Wait a minute," Freddy said, and jerked his finger at the front of the Ford for emphasis. "There isn't any gas in the carburetor. You'll run the battery down."

"Maybe not," Neal said, and pointed to the phosphorescent hands of a clock inside the station. "We don't have time to prime it. It's almost five AM. We got four hours to make it back to the Burp and collect the bet."

Sometimes when the Ford ran out of gas Neal had closed the hand choke and the engine had sucked gas into the empty fuel line and the engine had started, but this time it didn't. The battery had died. Neal sat behind the wheel in stunned silence. His wild ideas usually worked. This time his usual gaiety from getting away from the cops was withering away.

"We can still push-start it," he said. "But we're gonna need more gas."

A skinny black cat with a huge rat in its mouth raced out of the dark night and vanished under a dilapidated car sitting next to the gas station's big door.

Neal glanced right then left. "There's nobody around. Let's see if we can get some gas out of that car."

He jumped out of the Ford, ran around to the back, and popped the trunk open. Then he reached inside and snagged a siphoning hose. Walking past the car's window, he shook the end of the hose at Rafferty. "Midnight gas station at your fingertips."

Rafferty and Freddy followed him to the abandoned car. Before they got there, Neal had the gas cap off and the hose into the tank. Holding his ear to the tank opening, he rattled the hose. A disappointed look flashed from his face. Freddy knew that look, but hoped Neal didn't have the hose in the gas yet. "Is there any in it?"

Neal put the end of the hose next to his mouth and looked up. "I got one more trick up my sleeve." He blew into the hose. No sound of burbling bubbles from the hose being below the gas level came up the tank's pipe. He pulled the hose out and felt its end. "Dry as a popcorn fart." He leaped upright and took one step toward the Ford. A cop car swerved around the corner and screeched to a stop. As the first light of day streamed over the city, police car doors flew open. Two uniformed policemen jumped out with guns drawn.

They yelled, "Hands up!"

Rafferty whirled around and faced the police. "I guess we're going back to see the great walking stomach."

Neal, Rafferty, and Freddy threw up their hands and surrendered. Under a light blue sky turning orange behind the buildings to the east, Freddy looked up at the lighted clock on the gas station wall. It was five AM.

CHAPTER 6

While Swill wore a shiny new smirk, Blondie leaned against the wall in the shabby office and watched Doughnut enter. Sweating and out of breath from the strain of walking the short distance from the car to his office, Doughnut set a bag of powdered doughnuts on the corner of his desk and plopped his lard butt into the chair. Exhaling a great breath, he let his heavy frame sag into a blubbery slump. He took a doughnut from the bag, jammed the whole thing into his big thick-lipped mouth, and swallowed it. Then he opened the bottom drawer to his desk and pulled out a bottle of scotch. He stuck two fingers and his thumb into three water glasses, lifted them, and set them on the desk. Referring to police officers — bt's or bird turds — who are never let in on family secrets but are led to believe they are part of the mob, Doughnut waved his hand in the air.

"While we're waiting for our wayward bt's to get back," he patted his stomach, "let's have a little refreshment."

He poured large slugs of scotch into the glasses. Then, the three men clinked their glasses together; and while Doughnut and Swill threw the scotch down their throats, Blondie tilted his glass to his lips, but didn't drink. He stared at a sawed-off shotgun sitting on the shelf just behind the shoebox.

Twitching his trigger finger, Swill followed his stare. "We gonna blow their heads off?"

As if it were foul-tasting medicine, Blondie forced the scotch down. If he could pull this deal off, he would have enough money to keep himself out of

83

the system for life. But there could be a problem. With that much money to turn, he wondered if the cops would stay bought. Usually they would, but he could never be sure. His friend, Freddy, had trusted the men in the Arm, but when they sold him out, he lost all his money and Blondie's, too.

Even though Freddy had lost all their life savings, Blondie had learned a great truth: Wise guys and criminals don't think up colorful phrases to warn you. It takes too much time. If you don't do what they want you to do, they kill you, your best friend, your wife, your kids, your mother, and even your grandmother. Sometimes as a nudge to get their point across, they will give a guy a break and only slash across his face with a razor.

In reality, no one in the Arm could be trusted. In order to be free of the Arm and its influences, Blondie had to learn to live differently and join the herd of humanity where his own pleasure was not the only consideration. He hoped he could muster all his knowledge and use Doughnut and his thugs, who did not have the slightest idea about or care about the true nature of the world, and outsmart them. If he could, then he could begin to become a normal human being.

Swill swished past Blondie and reached up for the sawed-off shotgun.

Blondie waved his hand down. "No need for that. When the cops bring those kids get back, we're still going to need them to run ahead of the real deal."

Swill never liked to be told what to do, especially from a new man like Blondie. He flicked his own chest with his trigger finger. For a tense moment, he stood eye to eye with Blondie. Doughnut cleared his throat. Swill backed off, but he reminded Blondie of the soulless prick who'd told him his best friend, Freddy, had died in a plane crash in Lake Erie, and that his body couldn't be recovered because the internal gases that would make his corpse float would not form in the cold depths of the lake.

Blondie and his childhood friend, Freddy, had believed the Arm established an unbreakable code: harming a man's family was unthinkable, and double-crossing your friends was not even an option; and they had lived by this code. So, Blondie had believed that his friend's death was accidental and went along with the new bosses of the Arm. But after the winter thaw, his friend's rat-gnawed and decomposed body was found in the Cleveland sewer system. Too late, Blondie realized there was no code, and it would only be a matter of time before he would end up in the sewer system, too.

Before Freddy was murdered he and Blondie had discovered a great treasure that could be had by someone smart enough to take it. But after Blondie saw Freddy's mangled body, he wasn't sure of what to do. To ease his mind he went to the church that had sheltered him on many a cold snowy night when he was a kid, but the doors had been locked because someone had stolen the Blessed Sacrament.

This ruined the trust he had that criminals would never do anything against a church. It dawned on him that there wasn't a trace of good in the type of people who steal and kill for a living. They were rotten through and through. He no longer wanted to be a part of the mistakenly glorified lifestyle, and revenge was a part of that. But he didn't want revenge. He wanted out. So, he had put the first leg of his and his dead friend Freddy's plan into action: He left for Buffalo and Doughnut's office.

Doughnut eased his heavy frame back, and the chair moaned. He threw another doughnut into his mouth, and played with a metal fingernail file.

Swill and Doughnut tried to project images of the square-jawed gangsters in the movies, but Blondie knew the Arm didn't operate like that. After spending a brutal childhood in the windy city of Chicago, he'd spent his teenage years in Youngstown, Ohio, known as Bomb town; a place regarded as mob territory, but the real vacationland was miles down the road in Hall's Corners. There, outside of the jurisdiction of the local police, what grew from a brothel during the hard times of the depression had grown into the safe haven known as the Jungle Inn Casino. It was the capital of thugs and racketeers, run by a group of men with names like Capouto, Dupty, Flannigan, and Farah, but actually this 'place to be' was operated from the shadows by Vincentio James (Blackie) Licavoli. Blackie was the unseen leader of the Ohio rackets along with former Buffalo kingpin Joe DiCarlo. They dominated the Youngstown scene for many years.

The Jungle Inn attracted mobsters from all over the country. And common working people, with a need for action, swarmed to the inn every night, ate dinner, played bingo, or gambled at the tables. The inn had second floor machine gun turrets above the bar and slot machines. Although closed down in

1949 it had planted the seeds of the thrill of gambling.

Right down the road, in Brookfield, notorious bank robber John Dillinger was a visitor to this community. Because of its easy access to whiskey and gambling during the 20's and early 30's it was known as 'Little Canada'. FBI Director J. Edgar Hoover said Dillinger was a cheap, boastful, selfish, tight-fisted, pug-ugly gangster, but local residents fondly remembered him as 'a regular fella' who dealt cards for chuck-a-luck at the Green Parrot Inn. Its four thousand square-foot casino was surrounded with walls lined with steel plating three-quarters of an inch thick. The steps that led upstairs to the club had a buzzer, and the doors were opened and closed electronically. Before patrons were let in, two big fellas with machine guns frisked them. Dillinger's boss, 'Legs' Diamond, was killed by the mob that was backing him in the club in the '49' district of Masury, named after the streetcar stop there.

Just a jaunt down the road, establishments like The Gray Wolf Tavern, Pete Myers's place, and The Clover Club, with its nearby green cement-block house of prostitution still operated without interference. In this area, instant-win gambling tickets with a black bulldog stamped on brown paper and a security string sewn down the side, were manufactured and sold to small-time operators. Moonshine runners, cops, mill workers, and gangsters drank and gambled, shoulder to shoulder in a relaxed atmosphere where everybody kept their mouths shut and never told a damn thing to the feds or some nosy bastards looking for a reputation.

On his way to visit Masury and the surrounding safe haven, John Dillinger would stop in the Pennsylvania town of Farrell and rob the old Gulley Bank. After he raced over the state line into Ohio, at a time when lawmen couldn't pursue a criminal across state lines, he would spend most of the money on gambling. Then on his way out, he would cross back into Pennsylvania, rob the Gulley Bank again, and be on his merry way.

Even though Blondie knew much about the workings of the Mafia, because he wasn't Italian, he could never be made, or take the oath to enter the honored society of Cosa Nostra, which stated that you come in alive and you go out dead; and that the gun and knife are the instruments by which you live and die. On top of that, the Cosa Nostra always came first, above everything else, including family, country, and even before God. When summoned, the members were required to come, even if their mother, wife, or children were on their death-beds. Violation of the oath meant death without trial or warning.

Swill and Doughnut were not even the lowest ranking of all the men in the Mafia that were called soldiers. They were only nonmembers working for a soldier. Soldiers avoided the word Mafioso and usually referred to another insider as a 'wise guy' or a 'made guy'. Being outsiders, Doughnut and his gang had no idea where Hubbard or Masury was. These places weren't as wide open to gambling as they had been when the Jungle Inn operated at Hall's Corners, but Blondie figured that moving to Hubbard or Masury would be better than staying in Buffalo or Chicago. If he could pull off this one last moneymaker, he would go find a little place in the area. Maybe even buy the little house where Al Capone used to hide out. In a peaceful neighborhood, he could live like a human being, maybe even stay in one place long enough to have a sprinkler going on the front lawn. Maybe even plant a little garden in the back yard and run a bug-number lottery on the side. He would no longer be a pathetic man with no power and no life. But to pull it off he needed these kids, especially the one that looked like dead Freddy. And Freddy had almost gotten away. To keep his plan in action, Blondie would have to do some smooth talking.

Bam! The outside door to the building slammed open.

Doughnut jumped up. "They're back."

Powdered-sugar doughnut crumbs sprayed from his mouth. Expecting Neal, Rafferty, and Freddy to walk through the door, Doughnut got ready to put on a front. He swept the empty glasses into the drawer and put the half-empty bottle of scotch in the bottom drawer. Then he slouched in his chair, balanced his feet on the desk, clipped off the end of one of his expensive cigars, and lit up.

But his displayed indifference didn't fool Blondie for an instant.

When the office door opened, Doughnut jerked upright. A brute with a canvas bank bag walked in. Doughnut stiffened and took the cigar from his mouth. A bug-eyed, acne-scarred man with sturdy straw hair and a hard mouth stood before him. The man peered through diabolical eyes that established dominance over the room. As if he were waiting for a reason — any reason — to pounce on someone, he

89

aggressively leaned forward. When he moved his shoulder, a great mass of muscle shifted under his suit coat. Here was a body of enormous strength. It wasn't bad enough that Mother Nature had played a cruel trick with the man's face, his nose looked as it had been split open in a knife fight and resembled a vagina.

"Sorry for the hold up, Nose," Doughnut stammered, and smiled a weak smile. "But we seemed to have had a little problem."

Nose gave Doughnut a heavy-lidded stare and held it. "You got a bigger problem than you think." His voice chilled the air. He growled and threw the bank bag on the desk. "You think you're some kind of a comedian?"

Doughnut wasn't used to being pushed. He started to call the man by his behind-the-back name; 'cunt-nose', but the cement tone of Nose's voice made him back off. He innocently swept his hand at him. "What are you saying?"

"This is the penny ante dope bag those kids were supposed to get."

Doughnut's usual atmosphere of whisky and fun diminished. He leaned over. Acting as if the answer were in there, he opened a desk drawer. "Damn! It is." He straightened up. "If the Mafioso finds out, we're in trouble."

Nose stepped toward him. "No shit."

"We'll get it back," Nose said and held up his hands. "Our rent-a-cops are on their trail as we speak."

Nose's face tensed. "That bag would've made us enough money to take it easy for a long time."

Doughnut held his scotch glass in his shaking hand and stiffened.

CHAPTER 7

The two rent-a-cops escorted Freddy, Neal, and Rafferty back into the hall of the red brick apartment building. Trying to make something happen so they could escape again, Rafferty held his nose and complained. "Let's go outside. This place smells like drunks and pee."

Freddy resisted the cop's pushing. One of the cops jabbed him in the back with his nightstick. "Keep moving."

Waving his arms in the air, Neal cut in front of Freddy and Rafferty. "Right, right, right, of course," he said, and they walked down the hall until the cops stopped them at the door to Doughnut's office and pushed them inside.

Standing in front of Doughnut's desk, Freddy glanced at Blondie. At first Blondie didn't acknowledge their presence. He leaned against the wall with his legs crossed at the ankles. Then, as a trace of a grin flickered on his face, he nodded to Doughnut. Doughnut placed his hands behind his head, leaned back and stared at Neal.

"I see you're back," he said, lifted both of his chubby hands, and pointed to the two cops. "Make sure they don't run again."

"They ain't goin' nowhere," one cop said and jingled Neal's car keys. "I got these."

The other cop held up Neal's bongo board and the round cylinder that went with it. "I found these things in the trunk."

Doughnut stared at the cylinder. "What's that for?"

The cop shrugged. "I don't know."

Doughnut motioned to the door. "Throw that junk over in the corner, go outside, and close the door."

The cop threw the bongo bard and the cylinder into the corner.

Neal bent over, scooped up the board, and held the cylinder on the floor with his foot. "Gentleman, don't break this thing."

With confused faces, the two cops went out the door and closed it behind them. With the cops gone, Swill cast an evil eye toward Neal. "Hey, go-fuck-myself?" He jerked his fist at the bongo board in Neal's hand. "I ought to break that thing over your head."

In an instant rage, Blondie whirled toward Swill. "Back off!"

Swill backed into the corner and hunched down. Like a wild animal waiting for the opportunity to kill, he waited.

Doughnut smiled once and continued. "Did you guys deliver the package?"

"Ah, ahem, ah, yes," Neal stammered. "Of course, we were going to do just that." He smiled a big innocent smile and held it. "Not being from around here, you see, we go lost. Then we had a little problem. We seemed to run out of gas."

"Yeah," Rafferty said, and looked at the closed office door. "We would've made your delivery, but those cops picked us up." Looking directly into Doughnut's face, he smiled an exaggerated smile.

Doughnut beamed a bigger smile than Rafferty's right back at him. "Wouldn't you guys like to be rich?"

93

Rafferty's smile faded and he dipped his head. "Who wouldn't?"

Slowly shaking his head, Freddy muttered, "We're not going to do anything to get our asses thrown in jail."

Doughnut gestured to the door. "My friends outside wouldn't take innocent boys to jail."

Freddy was waiting for Doughnut to ask what happened to the money and the canvas bank bag they had hid in the spare tire. He knew it was the only reason they were still alive. If Doughnut found out where the bag was, they wouldn't have anything to bargain with. He decided to play it by ear.

"From what I've seen," he said, "your friends will take us anywhere you tell them to."

"Come on, Freddy, old buddy," Blondie said. "There's no need to think like that. Your friends seem intelligent. Do we have to explain it to them?"

Doughnut leaned forward. "Freddy, didn't you tell them?"

Freddy still didn't know what Doughnut was talking about, and he still didn't know who the other Freddy was.

"Come on, Freddy," Doughnut said, lifting his hand up. "Let your buddies in on it. We'll give them the same deal everyone else gets."

"What deal?" Neal asked.

"If, by some very slight chance you get caught, and after you have done a little stretch of time and kept your mouths shut, you'll be on easy street."

Freddy didn't like what he was hearing. "Why do we have to go to jail? We didn't do anything."

Doughnut dismissively waved his hand down. "Nobody said you did."

Directing a penetrating glare at Freddy, Blondie reached inside his suit jacket.

Freddy tensed for the worse.

Instead of a gun, Blondie pulled out a little bottle and tapped four aspirins into the palm of his hand. Then, he dry-swallowed them all and leaned against the wall. "I know you guys aren't above taking something that isn't yours."

"Oh, no, we'd never do that," Neal protested.

"Are you sure about that?" Blondie said, and then, as if he were trying to read everyone's minds, his eyes swiveled from face to face. "What about that flag the bum in the alley saw you try to steal?"

"Ah, man." Neal moaned. "That was just a joke."

"That Ford you're driving is a joke," Blondie stated and stared at Neal.

Neal met Blondie's angry stare. "That Ford can outrun any piece of junk you guys got."

"I don't mean to put your little ride down," Blondie said, and relaxed his stare. "But if Freddy would have told you guys what he knows, you'd be driving something as nice as a '57 Chevy."

Neal and Rafferty cast a questioning look toward Freddy.

Freddy leaned back. "I don't know what you're talking about."

Blondie sighed and nodded. "If Freddy won't tell you, then maybe I should."

Freddy figured Blondie was pretending to be helpful so they would let their guards down and tell him where the bank bag was. But Freddy wasn't going to let him know he was on to him.

"Go ahead," he said. "I'd like to know, too."

95

Blondie uncrossed his legs and stepped away from the wall. "Look!" he shouted, and turned serious. "If you guys want to get big money, you have to be big enough to find things that little people would never think of finding."

Freddy heard the word 'find', but knew the word should have been 'steal'.

Neal was all ears. "Big money to find what?"

Excitement filled Blondie's voice. "Find something big, like America."

Neal tilted his head to the side. "What are you talking about?"

Doughnut gave Blondie a menacing look. "Yeah, tell him, mister know-it-all."

For a moment, Blondie wavered, but recovered. "You think the Indians gave America to anyone? A couple of guys organized and got it the good old American way. They stole it and then said they discovered it."

"That's not really what happened," Freddy said, and Doughnut let out a big horselaugh.

Pounding his fist on the desk Doughnut pointed at Blondie. "This guy's school learnin's killin' me." Waving his hand in a circle, he encouraged Blondie to continue.

"No, that's really what happened," Blondie said. "And to top it off, they got some lady to sew them a flag. Now everybody thinks they were heroes."

Doughnut let out an exaggerated laugh. As if they were trying to be polite, Neal and Rafferty laughed with Doughnut. When Doughnut saw them laughing, his face turned stone serious.

"I'm Mafioso," he snapped. "You boys think you can laugh at me?"

96

Freddy knew Doughnut had done this on purpose to show his absolute control; and even though it was an act, hostile tension flared up and filled the room. From a crouching position, Swill cleared his throat. He sounded like a croaking bullfrog sitting on a lily pad about to snatch an innocent fly and end its life.

Rafferty covered his mouth.

Neal cut his laughter short. "Ah, ahem, ah, yes, I mean, no." He paused. "No, of course not. We're not laughing at you."

Doughnut leaned forward. His enormous weight caused the chair to tip toward the desk so fast that he had to slam his feet on the floor to keep from slipping out of the chair.

Squinting at Blondie, he balled up his fist and clinched it solid. "Blondie, I've had enough of your schoolboy stories. Let's cut the crap." He jerked his finger to Neal. "What did you boys do with the bank bag you were supposed to deliver?"

Neal lifted his arms in a puzzled gesture. "The last time we saw it, it was right next to the envelope of money sitting on the front seat of the Ford."

"If that's true, then why didn't you bring it with you?"

Referring to the cops, Neal jerked his head back. "Your friends behind the door wouldn't let us."

"That's right," Freddy added. "No one can trust a cop. Maybe they took it for themselves."

Rafferty stepped forward. "What was in that bag anyway?"

As if he were looking for an answer on whether to believe Neal, Doughnut studied Blondie's face. In a sudden silence, somewhere outside the door, that faint sound of dripping water plinked onto a metal surface, again.

Blondie broke the silence. "A lot of things could have happened, ya know, but we know, and you know those things didn't happen." He paused for effect. "Now did it?" He looked directly at Neal.

Neal didn't stutter or go through his usual routine of searching for the right words to sooth the situation. He came right out and said it. "We don't know what happened to your fucking bag."

"That's right," Rafferty added. "Ask one of your phony cops what they did with it. They probably got our money, too."

In one motion, Swill sprang up from his crouching position in the corner. "Our cops don't steal from Mafioso!"

Red faced, Swill reached up on the shelf, and grabbed the sawed-off shotgun. Freddy looked to Neal for a sign. Neal barely nodded, but he had that look in his eye. Freddy didn't know what Neal was going to do, but he knew he was ready to do something.

With his bongo board in his hand, Neal reached up and swept the shoebox full of money off the shelf. Green bills flew into the air and came down on Swill like a green blizzard.

With money swirling around his head, Swill waved the Sawed-off shotgun wildly, but didn't fire.

Neal jumped up on the desk and whapped Doughnut in the chest with the bongo board. Doughnut went flying backward. His feet flew up. Oomph! He landed on his chair. The chair broke under his weight. Thud! The back of his head hit the floor. Freddy bent his knees, grabbed the wooden cylinder of the bongo board, wound up and flung it at Swill. It hit the shotgun and knocked it from his hands. As if he'd had a running start, Rafferty dove and barely missed hitting his head on the corner of the desk. His foot managed to get traction and propel him forward. He landed with his hand on the shotgun; and with all the finesse of a flat tire, he thumped into the wall. The shotgun fell from his hand.

Blondie deftly swooped it up and pumped a shell into the chamber. The office door sprang open. Two cops stood with pistols drawn. A deathly silence cloaked the room. Standing with his back against the wall, Blondie waved the shotgun around. "Okay! The show's over!"

With pieces of splintered wood from the broken chair around him, Doughnut lay on the floor. Rubbing his head with his balloon stomach facing the ceiling, he looked like a turtle stuck on its back. With much effort, he managed to struggle to his side. Reaching up for the edge of the desk, he inched himself to his feet. Seeing that Blondie and the cops had the situation under control, he grunted and nodded with approval. Then he glared at Freddy.

"Freddy, I don't care what you and these little bastards did with that goddamn bag," he spat out. "You're all going to pay."

Swill smiled. Without warning, Whap! He backhanded Neal.

With his face flushed with rage, Neal lifted the bongo board to strike back, but Freddy nudged him on the shoulder and pointed to the shotgun in Blondie's hands. Neal let the bongo board fall to the floor. Swill grinned and wound up for another strike.

Neal tensed for the blow, but Swill only laughed, opened his clinched fist, and dropped his hand.

Doughnut jerked his thumb toward the two cops at the door. "Take these assholes to the back room. Maybe a few days in the shit hole will refresh their memories."

Freddy saw it first: an opening between the two cops. It was just big enough to dash through, and the doorway would stop any pellets coming from the shotgun. Swill probably had another gun, but it was probably some cheap junk only good for close-in work; and they wouldn't shoot to kill any of them until they knew where the all-important bank bag was. Freddy figured that if he could get outside, he could hide in the darkness and come back in the daytime when these assholes were asleep.

With Neal and Rafferty blocking Blondie's view, Freddy leaped between the two cops. To his surprise there was no resistance. The end of the hall and the door to the concealing darkness of outside was just a sprint away. Like a runner taking off after the starting gun had been fired, he burst toward freedom.

He didn't know where it came from, but the handle of a gun appeared right in front of his face. He tried to swerve out of its way. Thump! The gun barrel collided on the side of his skull. A bright beautiful star, like the center light of a fabulous firework, brightened his mind. As it sparkled away through the fog, he caught a glimpse of the dirty tile floor coming up to meet his forehead. Then it was dark.

CHAPTER 8

As if it were far away, the sound of dripping water plinking onto a metal surface awoke Freddy. Then a heavy, musty stench of mold welled up to greet him. He opened his eyes. Neal and Rafferty were looking at him.

"It's about time," Neal said and smiled. "We thought you were never going to come to."

With his head throbbing, Freddy felt the side of his skull. A lump the shape of a gun barrel had formed. In the dim light he looked up. Like an ominous cloud, a dirty-gray ceiling hovered over his head. At random locations, spiders had spun their entrapment webs in hope of victims. One web wrapped around a rusty bolt that protruded from the ceiling. Old cement blocks that looked to be twelve inches thick formed the walls. Skinny beams of light streamed in from a crack in a boarded-up window. In front of the boards, iron bars, half an inch thick, blocked escape. The only exit was a metal door. Rust had attacked the lower portion, but the steel was so thick that it would take years for the rust to weaken it.

Freddy turned to Neal. "Is that door locked?"

"Oh, why yes," Neal said, in a sarcastic tone. "No need to be afraid of burglars. Doughnut and his friends locked it right after they threw us in here."

Rafferty whapped the door with his hand. "I heard a big metal bar clank down right after it slammed shut."

"How long have we been in here?"

101

Squinting one eye, Rafferty looked to where the plinking sound was coming from. "Long enough to go nuts from whatever's dripping."

Neal rubbed his ears. "It's just loud enough to agitate you. But time moves like a snail when we're cooped up, and we can't see daylight. So, I really don't actually know how long we've been in here."

"This place smells like mold. Are they going to let us out?"

Rafferty stared at the dirt floor. "They said we're gonna stay here until we tell them what we did with that bank bag.

"That's nice," Freddy said. "If we tell them where the bank bag is, then they have no reason to keep us alive. If we don't tell them, we stay in here and rot."

Wondering what to do, Freddy looked to Neal. As if he were crying, Neal sat on the dirt floor with his knees almost touching his chin. His usual energy seemed to have been drained. Freddy didn't think Neal had a plan to escape, but he asked anyway. "How are we going to get out of here?"

Neal put his hands on his knees and rose. Then he waved his hands in the air. "We've been in here long enough to lose the bet at the Burp, but so what? We've been in worse situations than this." He pointed to his head. "We're just gonna have to think our way out."

As they sat on the dirt floor thinking, the irritating 'plink!' of water disturbed the silence. Outside, the sound of the wind shrilled through a crack in the hinged side of the door. A rubber seal shuddered and caused occasional shards of sunlight to flit onto Neal's hand, but the skinny beams of light no longer streamed in from the crack in a barred window.

Rafferty kicked at the bottom of the door. "Maybe we could get this thing open."

Neal held up his thumb and pulled his hand back. "If we could pry it open, that would be one way out." He started ticking off choices on his fingers. "The window has bars, but they're not that thick. Maybe we could bend them." He ticked another finger and turned his foot sideways. He rubbed the edge of his shoe along the dirt floor. "We could tunnel our way out, but we don't have anything to dig with."

Rafferty pawed at the floor with the toe of his shoe. "In the movies, guys in prison dig their way out with a teaspoon."

"Yeah, they do," Neal said. "But it takes years. And we don't have a teaspoon."

Freddy studied the bars on the window. "Maybe if we all pulled, we could bend those bars."

Neal nodded with hope. "If they're not made out of alloy steel, we might be able to do it."

Freddy got up off the floor. His head hurt but subsided. He stepped to the bars, grasped the bar in the center, and pulled. The bar didn't even budge.

Neal got up and grabbed on. "Let's both try."

They both pulled. The bar stayed solid.

Still holding onto the bar, Neal looked over his shoulder. "Okay, Rafferty get up here and show us how strong you are."

Rafferty squeezed between Neal and Freddy, and together they pulled. The bar stayed solid.

Neal backed off and brushed his hands together. "Okay, that was just a warm up. This time on three, we'll all pull at once.

They all re-gripped the bar. "Okay," Neal huffed. "One, two, three."

They all pulled. Grunting with all their might, their feet lost traction in the dirt floor, and the bar stayed still.

Neal let out a disgusted huff. "There has to be a better way." As if he sensed something on the other side, he looked at the door. The steel bar outside clanked up. The door opened. Unaccustomed to the bright light, Freddy squinted. Doughnut and Swill stepped into the doorway. Blinding sunlight bathed their bodies in white light and outlined them into dark silhouettes. Blondie and another man, who had a weird split nose, blocked the light. The man with the weird nose carried in a wooden chair and set it in the center of the room.

Doughnut smiled at Rafferty and gestured toward the man with the weird nose. "Here's someone I'd like you to meet. All his friends call him Nose."

Trying not to look at the man's ugly nose, Rafferty extended his hand in friendship. "It's a great pleasure to meet you, Mister Nose. I'm grateful for the opportunity to thank you in person for giving us the job of delivering the bank bag,"

"Yes," Neal added, catching on to Rafferty's attempted phony friendliness. "We're sorry we couldn't deliver it like we wanted to."

Nose glared at Rafferty. "Don't feed me that shit." He put his hand on Rafferty's shoulder and pushed. "Have a seat, young fellow."

Rafferty shrugged Nose's hand from his shoulder, bowed at the waist, and sat down. "Why, thank you." He put his hands behind his head, leaned the chair back on two legs, and smiled his ear-to-ear smile.

Nose grabbed him by the front of his shirt and pulled. The front chair legs smacked down onto the dirt floor and Rafferty's smile vanished. Nose let loose of his shirt and shouted directly into his face. "You laughing at me?"

Rafferty stood up. "I'm not laughing at anybody. I always smile."

"That's right," Neal said, coming to his defense. "His nickname's Smiley."

Nose jerked his finger toward the chair. "I don't care what they call you. Sit your ass back down."

Rafferty stared at Nose's battle-scarred face. "That's okay. I can stand."

A crazed look filled Nose's face. "Get the fuck in that chair."

Rafferty bent to sit, but before his butt touched the seat, Swill stepped out of the light and pushed Rafferty down into the chair. Doughnut jerked his head toward Nose. Nose threw a coil of rope. It sailed toward Doughnut's hands. Doughnut caught it and faced Freddy and Neal.

"Okay, fellows," he said, "your friend's in the hot seat. Either he is going to tell us what you did with that bank bag or one of you are."

Shrugging, Neal shook his head. "Like I told you before, we left it in the Ford and your stupid cops got it. And they got our money, too."

Freddy figured Neal knew if Doughnut let them into the Ford to search for the bag, he could distract

105

them while Neal started the engine. The Ford could outrun any police car they sent after them, and they would be gone before these un-mechanically inclined assholes knew what was going on.

"Yeah," he said. "Why don't you just let us go out and see if it's in the car?"

Blondie shouted from the doorway. "We looked! It's not there."

Doughnut jerked his finger toward himself. Blondie threw him a suit coat. It flew into the air and landed on the floor. Freddy bent over and reached out to pick it up. Swill grunted. As if he had been shocked, Freddy jerked his hand back and stood upright.

"Don't be afraid of it," Swill said and pushed Freddy toward the suit coat. "Your friend looks cold. Pick it up and put it on him."

Freddy snagged the coat off the dirt floor and draped it around Rafferty's shoulders.

Doughnut stood in front of Rafferty and grabbed the suit coat by the lapels. Smoothing out the shoulders, he smiled. "Now all your friend needs is a necktie." He uncoiled the rope and put the center of it around Rafferty's neck. Then the tied it in a single knot. "Okay gentleman, here's where we find out what you did with that bank bag."

Neal grabbed the end of the rope and held it toward Doughnut. "Here, take this thing off. Like I said, we don't have the bag."

Nose reached under his arm for his gun. With his other hand, he jerked the rope out of Neal's hand. Neal backed off. With Nose keeping Neal and Freddy at bay, Swill grabbed one end of the rope and Doughnut grabbed the other end. Together they pulled. The rope tightened around Rafferty's neck. He gurgled and choked. His hands flew up and tugged at the knot. Doughnut and Swill pulled harder. Rafferty's face turned an unhealthy purple, and his eyes bulged. Keeping one hand on the rope around his neck, he reached out for help.

Freddy reached for Rafferty's outstretched arm and pleaded, "Don't kill him, please."

An annoyed growl rumbled from deep in Doughnut's chest. "Take that hand down," he told Rafferty. "Or we'll really tighten it."

As if he had succumbed to the fact that he was going to die, Rafferty lowered his hand from his throat.

"Cut it out," Freddy begged. "He doesn't know where the bag is."

"Yeah," Neal added. "Why kill an innocent man?"

"Oh," Doughnut said and his eyes went wide and his eyebrows lifted. "Are *you* going to tell us where the bag is?"

The rope slackened. Freddy hoped that they weren't going to strangle Rafferty, and that they were trying to make Neal feel ashamed for letting their friend suffer so they would tell them where the bank bag was. Fighting back tears of fear, Rafferty pried the rope loose from his neck and gasp for breath. He tried to talk, but only gurgling came out.

"You bastards," Neal said with a rage-filled face. "You broke his throat."

"Well, if he can't talk," Doughnut said, and pointed to Neal, "you'll have to talk for him."

Fighting a growing rage, Neal jerked his hands up and down. "We don't know where the bag is." He jerked his clinched fists. "We just don't know."

To get everyone's attention, Blondie cleared his throat. "Maybe if we let the boys think about it for a while, the next time we come in, they'll remember."

Doughnut smiled and dropped his end of the rope. Swill grinned fiendishly. Then he gave the rope one violent jerk. Rafferty flew off the chair, landed on the dirt floor, and lay there with his eyes tightly shut. Fighting back the pain, he curled into a fetal ball. Swill dropped his end of the rope and let out a drunken laugh.

Doughnut turned friendly. "You boys look a little peaked. Would you like something to eat?"

"Ah, um, ahem, why yes," Neal muttered. "We were going to request a few morsels. Not that we're hungry, you see. Not to be rude, you know. Just to be polite, we'd like to accept your hospitality."

"It would be a great party," Doughnut said, and motioned to Nose. Nose handed Doughnut a bag of powered doughnuts, stepped back into the doorway, and was gone. Doughnut took a doughnut from the bag and threw it into his mouth. "And we'd like to throw a party for you," he said, with white powder puffing from his mouth. "But first, we'll have to know what you did with that bank bag."

As if he were a great chef, Swill put his fingers to his lips, kissed them, and jerked them away from his face. "Tell us where that bank bag is. We'll bring you a banquet."

While Freddy and Neal watched in hunger, Doughnut jammed doughnuts, one by one, into his mouth until the bag was empty. With white powdered sugar around his mouth, he looked to Neal and smiled. "Want a doughnut?"

Neal didn't answer.

Doughnut threw the empty bag on the floor, mashed it with the heel of his shoe, ground it into the dirt, and laughed. Shooing Swill and Blondie out the door, he said, "We'll leave the chair and rope here. It might refresh your memories."

The door clunked shut and the steel bar clanged into place. They were locked in, again.

In the silence, the plinking grew louder. Freddy and Neal took the rope out from around Rafferty's neck and sat him on the chair. Rafferty shook his head. "Damn, are you guys trying to take those grumpy pricks' place, and start pulling the rope?"

Rafferty had just about been strangled to death and he was making wise cracks again. Freddy smiled. "I don't think so. But when they come back, I think they'll put me or Neal in the chair."

As if he could feel the rope already, Neal rubbed his neck and looked at Freddy's suit coat. "I'm the only one left that doesn't have a suit coat. We better find a way out of here before they give me one."

Rubbing his red chafed neck, Rafferty nodded. "I never did like wearing a tie. But one good thing: when they pulled that rope, I couldn't hear that damn plinking."

Freddy grabbed the end of the chair. "Okay, Rafferty, get off."

"I just sat down."

"Come on, you guys," Freddy said and picked up the chair. "Maybe this thing can bend those bars."

Neal jumped to the window. "Put it here," he said, and guided the chair leg between the bars. They all pulled. The bar began to bend. Then, crack! The chair leg broke.

"Damn," Neal said. In anguish, he turned away from the window.

Rafferty forced a grin. As if he had just broken his favorite toy, he sat on the dirt floor with a fake pouting expression. "Now we don't have anything to sit on."

Freddy looked at the rope. "Maybe we could build a swing and sit on it."

Holding the broken chair leg, Neal looked at the bottom of the steel door. The dirt floor ran right to it. "Let's use this broken leg and dig under the door."

The broken chair leg was bigger than a teaspoon. Freddy lit up with excitement. "Okay. We'll take turns."

Neal took the broken leg and scraped it across the bottom of the door. A few inches of dirt moved. He cleared it away with his fingers. "There's a cement pad right under this thing." He stopped digging and sat on the dirt floor. Studying the chair leg in his hands, he leaned back against the wall.

Rafferty stared at the door. "What do we do now?"

Leaning back, Neal hooked his thumbs in the side of his pants pockets. "Those guys are too dumb to be real gangsters. It should be easy to outsmart them and get out of here."

Wondering what he could do with them, Freddy studied the chair leg and the rope.

Rubbing his neck, Rafferty said, "That rope really put some torque on my neck and they hardly pulled."

"Yeah," Neal said. "Too bad we don't have a mule or a four-wheel drive jeep. We could pull those bars right out of the wall."

Freddy looked up at the lone spider-webbed bolt hanging down from the cement ceiling. It was rusted, but thick.

"If we had a pulley system," he said, we could leverage those bars out with that rope."

Neal stood up and looked at the bolt. Then he looked at the bars in the window, then back at the bolt. Turning the chair leg as if he were trying to gather a windblown thought, he moved his head from side to side. Then, singing his up-beat tune, he tapped his foot. "Dit-a, dit-a, plonk-oh! Dit-a, plonk oh!" He held up one finger, smiled, and rubbed his chin. "During the war, my uncle used to pull jeeps out of ditches."

Rafferty ran his fingers through his hair and stared at the bars. "Well, plonk-oh! The next time we get close to a phone, give your uncle a call."

Neal stared down at Rafferty. "Don't you get it? Dit-a, dit-a, plonk-oh! He used a rope to pull the jeeps out."

From his sitting position, Rafferty looked up. "How many guys did he use?"

"Two or three." Neal picked up one end of the rope and looped it around the bars. "It's just like winding up a model airplane."

Freddy knew that when a model airplane used a rubber band and the propeller was twisted, the rubber band stored enough energy so that when the

111

propeller was let loose the plane would fly. If they looped the rope around the bars and the thick bolt in the ceiling and put the chair leg in between the rope and twisted, it might create enough torque to bend the bar.

He jumped up. "That might work."

He took the other end of the rope, batted the spider webs away, and wrapped the center of rope around the bolt in the cement ceiling. Holding the rope taut, Neal tied the two ends of the rope together. Rafferty placed the chair leg in-between the rope.

Neal started to twist the rope with the chair leg, but stopped. "Wait a minute," he said. "This leg wasn't strong enough to bend those bars. It'll probably break if we get too much torque on it."

Freddy gestured to the broken chair. "So, we'll use the three legs that are not broken."

Rafferty broke off the other three legs, and they put all three legs in-between the rope.

Neal grabbed onto the legs. "Once we get it started, we can't stop. If one of us lets go, these legs will knock our blocks off."

Rafferty and Freddy nodded that they understood, and they began twisting the rope. Four twists and the rope fell off the bolt.

"Wait," Freddy said, and picked up the back of the broken chair. "Rafferty, put the rope back on."

Rafferty did, and Freddy held the rope in place with the back of the chair. "Okay, you guys keep twisting. He pushed the rope tighter against the bolt. "When it gets tight enough so it won't fall off, I'll jump in and help twist."

They twisted and twisted. The bar would not bend. They twisted some more. The rope was at its breaking point. Their feet slipped and slid on the dirt floor.

"Damn," Neal huffed. "That's only one bar. It should've bent by now."

"Must be alloy," Freddy huffed back, and pulled on the chair legs.

Neal put his shoulder under the chair legs and pushed upward. The bar did not bend, not even a fraction of an inch. Freddy and Rafferty maneuvered part of their shoulders under the opposite side of the chair legs and pushed. The bar stood still. Neal reached over and pulled one time on the chair legs.

Whoosh! The whole frame of the bars pulled out and thumped onto the floor. As years of gray dust billowed around the windowless hole in the wall, somewhere in the distance, a lone dog barked once. They covered their faces with the tops of their T-shirts and waited for the dust to settle. All was silent except for the plinking. Neal brushed the dust from the front of his T-shirt and looked toward the bar-less window. With a big smile on his face, he swayed his hips as if he were on his bongo board.

"Dit-a, dit-a, plonk-oh!" he said. "It's time to go home."

CHAPTER 9

After Blondie left the room where Freddy and his friends were locked in, he walked through an alley strewn with wind-blown newspapers and trash. A few blocks down the street, he short-changed a gray-haired Chinese street vendor for a hot dog and didn't feel guilty.

Walking back to the apartment building and eating the dog, he thought about the story of the man who had cheated a lot of kids by hanging onto the end of the hotdog with his little finger. When the kid pulled the empty bun off of the hotdog, the guy dropped the hotdog back into the pot and told the kid that he must've dropped the hotdog somewhere. Blondie didn't know if the story was true, but he didn't trust anyone. If that story was only half true, that guy must have sold that same hotdog four or five times.

Preying on the innocence of hungry children was a cruel thing to do. And it was even crueler for Swill and Doughnut to pull an Italian rope trick on the locked up kids. For a weak moment Blondie considered that they might be just children, but then again they were too old. They were young adults. And in this world there was no such thing as an honest adult. He didn't like it, but the next kid to get the rope trick would be Neal. If he didn't talk and got the suspended sentence, Freddy would be next. More and more, Freddy reminded Blondie of his dead friend. And he didn't know if he could stand by and let Doughnut and Swill strangle Freddy. But that bank bag had the key and a coded message that could be worth millions.

At first Blondie had speculated about how great life would be if he could pull off this one last caper. But now bothersome things were wearing him down. He was tired of the gun-toting half-wits of the mob, and he was tired of always looking over his shoulder. Cemeteries were full of people who followed the mob's every wish and went from one hell to another. He wasn't ready for another fresh hell.

With a cold wind scuttling papers along the gutters, he stopped at the apartment building. From the outside, it looked like other turn-of-the-century buildings. Its crumbling, red brick walls climbed pitifully toward the dirty sky. Thinly tarred-roofs allowed cold rain to crawl down into the interior like weary tears that no one cared about. It was just another slum in the dead end of the city. Inside, it was rundown just like the outside. Odor from urine in corners and down the stairwells hovered in every room. Brown tiles that remained on the floors were loose, or bubbled up from overrun toilets. Walls, thick with dirt and grime embraced the dirty-clothes odor of poverty.

The building reminded him of his early life and caused him to be envious of Doughnut's easy childhood. Doughnut never had to survive in the streets. He'd never had to fight to have a moldy crust of bread to eat. Doughnut's lavish childhood had managed to produce a half-witted leech, who didn't know the real streets of any city from his fat ass.

Blondie had never had a chance to be a child. Although it hadn't bothered him at the time, he had looked like a grotesque creature that had escaped

115

from a mental institution. After his mother died, he tried to keep the damp of the night off his body by sleeping on benches under the cover of trees. In winter, although he wrapped himself in rags, he coughed and shivered through long nights of semi-sleep. As an eleven-year-old man, scabs haphazardly covered his filthy body. Fever blisters made his nose and lips swell and made his face look like he was the beginning of a new Elephant Man.

Before he had met Freddy, the only man who had come close to being a father was a stranger who would leave change under a loose brick in the bottom step of a rundown apartment building. Regular bullies of the street were much stronger than he was, but he took pride in controlling situations by outsmarting them.

Freddy had always said, "Why use your body when a few well-placed words will do the job."

A cold breeze spun around a corner and swished down Blondie's back. It renewed old feelings of his cold hungry days in Chicago, and it chilled his entire body. He shook off the feeling, immediately regained his tough edge, and walked into the building.

In his office, Doughnut was sitting in a bigger chair than the one he had broken. Rolling a fat yellow candle in his chubby fingers, he leaned back and talked toward the ceiling. "You know, delivering that little bank bag would have been the easiest money we ever made."

"Yeah," Swill said. "And it still will be. All we got to do is get those kids to tell us what they did with the goddamn thing."

"I think Freddy would have told us if he knew," Blondie said. "Maybe one of your great rent-a-cop friends took it."

Doughnut leaned forward and raised an eyebrow. "I don't think so. Those lazy cops have a good life. They wouldn't want their weekly paydays to stop."

"I think you right," Blondie said with a slight bow of his head. "If they got that bag and tried to sell it to the wrong people, they wouldn't need weekly paydays in the cemetery."

Swill pursed his lips in a businesslike manner. "If the Detroit Purple Gang had anything to do with it, there's a bomb in the damn bag."

Doughnut waved Swill off. "I don't know what was in it. But I'm pretty sure there wasn't any dope in it. And even if there is, those dumb cops don't have the connections to sell it to our fence." He shifted in his chair and grunted. "Even if Freddy doesn't know where the bag is, I think those other two kids hid it somewhere." He looked toward the door. "You sure you checked out that Ford?"

"Checked every inch," Swill said. "The cops helped, too. We couldn't find a damn thing."

"Did you check under the floorboards and under the dash?"

"Yeah, we did," Swill said and belched out a sickening huff of beer breath. "We even checked between the fenders. Hell, we even cut into the seats."

Blondie looked at Doughnut. "How long you gonna let those kids sweat out another rope trick?"

"Relax," Doughnut said. "Swill knows what to do."

Swill held out his arm. "We weren't doing it right. A few broken ribs, cigarette burns, and a couple of knees in the balls will cause enough pain to make those kids talk."

Blondie pulled a wooden chair away from the wall, leaned on it, and looked down. "I don't know," he said, without looking up. "These guys didn't break when we almost strangled their buddy. They seem pretty tight. They might just give up and die."

Doughnut breathed in. His stomach ballooned out. Then he let out a disgusted breath. "Let them starve for a while." His eyes lit up. "Or better yet, maybe we'll give them a late night visit. A rope trick in the dark ought to scare them into telling where they put that bank bag."

Blondie sat on the chair and folded his hands behind his head. "I don't know about that, but we better find out pretty quick. The fix at the fire department is only working tomorrow. Then he's going on vacation with the money we paid him to say the fire was electrical."

Doughnut waved his hand in the air. "If he's not there, what's the difference?"

Blondie leaned back on his chair and balanced on its two back legs. "That gas and kerosene is hard to disguise. That other fire marshal is as straight as they come. If he says it's arson, we won't get a dime."

Doughnut jumped up and yelled in Blondie's face, "We already fucked up one deal." He clutched Blondie's forearm and pulled.

Blondie's chair slammed down on the front legs. He grimaced with pain and surprise.

118

Intentionally inflicting pain, Doughnut viciously squeezed Blondie's arm. "I don't want to do it again."

Blondie wanted to grab Doughnut by the throat and jerk his fat ass to the floor. But Doughnut was self-destructive. Someday this loser would bring punishment down upon himself, and it would be much worse than anything Blondie could do to him. That and the thought of what the bank bag would bring kept his temper in check. He gritted his teeth, and stared right into Doughnut's bloodshot eyes. "What if those kids never tell?"

Maintaining pressure on Blondie's forearm, Doughnut sneered. "Those kids are lying. Liars make me edgy."

Blondie reached for the sky. He wanted to make a fist and bring it down on the bridge of Doughnut's nose. Doughnut looked up at his hand. Swill reached up for the shotgun. He looked anxious to use it. Fighting back a rising anger, Blondie yawned as if he were stretching and didn't feel the pain Doughnut was inflicting in his arm. For a tense moment he stared at Doughnut and didn't give an inch.

Doughnut released his grip, and his lips twisted into an enlightened smile. "Hell, Blondie, if they don't tell, we'll cancel their suspended sentences with the rope and just let them burn."

Blondie was in too much pain to speak, but he nodded, leaned back into the chair, and balanced on the rear legs, again.

"Yeah," Swill said, and took his hand off the shotgun. "With those suit coats, two of them are already dressed to kill."

Doughnut reached into the top drawer of his desk, took out a candle, and place it on his desk. "Next time we visit the boys we'll give that other kid a suit coat, too. We wouldn't want him to feel left out."

A faint thump echoed through the walls, followed by a single bark of a dog. Swill jerked his head toward the sound. "What was that?"

Blondie wanted to say, "It's probably that single marble rolling around in your head," but he didn't.

Doughnut reached in the drawer for the bottle of scotch. "It's that dog chasing that cat again."

Like a man on a desert dying for a drink, Swill watched the bottle of scotch. "Yeah," he said. "That dog's a mean little bastard."

Doughnut pulled out three dirty glasses and poured generous portions in each. Swill scooped his glass up and drank it down.

Blondie picked up his glass and took a small sip. "How's that candle work?"

"Easy," Doughnut said. "Let me show you."

CHAPTER 10

Imprisoned in the room, Freddy, Rafferty, and Neal watched the window opening where the bars had been pulled out and waited for the dust to settle. Instead of a bright beam of sunlight bursting through the new opening, a hazy light crept in and flung shadows into gray corners.

"Where's the sun?" Freddy asked, and musty air floated into their faces.

Neal looked down. "There's still light coming under the door."

Rafferty looked at the bottom of the door. As if it were moonlight, shadowy blue light crept beneath it. He opened his hand and gestured toward the light. "Is it getting dark already?"

Neal pointed to the window opening. "Let's go through that window, and find out."

One by one they pulled themselves over the bottom of the window opening and swung their feet down until they touched a concrete floor.

Standing up and looking around, Neal grabbed his nose and shook his head. "We're not out," he whined. "We're in another stinking room."

Freddy breathed shallow and searched his mind. "What's that smell?"

"I'm not sure," Neal said, and sniffed. "That mold smell got my nose all messed up."

The sound of plinking water grew.

Rafferty shrugged and looked toward the sound. "At least we can find out where that mind-peckin' dripping's coming from."

Freddy took a few steps and stopped. Behind cobwebs dangling from the ceiling, another steel door was right in front of him. "We might have to go back and get that rope and the chair legs."

"Ah, um, ahem, ah, of course," Neal said. "But wouldn't it be easier if we checked to see if the door's locked?"

Rafferty whisked the cobwebs away, grabbed the door handle, and pulled. It opened a crack. He looked into Freddy's face and joked good-naturedly. "Dumb ass."

"Open the damn thing," Neal said. "I want to get out of this stinking place."

Rafferty peeked through the crack, smiled, and pulled the door. Creaking on its hinges, it opened wide. From out of a narrow hallway, draped in murky shadow, a familiar but unrecognizable odor blasted into their faces.

Rafferty wrinkled his nose and waved his hand in front of his face. "What' that smell?"

Neal pushed him aside. "Let's go find out."

Rafferty and Freddy followed Neal through the door and into a narrow hallway. Up above their heads in the rafters, what looked and sounded like water plinking, something dripped onto a metal plate. With each plink it splashed onto the rafters and up onto the bottom of the wooden flooring, slowly saturating each board.

Neal snapped his fingers. "That's kerosene."

Freddy pointed to a whisky bottle. "Look."

The bottle was tied between the rafters with a rusty wire that held it at an angle that allowed kerosene to slowly drip from a small hole in the cap and onto the metal plate. "They must move that thing every few hours. It's almost empty. But they

122

got most of the wood floor saturated with kerosene."

Neal looked a few yards in front of him. A set of steps led to a closed door. A red five-gallon gas can sat next to the first step. Stacked next to it was a pile of rags. Right above the pile, the door of an electrical fuse box hung open.

Neal went to the gas can and lifted it. It was full. "I'll bet this is our gas they siphoned out of the Ford."

Freddy looked at the rags. "This looks like a good place to start a fire."

The plinking stopped.

As if he had a headache and it just quit aching, Rafferty rubbed his forehead. "It's about time that thing quit." He walked down the hallway, stopped, and leaned against the wall. Neal looked his way. Rafferty put his finger to his lips and waved for them to come. Neal and Freddy tiptoed to him. Pointing to the wall, Rafferty cupped his hand against his ear and whispered, "Listen."

Freddy and Neal cupped their hands to their ears, held them against the wall, and listened. On the other side of the wall, Doughnut was talking.

"Now you take this candle," he said. "It's like a timer. The longer you want to take for the fire to start, the longer you let the candle burn."

"How's one candle gonna burn down this whole place?" Swill asked.

"It isn't," Doughnut said. "That gas you guys have been taking is right under the fuse box. We just stick a wick in the bottom of the candle and when it burns down to it, it lights the fuse." His

123

voice grew with excitement. "Then, the whole pile of rags goes up and then the kerosene takes over."

With great expectation in his voice, Swill asked, "How soon will we get the money?"

Something clinked on the glass ashtray on Doughnut's desk. He grunted. "It'll take us a few weeks to collect the insurance money."

"Speaking about money," Blondie said. "When are we going to visit those kids again?"

"After it gets dark," Doughnut said, with a superior air. "Make sure you got a suit coat for that other kid."

The metallic sound of a shell being chambered into a pistol cracked. Swill laughed with cruel delight. "That ass hole that told me to go fuck myself will be the next one we invite to our little necktie party."

"There was a lot of money in that envelope," Blondie said. "And it's a lot to lose. If they don't talk, are you sure you still want to let them burn?"

"If they don't talk," Doughnut said, with a spasm of amusement. "Mister go fuck yourself will be dead. And if we let them all burn, it'll save us some cleanup work."

Swill let out a weird giggle. "If things get tough we could get the fire jerk to say that those dumb ass kids started the fire."

The ashtray clinked again. "We'll set the candle to start the fire around five in the morning," Doughnut said. "Most of the firemen are sleeping then."

Blondie said, "Where are we going to be when the fire starts?"

Doughnut grunted with anticipation. "The first batch of doughnuts comes out of the oven at five." His voice rose with mischief. "We'll be at the doughnut shop with all our rent-a-cop friends."

Neal leaned away from the wall, turned, and motioned for Freddy and Rafferty to follow. When they got back to the window opening, he looked at it with a determined air. "We have to get out of here before I get a new necktie."

Rafferty turned toward him in tortured wonder. "How?"

"That's a good question," Freddy said. "If we wait until they light the candle, it may be too late."

"Neal looked to be in deep though. "If we do get out, they might catch us again. We need something to keep them and their rent-a-cops busy long enough so we can put some miles between them and us."

As if he were lighting a Zippo lighter, Rafferty made a fist and flicked his thumb up. "A good fire would keep them busy."

"Very funny," Freddy said, and then something occurred to him. He looked at Neal. "Are you thinking what I'm thinking?"

"Sure, we start the fire early and burn to death."

Freddy smiled. "Not really. We start the fire early, but they won't be expecting the fire to start early. We'll have a good chance to escape in the commotion."

Neal's eyes lit up like a slot machine about to pay off. He snapped his fingers and swayed his hips. "Dit-a, dit-a, plonk-oh! Let's do it."

He stepped away from the window opening and held up his hand. "Wait," he whispered. "Someone's coming."

Neal, Rafferty, and Freddy scampered to the sides of the hallway next to the steel door that led to the room with the gas can. They crouched down and watched through the crack in the cement block wall.

A brute with a hard brown athletic profile and a split nose walked down the steps with the candle in his hand. It was Nose. He took one of the kerosene-soaked rags, made a long wick, and snaked one end of it into the five-gallon gas can. Then he took the candle and placed it on the step. Making sure the other end of the wick was secured to the bottom of the candle, he took out a match and lit the candle. Shaking his hand to put out the match he hit the candle. It fell over, but he quickly picked it up before it could set the wick on fire. He let out a sigh of relief. In the candle's orange glow, his glowing devil-orange face broke into a diabolical smile. He turned, walked up the steps, and closed the door.

After Neal, Rafferty and Freddy tiptoed back to the window opening, Rafferty breathed a sigh of relief. "Looks like we're getting an early release."

With smiles all around, they made their way to the lit candle.

Standing in front of the candle, Rafferty said," Wanna sing happy birthday before we try to get out of this dump?"

Neal reared his foot back. "I'm sick of this place. We ought to knock that candle over right now and take our chances in the fire."

Freddy pushed him away. "No, wait." He looked at Neal as if he were crazy. "I'll go up to the top of the steps and see if we can get out the door."

Rafferty bowed at the waist. "Be my guest."

Freddy shook his head in disbelief. Neal had almost kicked over the candle before he knew if they could get out before they burned to death, and Rafferty was joking as if he didn't have a care in the world.

Being careful not to step on a creaking board, Freddy worked his way up the steps. At the top, he could see through a little window in a metal door. At the end of the hall, another door was closed. A few yards in front of the door, Nose sat in a chair holding a ring of keys on his lap. His chin was almost touching his chest, and his eyes were closing and opening. Freddy kept watching, but he had to rub his eyes to make sure he was seeing what he was watching. Nose's split-open Nose looked like a vagina. Nose reached up and rubbed his split nose, and his eyes shut. Then his hand slipped off the keys and fell to his side. When he turned, the keys clinked on the floor. His eyes jerked open. With his head drooping, he bent over to pick up the keys. Instead, he sighed and leaned back. In a few seconds he was asleep.

Freddy tried the doorknob. It turned freely. The keys lay on the floor waiting to be taken. He made his way back down the stairs and stopped at the candle.

Neal spoke first. "What did you see?"

"The door's unlocked, but there's a guard by the door. It's Nose." Freddy shook his head and grinned. "I hadn't noticed it before, but he has a

127

nose that looks like a cunt, and he just fell asleep. I think if we wait a few minutes we can sneak past him."

Neal gazed at the candle. "After we sneak past pussy-nose, then what?"

"There's another door at the end of the hallway. I don't know if it's locked, but Nose dropped the keys on the floor."

"Those have to be the keys to the door." Neal looked up the steps. "You guys ready?" He wagged his finger in the air. As if he were on his bongo board, he swayed his hips and sang, "Dit-a, dit-a." He kicked the candle over. "Plonk-oh!"

The flame sputtered and almost went out. Then the fuse sparkled and the pile of rags ignited with a *fwummp*. Freddy jumped on the fire with his feet, but it was out of control. From the top of the stairs, a muffled grunt came through the door. Neal shrugged and went up the steps.

Grinning and snickering to hide his nervousness, Rafferty looked at Freddy. "We're not even sure if there is a way out and he's got the place on fire."

Freddy glanced at the five-gallon can of gas. "We might need that."

Rafferty reached down to grab the can of gas, but hesitated. "If we don't get out of here, this is the last thing we'll need."

Freddy picked up the can. "If we do get out, we're not going anywhere without it."

They rushed up the stairs.

CHAPTER 11

After a few quick leaps up the steps, Freddy and Rafferty stopped next to Neal. Flames had licked their hungry way along the kerosene-soaked floor rafters. Like thousands of orange hooked fingers the flames were crawling up the cellar steps. Neal opened the unlocked metal door and looked down the hallway. Nose was still in his chair sleeping.

Looking at Freddy and Rafferty, Neal held his finger to his lips. "Wait here." He tiptoed to Nose and picked the big ring of keys up off the floor, but Nose moved. Neal froze in place. Waiting at the top of the stairs, Rafferty and Freddy waited to see if Nose would wake up.

Holding the gas can in his hand, Freddy whispered in Rafferty's ear. "I don't care how big he is, this thing's heavy. If he wakes up, grab the handle; we'll use it to bash his cunt nose in."

Rafferty suppressed a giggle. "It's already bashed in."

Nose let out a slow snore. Quick-footed Neal raced down the hallway and stopped under the nicotine-coated red exit sign. He quietly rolled the big ring of keys in his hands and tried to unlock the steel door.

Rafferty put his hand on Freddy's shoulder. "I think he's got it open."

Together they went through the door at the top of the stairs and closed it behind them. When they started to tiptoe past Nose, he reached out. Freddy and Rafferty stopped. Nose drew his hand back and scratched his arm. Rafferty dropped his hand from

129

Freddy's shoulder. They both scampered to the door below the cracked red exit sign and stopped. Neal didn't have it open yet.

While Rafferty paced back and forth with quick waltzing steps, Freddy set the gas can down on the floor. Impatiently waiting for Neal to open the door, he looked back down the hall. The growing fire's orange light brightened the little glass window on the cellar door. A weird feeling of revenge crept up Freddy's spine. Even though there was a good chance he would be burnt to death, coldness flowed into his body.

He shook it off and looked to Rafferty. "If we get out," he whispered, "those goons will wake up. They'll collect the insurance and think we're dead."

Rafferty smiled the first real smile since he got out of that chair. "They'll think we're dead, but they're not going to collect anything." His smile disappeared. "When the place burns down the fire marshal will know it was arson." He jerked his thumb toward his chest. "Because I'm turnin' them in."

Neal tried another key. It didn't fit. "You can do that," he whispered. "But before we make a call," he looked at the gas can, "we got to get out of here and get that gas in the car." Rolling the ring of keys in his hands, he searched for a key that would fit the lock. In his haste, the keys hit the doorknob and jingled with a gentle Christmas sound. All escape efforts stopped. Heads snapped sideways. Nose grunted and scratched his weird nose, but his eyes stayed shut. Neal picked a key out of the jumbled mess and inserted it into the lock. It wouldn't turn.

130

Bam! The door at the top of the cellar steps flew open. Blondie ran out of the smoke and fire, and stopped.

Nose jumped up. Jerking his sleepy head from side to side, he reached for his gun. "What the hell's going on?"

Coughing with his hand over his face, Blondie pointed to Freddy. "They're trying to get away."

Nose looked at Freddy and the others, and then looked back at the open cellar door. Flames licked around the doorframe, and a steady stream of smoke crawled out the top. Taking a deep whiff of the smoke, Nose wrinkled his split nose. "That candle wasn't supposed to start until five in the morning."

With his eyes watering from the smoke, Blondie nodded.

Rafferty hesitated, but then spoke anyway. "Maybe you slept right past five."

Nose looked at his watch and then cast a menacing stare in Rafferty's direction. "Maybe I should knock that smart mouth off your ugly face."

With sweat beads forming on his forehead, Blondie coughed and looked back at the cellar door. It was engulfed in flames and the smoke was coming down to head level.

"Ah, um, ahem, ah, of course," Neal said, trying to act calm. "Don't you think we should get outta here?"

Nose rammed the barrel of the gun into Neal's stomach. Neal grunted and pointed to the smoke billowing above his head.

Nose paid no attention. "We're getting out of here." he sneered. "But you're not." He shoved Neal toward the cellar door, lifted his sweaty hand, and

131

waved the gun at Rafferty and Freddy. "You too, get your asses down that cellar."

Freddy took one step toward the flaming door and stopped. His eyes met Blondie's. For a moment, a trace of compassion seemed to come from Blondie's face. They seemed to know each other. But just as fast as it had appeared, Blondie's compassion faded. He pushed Freddy toward the cellar door. "Move it, buddy."

As if herding cattle into a slaughterhouse, Nose pushed Neal, Rafferty, and Freddy past Blondie and toward the billowing smoke and flames.

"You're fucking crazy!" Neal shouted, but Nose pushed him harder.

Neal stumbled to the flaming door and dropped to his knees. Then Nose pushed Rafferty toward the door. Rafferty buckled at the knees and dropped down gasping for breath. When Freddy felt Nose's hand on his back, he braced for the push. But it didn't come.

Whap! It was the unmistakable sound of someone being hit on the head. Nose's limp hand slid down Freddy's back. He turned around. Blondie was standing there with a blackjack in his hand. He had whapped Nose up the side of the head and knocked him cold. Figuring that the whap had been meant for him, but somehow had hit Nose instead, Freddy held up his arms in front of his face and braced for the pain.

"I'm not going to hit you," Blondie said, and stepped back toward the door at the end of the hallway. He jerked his arm toward the door. "Let's go."

Freddy couldn't believe this tough gangster was going to help them. Crawling on all fours, Neal and Rafferty plodded past Blondie and went to the locked door. With the flames and smoke licking closer, Freddy just stood there.

From his hands and knees position, Neal lifted his arm and motioned to Freddy. "Get your dumb ass down here. He's trying to help us get out."

"I don't know what I'm doing this for," Blondie said. "But you better move your ass before I change my mind."

Freddy ran to the door. The smoke burned his eyes. He couldn't see. Neal reached up and pulled him down. "The air's better down here."

Standing, Blondie reached for the door handle. Neal reached for the ring of keys and lifted them up so Blondie could grab them. But he didn't. Instead, he kicked the bottom of the door and pushed. The door opened. As if they were standing with their backs in front of a gigantic furnace, a rush of heat blasted behind them.

Neal grabbed the can of gas. Blondie grabbed Nose by the shoulders and pulled. As he was dragging him through the door, Freddy heard something clunk in front of him. He looked down. Nose's gun had fallen to the floor. Freddy reached over, grabbed it, and stuck it in the belt of his pants.

Neal stood in the doorway and shouted, "Quit screwin' around, Freddy, and get the hell out!"

On all fours, Freddy and Rafferty rushed out the door, and Neal slammed it shut.

Halfway down the steps, Freddy stopped next to Blondie. "You need any help?"

Dragging Nose down the stairs, Blondie flicked his head toward the end of the hall. "No! Get out of here while you can."

CHAPTER 12

The flames from the growing fire could not be seen from outside the red brick apartment building, but in the dark parking lot Neal's '40 Ford sat in a moonlight shadow like an isolated island of hope. Freddy, Neal, and Rafferty ran up to it and stopped.

Neal gestured to the gas can in Freddy's hand. "Get that in the tank. I'll get the door open."

Freddy stood at the driver's side back fender and unscrewed the round gas cap. Tilting the small end of the five-gallon can into the opening, he watched Neal. Neal frantically try to unlock the door by using every key on the ring of keys, but none were fitting.

Rafferty nudged him on the elbow. "Too bad you can't hot wire the door to open."

Freddy put the gas cap back on the Ford, set the can down, and squeezed through the two cars. Then he crawled into the open window on the passenger side. "This works just as good." He unlocked the driver's side door.

Neal flung the door open. "If they didn't find my secret kill switch when they towed it here, the never got it started." He bent over and felt his hidden switch. "It's still off."

While Freddy jumped into the back and Rafferty slid into the front seat, Neal turned the kill switch on, placed the ring of keys on the front seat, and crawled under the dashboard. With his left hand, he pulled the three ignition wires down from under the dash, but stopped and looked to Freddy. "Did you leave some gas in the can to prime the carburetor?"

135

Freddy lifted his hand and held his thumb and forefinger an inch apart. "Just a little."

They both got out. Freddy opened the hood. Neal took off the air cleaner. Freddy tilted the gas can, and let a trickle of gas flow into the carburetor.

Neal crawled back under the dash. "Okay, let's see if this baby starts."

As Freddy closed the hood, movement in the shadows beside the apartment building tweaked his sense of menace. In the next instant two shadows emerged from around the corner of the building. Before he could warn anyone, Rafferty came around the side of the car, punched him in the arm, and whispered, "Somebody's coming."

Freddy crouched down, made his way into the back seat, and silently closed the door. Rafferty stepped over Neal's feet and crawled across the front seat, but Neal stayed on his back and kept on working on the wires. Lying on the seat, Rafferty grabbed Neal's arm and shook it.

Neal stopped working and looked up.

Rafferty pointed in the direction of the two men and whispered, "They must've woken up."

Neal slid out from under the dash and crawled under the steering wheel. Then he silently pulled the door closed, poked his head under the dark concealment of the dash, and curled into a ball. Rafferty slid down onto the floor and curled up next to him. Freddy flattened out on the floor behind the front seat and faded into the darkness. All movements stop.

The two men walk up to the car.

One spoke. "Doughnut wants us to dump this car in the river before the cops have a chance to tie it in with the bodies."

"Yeah, but we'll need some gas. Those kids ran this thing bone dry. The tow truck driver was supposed to fill the tank, but after Doughnut stiffed him for the tow, he got mad and told Doughnut to stick the car up his fat ass." The man let out a he-haw laugh. "He said the car would probably fit, too."

Thump! Something hit the car. Freddy kept his head down, but squinted toward the rearview mirror. A hand as big a boat paddle was resting on the trunk. If the man that the hand belonged to looked in the car, he'd see that big ring of keys lying on the front seat. Freddy flattened more, but he felt he could be seen. Although it was impossible, he tried to crawl through the floor. The car tilted sideways. He figured the man's gigantic foot was resting on the bumper.

"Looks like Swill already dumped some gas in this thing," the man said. "The empty can's still here."

"That saves us a trip," the other man said. "Too bad Freddy couldn't play by the rules. Him and his buddies are ashes."

The vulture shadow of the other man loomed outside. "I guess Swill's gonna drive this thing to the river and shove it in." His shadow crawled across the window. The car tipped back to level.

"Too bad," the man in front of the Ford said. "This *is* a nice car."

Freddy heard the other man laugh. "Let's get back to the party. I hear they're roasting Freddy tonight."

Freddy lifted his head and looked out the window. The men laughed in each other's faces and slapped each other on the back. Not noticing the growing orange light from the second floor, they dissolved into a dark doorway. Freddy leaned over the front seat and whispered. "They're gone."

Neal uncurled from the ball he was in and came back to life. Trying to start the Ford, he reached under the dash and grabbed the three ignition wires.

Rafferty glanced at the growing fire inside the building and then back at Neal. "Hurry up. We got to get outta here before they see that fire."

Neal twisted the wires together. Nothing happened. He reached up under the dash and wiggled the kill switch. The engine moaned and backfired once. The wires sparked sporadic-orange and flew apart. He twisted the wires together again. The engine caught. The custom exhaust pipes resonated with that unmistakable boulevard rumble and then calmed to a smooth purr.

Freddy looked back at the building. Nothing was moving except the licking of the growing orange flames. Neal hooked the transmission into low gear but didn't let out the clutch.

Aggravation filled Rafferty's face. "Now what?"

Neal placed his hand on the door handle. "I wonder if we have enough time to go back in and get my bongo board."

Freddy pointed at the flowing flames. "It's probably toast by now."

Neal shrugged. "Let's see if we can get away this time."

As he pulled away, nice and easy, they all held their breaths. After the building was out of sight, they breathed easily. With the threat of being burned alive gone, as if they were on a joy ride for the evening, they cruised down the street.

When Freddy had been locked in that room, time had dripped by. Now he felt the need to run, to move fast, and to get away. He reached over and tapped Neal on the shoulder. "Why are you driving like we're in a funeral? Come on! Punch that thing to the floor."

Rafferty spun his hand in encouragement. "Let's get moving."

Neal slowed the car even more, a big grin on his face. "I lost my bongo board, but if we get that Canadian flag for a souvenir, we'll be able to sucker those guys at the Burp into another bet."

He stopped the Ford right in front of the iron picket fence. Up on the porch, still attached to slanted flagpole, the Canadian flag still waved. With the engine running, porch lights being flicked on, and the pit bull barking, Neal ran up the steps and cut the rope to the flag. The rope slipped up the flagpole and slipped off the top. As if the Union Jack flag were a big red white and blue striped leaf, it fluttered to the ground. Looking like it wanted to play, the pit bull jumped up and nipped at Neal's rear end. Just before the flag touched the ground, Neal caught it and ran to the car. He jumped inside and slammed the door. With the dog outside yipping and whining, he stuffed the flag under the seat. As if he had all the time in the world to get away, he laced his hands behind his head and leaned back. "Money in the bank."

"Okay, smart ass," Rafferty said. "You think we can get going now? Or do you want to go back in Doughnut's office and ask him for a suit coat like ours?"

Neal looked toward the glowing apartment building. "I would, but those suit coats are probably stolen. I never did like hot merchandise." He paused. "We got to make that phone call before the place burns down."

CHAPTER 13

Blondie's arms ached from dragging Nose down the stairs. But he kept pulling until he was in front of Doughnut's office. Then he lowered him onto the dirty floor, opened the door, and walked in. Under a urine-yellow glare from a cheap light bulb, Doughnut was slumped in his big comfortable chair. As if he were dead, his head was flopped over to one side. At first Blondie thought Doughnut had been shot, but the slobber coming out the side of his mouth and the empty scotch bottle on the desk, told Blondie the great wanna-be mob boss was drunk. Swill was slumped down in the corner. With eyes closed, he talked to the sawed-off shotgun.

At first, Blondie couldn't believe it, but like the dumb asses they were, they had been celebrating about the riches they were about receive from the fire insurance before it was collected.

Blondie reached down and shook Swill's shoulder. "Come on. Wake up! The place is on fire. You got to help me get Nose out of here."

Swill's bloodshot eyes flew wide open. He swung the shotgun up and stuck it in front of Blondie's face. "You don't tell me what to do. I'll blow your goddamn head off."

Swill pulled the trigger. Click! The gun didn't go off. Grinning like a madman, he pumped another shell into the chamber, but Blondie grabbed the barrel and jerked it to the side. Boom! The gun went off, sending a close pattern of double-ought buckshot into Doughnut's face. Like a little kid that had been awaken from a deep sleep, Doughnut cried out and withered in the chair. Blondie had never seen anyone shot with a shotgun in the face this close.

Going into momentary shock, he relaxed his grip on the barrel of the shotgun. Swill jerked the gun. It flew out of Blondie's hands. Swill pumped another shell into the chamber. In one smooth motion, Blondie reached onto the desk, grabbed the heavy glass ashtray, and whipped it toward Swill. It caught Swill's jawbone. He crumpled into an unconscious heap.

Blondie scanned the office for help. No one else was around. He looked down at Doughnut's hamburger face. He exhaled a blood-bubbling breath, slid off the chair, and crashed onto the floor. When Blondie reached down to drag him out of the office and away from the growing fire, Doughnut was barely breathing. It would be a difficult task. Doughnut would need years of plastic surgery, probably have a nose uglier than Nose's; but Blondie decided to save him anyway.

As he bent over, Doughnut's earlier cutting words, "Don't question my authority, you asshole. I'm the boss here," rang in his brain.

"Who's the asshole now?" Blondie muttered, and straightened up to go. But if he did, he would be a heartless animal like Doughnut, and he didn't want to be that anymore. He bent over, lifted Doughnut by the arms, and dragged him to the door. Holding onto him with one hand and opening the door with the other hand, he pulled.

Boom! Doughnut's hand flew off and slammed against the wall. The end of his wrist was a bloody stump. As if there were a squirt gun inside his arm,

142

a severed artery allowed his heart to pump blood three feet into the air.

Blondie jerked his head toward Swill. He was upright and staggering. Where he had been hit on his jaw with the glass ashtray, a knot was forming, but he had the shotgun again. Blondie released Doughnut's arms. His blubbery shoulders smacked onto the floor. Blondie jumped into the hall and slammed the office door shut. He took one step and stood off to the side of the door.

"If it's all right with you, Swill," he yelled, "I'm going to let you be in charge!"

Boom! A spray of double-ought buckshot broke through the bottom of the door. Blondie looked down at Nose who was still on the floor. He was unconscious, and Blondie wanted to try to save him; but he would bleed to death before he could get the shotgun from Swill. He looked at Nose and thought about leaving him there to burn, but again, he couldn't bring himself to deliberately let another human being die. He didn't even want to let Swill burn, but with double-ought buckshot bursting through the door he had no choice. He remembered what his friend, Freddy, had told him the last time he had seen him alive.

"Don't think for a minute that those guys are human," he had said. "They're cold-blooded killers. They'll kill their own kid and then have a party. We can make a lot of money off these dummies. It'll be like mugging a blind man, but we'll have to watch our backs."

With smoke burning his eyes Blondie squinted down the hallway. Consuming everything in its hungry path, the fire swelled to a brilliant orange.

Blondie lifted Nose by the back of the shoulders and dragged him out of the building.

144

CHAPTER 14

Neal drove a few blocks away from the burning building, pulled the Ford next to a phone booth, and jumped out. Instead of slipping Canadian money, which he didn't have, into the coin slot, he placed a paper clip into the center hole of the mouthpiece and touched it to the bare metal on the keyway of the money box. He looked back at Freddy and gave him a thumbs-up. He had gotten a dial tone.

Freddy looked up and down the dirty street. Amber lights on rusty steel poles burnished the sidewalks and bathed old storefronts with antique light. A teetering drunk, with his pants hanging half down around his behind, staggered to the corner of an alleyway. When he placed his hand on the side of a red brick building to steady himself, he urinated on his shoes.

Rafferty threw him a taunting smile and turned toward Freddy. "I guess we're in a high class neighborhood."

Neal hung up the phone and jumped back into the car. He turned toward Rafferty. "I didn't make the call."

Rafferty's smile faded. "What? We wanted those guys to get caught."

Freddy leaned forward and popped his head over the back of the front seat. "Yeah, what's the deal?"

"If the fire department gets there too fast and puts out the fire and they don't find any bodies, then those guys will know we're still alive." His face broke into a radiant smile. "So if we were burnt to death and the fire got hot enough we would disintegrate. There wouldn't be any bodies left to find."

"That makes sense," Freddy said. "The hotter the fire gets the more believable it is that we died in the fire."

Rafferty stared at the phone booth. "Yeah, but even if we don't call and it looks like we burned up, Blondie probably told those guys we escaped. They'll still be looking for us."

"I don't think so," Freddy said. "Blondie let us go. If the other assholes find out what he did, they'll kill him. I don't think he'll say anything about letting us go free."

With a look of uneasiness, Rafferty looked to the road ahead. "You may be right. But I'll feel a whole lot better when we're out of here and Doughnut and his buddies think we're ashes."

Neal gestured toward Rafferty. "At least, you guys got nice suit coats out of the deal."

Rafferty smoothed the front of his suit jacket. "Nothing but the best for Freddy's friends." He jerked his thumb to the back of the car. "Hey, Freddy, they're probably having a fire sale. You wanna go back and see if we can get a suit coat and a tie for Neal?"

Freddy rubbed his neck where the knot of the Italian rope trick would have been. "No thanks."

Neal slipped the Ford into gear and eased out the clutch. When he turned right and pulled onto the main highway, he fanned his hand in front of his face. "Locked in that cellar got my lungs stunk up with that mold smell." He flipped the side wing window wide open, pulled into the passing lane, and tromped down the accelerator. A stream of air flowed into the car. "This isn't enough air," he said. "Hey, Rafferty, my window doesn't have a handle. Open your window, pop off that handle, and give it to me."

Rafferty grabbed the handle and jiggled it. "It's stuck."

Freddy needed those windows down, too. He hadn't admitted it, but the cellar's gloom had eaten away at his sanity like some kind of slithering fungus. Now he welcomed the fresh air cure that was right down the highway. It was nice to be back among the living, and that little stream of air was making him feel better already.

"Get that window down, Rafferty," Freddy said, and they wheeled around the slow moving car in front of them.

The headlights flashed inside the car and lit up animated figures of joyous people drinking green bottles of Canadian beer. Rafferty finally freed the handle and cranked the side window down. Clean wind rushed past Freddy's right ear and sounded like a huge seashell. He breathed deep and stared down the onrushing highway. Outside, a throaty noise roared from the Ford's exhaust pipes, but Freddy felt they were going too slow.

Rafferty jiggled the window handle off and handed it to Neal. Neal popped it on and wound his side window down. Refreshing wind blasted into both sides of Freddy's face. He drank it in, and the powerful hopped-up engine purred at a steady idle.

Rafferty leaned toward the windshield. "There's a straight road ahead. You can speed up any time now."

"I would." Neal wiggled the steering wheel. "But something doesn't feel right."

"That never stopped you before."

"Hey, that's right."

Neal tromped the gas feed to the floor. The car took off like a scared cat and pulled them into the wide open spaces of freedom. Freddy stared straight ahead. No restraining window bars blocked their view, and no steel door blocked their way. The long road welcomed them. Tires rolled and the Ford whipped around a bend and into a whirlpool of darkness.

As a clear country current of air glided through the open windows, time seemed to chatter. Shapes of things to come exploded over the dark horizon and boomed back at the little Ford. Intangible excitement of the moment bawled out like one of those World War II movies where the hero throws his arm forward.

"Follow me!" he commands, and charges into the battle and shines in the glory of it all.

It was great just to be alive. Freddy leaned back and closed his eyes. The excitement of the escape had waned. He felt like some kind of vibrating escape machine. He hadn't noticed it before, but his teeth were chattering. He looked at Neal. Hours ago, Neal had tried to see between the cracks in the boards behind the bars of that cellar window and joked about building a go-cart with a big engine and escaping.

Now he pounded his fists on the hard plastic steering wheel and shouted, "Yes! Yes! Yes! It's not a Corvette engine on a go-cart, but it just doesn't matter."

Freddy was glad they were leaving the prison of mold, plinking, and death behind, but he felt as if Doughnut's hands were pulling him back. An urgent need to streak past his controlling world ran up his spine. He shouted out from his perch on the back seat, "How fast are we going?"

Neal excitedly lifted his hands off the steering wheel and threw them into the air. With his voice vibrating, he said, "What's the difference? Just as long as were putting miles between us and them, it just doesn't matter."

Neal's sudden attack of excitement made Freddy uneasy. He had been so intent in getting away that he hadn't noticed the unfamiliar vibrations from speed. Now that he did, it scared him. He looked into the rearview mirror and saw the reflection of Neal's face. He looked really scared. It was as if he had kept all the fear bottled up and was releasing it all at once, and he didn't want to show it. Neal had always been the man who made things happen. Just to have something different to do, he would do almost anything; and the border was still a long way off. Freddy hoped Neal wouldn't pull off one of his famous nut house stunts just to hide his fear.

Neal cried out, "You don't have to live to tell about it, but I can't take it anymore." He slowed and pulled the Ford off to the side of the road. The vibrating stopped. "It feels like the whole front end's falling off. Maybe asshole Swill loosened the lug nuts."

Instead of getting out of the car and checking the wheel's lug nuts, Neal sat behind the steering wheel laughing.

149

Puzzlement filled Rafferty's face. "What's so funny?"

"Dit-a, dit-a, plonk-oh!" Neal sang. "I think those guys had a flat and changed the tire."

Freddy realized why the car had been shaking so badly. The bank bag and the envelope were inside the spare tire and the spare tire was on the car.

"No wonder my teeth are shaking out of my head."

Rafferty leaned back and threw his arm over the back of the seat in a relaxed pose. "Let's get out and change it."

"Change it into what," Neal said. "If Swill and his buddies changed it, the other tire's flat."

"We can't drive like this," Freddy said. "The whole damn car will shake apart, and if Doughnut comes after us we won't be able to gain any speed."

Neal nodded. "You got a point there, Freddy." He looked at Rafferty. "How's your tire pumping arms?"

Rafferty's face brightened with comprehension. "I think I'm about to find out."

Neal got out. They broke down the tire, took out the bank bag and envelope, and put them in the trunk. Then, they took turns pumping the tire up, bolted it back on the rear axle, and jumped back into the car. After shifting into third gear, Neal's scuffed leather-shoed foot slid across the black rubber groves of the accelerator and tromped it flat. Now the Ford smoothly churned on down the highway.

Neal shouted, "Man oh man, this thing purrs!" His face relaxed and that scared look was gone.

Although Freddy usually liked being on the edge, Neal's very presence kept people teetering on it. Freddy was weary; but wherever Neal was there would be no rest. The excitement of the journey would continue to stay alive.

Freddy closed his eyes and leaned back in the seat. Like a prisoner who had just been set free, he had gained a new appreciation for the little things in life. He realized there was too much to see, too much to miss. He couldn't sleep now. He opened his eyes.

As the Ford's yellow headlights bore into the black night ahead, its sergeant-striped red taillights whooshed behind. Crossroads and stop signs hid in the dark. Freddy's tired eyes couldn't adjust. He couldn't tell if what was zipping past were side roads or driveways. No streetlights were working in the dim mist of fog, but shaky shadows seemed to teeter into view then fade. It was a wobbly night, but they were leaping toward a great unknown where they could open the bank bag. Freddy wanted to drift off to sleep, but he felt like he was waiting for something to happen, he just didn't know what.

CHAPTER 15

After Blondie dragged Nose out of the apartment building, he propped him up against the concrete steps. With his chest heaving, Nose's dark eyes widened and reflected the orange dancing flames of the growing fire. Through great effort, his mouth formed to say something, cut nothing came out. As his chest rose and fell, he stared into the dark sky. If one of the pellets from the double-ought buckshot had entered his blood stream and went to his heart, it may have killed him. Blondie reached down to check his pulse, but red lines of light from approaching fire trucks shot through the black and orange night and flicked onto Nose's face.

Blondie let Nose's wrist fall to the ground and took off. Running away from the apartment, he looked back. Nose lifted his arm. Like a dying man's last thwarted effort to save himself, it flopped back down.

Blondie ran around three buildings and into a narrow passageway between two decaying buildings. Gasping for breath, he stopped. As he hung onto the iron railing of a filth-encrusted stairwell, the sickening smell of blood, urine, and relaxed bowels, wafted into his face and stayed there. He looked down into the stairwell.

Doughnut and Nose were good at instilling fear. Below his feet lay one of their warnings meant for those who did not do as they were told. The bodies of the three men, who had been in Doughnut's office, last week, were stacked in a heap with their throats cut. What at first looked to be rice around their mouths and noses were moving masses of maggots.

Blondie felt something brush his leg. He jumped back. The pit bull that had chased Freddy and his friends made its way to the bottom of the steps and warily sniffed at the outstretched ghastly blue hand on the man on the bottom of the pile. Without warning, an acrid taste filled Blondie's mouth. Before he could stop himself, he bent over and threw up.

For a long time, death hadn't affected him this way. Blaming death on someone else's ignorance had made him stay tough. But this time he knew it wasn't only Doughnut's ignorance. It was his own ignorance and inaction that had let Doughnut do it. He cussed himself for being so gullible.

Trying to make sense of the last few days, Blondie searched his mind to find an answer to his very existence. Before he had become street wise, people had looked at him as if he were a loser, and he had hated it. When he was a kid, he had believed in some kind of religion or code of ethics, but he went hungry. He found out that if you want to survive in this world, you got to throw the first punch; and it's got to be hard enough to knock them down. And when they're down, you can't be nice about it. Before they get up you got to stomp them.

The pit bull ran up the steps and sniffed at a garbage can. It caused Blondie to remember his hungry days of stealing food and holding up in some dark alley. Like an animal, his searching eyes would flick from right to left worrying that someone was just around the corner waiting to steal the precious food back. Back then he ate when he could, slept when he could, and drank when he could. He lived by no set schedules. After he had become as dirty and as vicious as he could, he lost sympathy for those wimpy people who weren't tough enough to help themselves and needed some kind of religion to help them through their miserable lives. If they didn't have enough balls to stand up and fight for themselves, like he had done, he wasn't going to feel sorry for them.

The constant pain of going hungry had caused him to mourn for himself, and he had allowed grief to degenerate into self-pity and chronic depression. If his deceased friend, Freddy, had not taught him the art of survival, he would not be alive. Looking at what this survivalist attitude had brought to the men lying dead beneath him, he wasn't sure of anything anymore. He was tired of it all. Staring at the dead bodies, he thought that a little education, discipline, and love, might have changed their lives, but it was too late for them. He turned away from the haunting sight and hoped it wasn't too late for him to change.

He scurried away from the stairwell, turned down another alley, tramped over a gum-spattered sidewalk, and stopped in front of a waistless, fat-necked prostitute. She tried to entice him by lifting her skirt, but it only revealed a set of bruised legs haphazardly spotted with scabs. Off to the right, just inside the reeking entrance of a vacant storefront, her pimp held his hand on a gun and looked out with rheumy eyes.

At another time Blondie would have grabbed the little creep by the throat and slammed him through the storefront window, but he was in no

154

mood for a confrontation. He turned and stepped across the street. Under a turbulent dark sky, he tried to make his way past a leaking fire hydrant, but a black limousine splashed by and sent a sheet of water onto the side of his face.

"Insanity," he mumbled. "Just plain ignorance. How did I ever get into this kill and be killed business?"

Beneath his anger, he had an icy confidence, and a clear head. He was already forming in his mind what he must do next. The first thing he had to do was find those kids and get that bank bag back. After being locked in that room and being shown the Italian rope trick, any normal kid would be afraid to go to Buffalo. Any normal kid would be afraid to put the bank bag in the basket. Any normal kid would hightail it over the border and never look back.

But Neal was driving, and he had not played by any rules. When it had been safe to go, he had pulled that do you like sex joke on Swill. When Swill stood there like a bear on its hind legs about attack, it hadn't bothered Neal. Neal was a kid who loved to do just the opposite. He wasn't normal. People like him always went like hell and went to the grave satisfied.

No matter what his friends said, Neal wanted the other half of the money wrapped in the 'New York Times'. He would go to Buffalo. He would drop that bank bag in the basket. He would stop at the newsstand and collect the other half of the money. Neal would make it possible for Blondie to lead a new life. With sirens wailing, red lights splitting the dark night, and a conglomeration of fire trucks racing toward the fire, Blondie slunk through the shadows of the slum apartment buildings and began to feel better.

CHAPTER 16

With the powerful Ford's V-8 purring down the road and Neal and his expert driving skills behind the wheel, Freddy should have felt relieved, but an unpleasantness hovered in the air. He should have been used to Neal's twists and turns and constant wealth of changes, but another one of Neal's on-the-edge feelings piled into his mind; and it made him wonder if he would ever get used to Neal's world, complete in itself and created with his own standards. A world that in one snap up of the moment could make just about anyone near him want to experience everything at the same time and cause them to hunger for his fantastic world and fly away on one of his crazy quests for a tiny piece of action people crave, but are too afraid to experience.

Freddy's body ached for sleep. He didn't know if he was just too tired to doze off or he was staying awake so he wouldn't miss anything. Almost in a zombie state, he stared out the window. They should have crossed the border by now, but he felt a familiar feeling. As the Ford's tires rumbled over a rough stretch of road and the floor trembled beneath his feet, he knew Neal was going to make something happen again. Freddy didn't know what it would be. It was always a mystery.

All of a sudden, like the disappointed feeling when a beautiful sunset blinks to black and ends a summer day, the atmosphere inside the Ford was advanced sad. Freddy was back in that moldy cellar of the apartment building. Sounds of something being dragged along the cement floor invaded his mind. From out of the darkness, a taunting voice whispered in his ear. "It's all your fault, Freddy. It's all your fault."

The projection of a magic lantern from his subconscious burned a weak beam. Behind it the ugly face of Nose jumped out at him and grinned fiendishly. If they were in some carnival watching a sideshow of freaks, he could see something like this happening, but they were in Canada. Neal's one wrong turn had put them right back in that cellar. Unwanted mind marauders invaded this gloom and filled his chest with strange emotion so awful that he woke with a jerk.

He looked around the inside of the car. If his name wasn't Freddy, they would have never been locked in that cellar. They would have picked up the Canadian flag, got the cup of coffee, made it back to the Burp, and collected the bet money. Still suffering from the horrors of the dream, Freddy waited for Neal or Rafferty to say, "It's all your fault, Freddy."

But they didn't. They stared straight ahead. Maybe they knew he couldn't help it that his name was Freddy. If they were okay with it, then he was okay with it, too.

As the Ford churned on down the highway, Freddy nodded off again. With sounds of screeching rubber blasting into his ears, the Ford came to a stop and he slid forward. A horn honked long and loud. A speeding vehicle whizzed past.

Neal gripped the steering wheel and exhaled a long whistling breath. "Damn! That was close."

As if it were a friendly reminder, Rafferty said, "You know you're supposed to stop for stop signs?"

Freddy jerked his head and looked out the back window. If Neal had gone through a stop sign the night had eaten it. Freddy couldn't see it. With the smell of burnt rubber invading the car, he wondered if they would wreck and never make it back to the illuminated land of bongo board bets and the easy life.

Neal hooked low gear. "Ah, ahem, yes." He turned to Rafferty. "Sorry for the sudden stop." He flashed a smile and held it. "But I stopped. Didn't I?"

"Ho, ho, ho!" Rafferty's merriment swelled. "You're so good you can even stop in your sleep."

Neal gave Rafferty a thumb's up, let out the clutch, and turned his attention back toward the road.

Outside, on Freddy's left, trees flitted past. On his right, heading to where they had just come from, the dim-yellow lights of an old bus, spewing diesel fumes, rattled past dark houses, and he was glad they were on their way home. As Neal tried to get the radio to work, tires spun in front of them. Tires spun behind them, and the little glow-in-the-dark needle on the speedometer climbed.

In the distance, oncoming headlights flashed out of the dark. In a stupor, Freddy watched them. The lights intensified to blinding bright. Then, like light through a fan blade, they zipped past, sending small spangles of yellow flickering into his night-adjusted eyes. When he looked back, the spangles disappeared into the small exhaust whirlwind trailing behind them.

Neal rubbed his hair with intense excitement. He talked fast. "Now we can just leave all that nonsense behind. Yes! Yes! We can make them eat our dust tonight."

Up ahead, a lone streetlight shone on a small washed out layer of yellow dirt that jutted across the intersection. The Ford's wheels flew over it. Freddy looked back. The yellow swish of two dust-filled tailwinds colliding filled the lighted air, making it look like gold.

Rafferty jerked his head from front to back. "Wow! Did you see that dust fly?"

Freddy thought their escape had happened so fast that fate had actually jerked them away from a burning death. Now it didn't matter if they wandered in the dust for a while. It was better than being locked in that cellar. Out-of-town suburbs, with little black trees, paraded past. In the continuing dark, a road sign flew by. Freddy couldn't read it. He tapped Neal on the shoulder. "Are we going the right way?"

"Who knows?" Neal said. "All the signs are metric." He shook his head and smiled. "But it doesn't matter. As long as I'm behind the wheel, we're getting closer to home."

Rafferty nodded in agreement. "Just keep on going."

Neal hunched over the steering wheel. "Nothing can stop us now. We can hit peak speed on our way to…"

He stopped in mid-sentence. Up ahead, the lights of the border crossing glowed. Military smugness of the concrete structure stood out like a shrine dedicated to the worship of some kind of government god. Fear of Doughnut's rent-a-cops waiting at the structure grabbed Freddy's chest like a rock crusher.

"Let's jump out and run into the weeds," he said. "We can cross the border where there's no guards."

"Have a little faith, Freddy," Neal calmly said. "We know you're not the Freddy the cops and Doughnut want."

"Those rent-a-cops might be waiting to jump out and nab us. What if those guards think I *am* the other Freddy?"

"No problem," Neal said, and lowered his voice. "We'll make something up."

As Freddy stared at the concrete structure, it looked cold and intimidating.

"They don't watch the entire border," he said and looked to his right. "They only watch it at the roads." He pointed to the forest. "If we jump out before we get to the border, we can get across through those trees."

Raising an eyebrow, Neal tilted his head to one side. "We could." Making a yes-and-no gesture, he wobbled his open hand in the air. "But I don't feel like walking."

"Yeah," Rafferty said and sat up straight. "That's a long way on foot. Let's take the chance."

Freddy rested his hand on the gun he had picked up before they escaped from the burning apartment building and looked out the front windshield. The border with its white gate, the crossing lanes, and the little guard shacks loomed in front of them. "I hope they don't find this gun."

Neal's head jerked around so fast Freddy thought it was going to snap off. "What gun?"

Freddy lowered his head and looked down at the back of the seat. "Nose dropped it after Blondie hit him. I found it on the floor. Should we turn around?"

Neal turned to the front. "We can't. And I hope those border guards don't find that thing." He let out a long breath of air. "If they do, they'll find that bank bag and the money, too."

Freddy reached across the seat and shook Neal's shoulder. "Turn around and let's get out of here."

Neal continued to drive. "If we turn around now, it'll look suspicious." He expelled his breath in a long sigh. "Let's face it, gentleman. We're here."

As the Ford cruised past the rear ends of two cars parked on a crooked slant, Rafferty grabbed the door handle. "Get ready to run."

Neal pulled into the first lane on the right. "This is it. If that Freddy guy is wanted by the law, we'll be in a place worse than that cellar."

As the car slowed, hold-your-breath-silence filled the air. Freddy looked to his right. Dressed in one of those off-green uniforms that broadcasted authority, a border guard slumped in a chair. With his mouth and fly open, he clutched a brown bottle that rested on the ground, and his right hand hung down listlessly.

"That guard must be drunk," Rafferty said. "Maybe we can ease on though."

The skinny door to the border shack banged open. A red-eyed, hat-less guard in a wrinkled-gray military uniform looked toward the sleeping guard. Then, as if he were hiding his identity, he dropped his bare head and frantically waved Neal on through. Neal held his arm out the window. With his thumb and fingers held high in the air, he signaled 'OK'. The bareheaded guard ran over to the sleeping guard and woke him.

Rafferty took his hand off the door handle, threw his left arm over the back of the front seat, and smiled at Freddy. "It's a good thing they picked tonight to celebrate."

Neal shifted the transmission into second gear. As the car rolled on down the highway, a look of enlightenment crossed his face. "See, nothing to it."

When he shifted into third gear, Freddy turned and watched out the back window. Behind them, the guards and their little shanties looked smaller and smaller until they disappeared into the dark. Freddy shook his head and whistled out a long breath. "The next time you want to go for a little jaunt across the border just to get a cup of coffee and a souvenir, don't ask me along."

"You don't have anything to worry about," Neal said. "If those guys were in with that Doughnut gang, then they think that Freddy guy that they think you are, burned up in the fire."

Rafferty flashed Neal an exaggerated dumbfounded look. Then, as if he were trying to get his addled brain back into working order, he shook his head and yelled out the open window. "Wherever you are, Freddy, you're a free man."

His voice echoed across the Peace Bridge and up into the heavens.

Looking at the powerful blue-black water that forced its way under the bridge and downriver, Neal said, "Maybe the next time, for some real excitement, we'll go over Niagara Falls in a coffee can."

Freddy peered out the side window. A white-tailed buck with a large rack of horns stood in a grassy field. Like brilliant sparks in the night, its reflecting yellow eyes flitted by. Then, the T's of the tops of telephone poles, mailboxes, trees, country fields, and bright streetlights in front of dimly lit houses, interrupted by dark nothingness, zipped past. Advancing through the pelting moments in the record of time, the Ford rumbled down the road and the collage of night sights vanished into the dark.

Finally at peace with the thought that at last they were back on the American road, Freddy let his shoulders relax and slumped down in the seat. Being back in the United States, moving non-stop, and traveling toward their old neighborhood of Patagonia, gave him comfort.

Neal stopped at an intersection. Freddy lifted his head from the seat. To ward off sleep, he blinked and wiped his eyes. Neal seemed too quiet. It gave Freddy an uneasy feeling. Up ahead, a right turn would take them home. But Neal went straight ahead.

Rafferty looked to his right. The road they should have taken passed him by. He looked to Neal. "What are you doing?"

With his mischievous grin, Neal waved off Rafferty. "Let's see what's just up around the next bend."

Freddy winced. "Oh, no," he slurred, and jerked forward from the back seat. "You're going the wrong way."

164

Grinning as if it were all a game to him, Neal shifted the transmission into high gear and barreled on down the wrong road.

"It'll be new." He waved his arm. "It'll be exciting. Man, oh man! We'll be there. We'll be in the great glimmering city of Buffalo."

Rafferty stared at Neal. "Don't even tell me you're going drop off that bank bag."

Neal turned to Rafferty. "Don't you want to see New York before you take a dirt nap?"

"Not really."

Neal reached over and shook Rafferty's shoulder. "Come on, man. Everybody's alive in New York. It's where everybody jumps. Maybe it's the same way in Buffalo."

Rafferty waved his hand. "All I ever seen in New York was broken down tenement houses."

Neal leaned back and his manner took on a significant air. "People can say what they want about New York, but the place jumps. It jumps twenty-four hours a day. In the morning, everybody's rushing to get to work."

A slow-moving Chevy's taillights beamed in front of the Ford. Neal passed it, and continued, "New York doesn't have slow people like the ones we just passed. Even at lunchtime everybody's in the streets rushing around digging everything. It's the place where you can watch big buses pull away from the curb and hear them groan. In the afternoon, kids are out of school, playing stickball or lounging with girls. They even have guys selling fruit and vegetables from wagons. It's the jumpingest town in the world. At night the lights come on and the pace is set. Those lights tell the world this is New York; come live here, man."

Freddy leaned over the seat. "Can't we go home first?"

Neal formed an exaggerated frown. "Are you trying to tell me you don't want to see what's happening in Buffalo and collect the other half of the money?"

Freddy was going to say something, but he knew better than to argue with Neal. When his mind was made up there was no way of changing it. As a last resort he asked, "What if we run out of gas again?"

Neal reached into his pocket and pulled out a Buffalo head nickel. "We'll put a nickel in the tank and let the Buffalo push it."

CHAPTER 17

On the outskirts of Buffalo, Neal pulled the Ford into a closed gas station. Under the dim light of a lone light bulb hanging from a metal pole, he got out and opened the trunk. Freddy reached in and took out the bank bag and the envelope.

Rafferty pointed to the bank bag. "You going to stand there and hold that thing or open it?"

"Neal's the locksmith," Freddy said, placed the bank bag on the bumper, and stepped back. "Okay, Neal, use your great master key."

Neal picked up the tire iron and arched back to break the flimsy lock.

Freddy stepped close and held up his hand. "Wait!"

Neal snapped at him. "What?"

"If Doughnut's gang is like those guys from Youngstown, they put bombs in things."

Holding the tire iron over his head, Neal studied Freddy, then the bag. He lowered the tire iron. "That bag's too little for a bomb." He lifted the tire iron but didn't strike.

While Neal held the tire iron in the air, Freddy shrank back. "Dynamite's small, Maybe there's a half a stick in there."

Neal raided an eyebrow and lowered the tire iron. "I knew that." He felt through the bag. "I don't think there's any dynamite in this thing. It's not round."

"Yeah, but," Freddy protested, "if they find out we opened it, we'll never get the other half of that envelope money."

As if he were weighing it, Neal held the bag in his hand. "So what? There's something heavy in this thing, maybe it's a bar of gold."

"It could be," Freddy said. "But if we drop off the bag, Doughnut and his buddies won't be after us anymore."

Leaning against the back fender, Rafferty crossed his arms. "They won't be after us anyway. They think we burned up in the fire."

"Maybe they do," Freddy said. "But Blondie still knows we didn't. And the only reason he let us go was to get the bag."

Neal jerked his finger at Freddy. "You got a point there, but I think he's a little smarter that those other jerks."

"It seems to me," Freddy turned his eyes toward the bag, "if we drop it off, Blondie will be happy. Then we'll get the other half of the money and we'll be twice as rich."

"And Blondie will have no reason to hunt us down," Rafferty added.

Neal seemed convinced. "Okay. We'll drop off the bag, get the money, and go home."

Freddy slumped with relief. "That's the best news I've heard all day."

In the city of Buffalo, few cars traveled the streets, but windows flashed neon beer signs signaling that the bars were still open. Neal downshifted and let out the clutch. The engine moaned. The exhaust pipes rumbled and protested the slowing. Neal pulled to the curb and stopped. Up ahead, at the red light on the corner of Main and Washington Street, a newsstand sat on the sidewalk. Under the slant of a corrugated steel roof, a naked light bulb illuminated stacks of newspapers and periodicals. Several yards from the stand, flattened cigarette butts circled a wire wastebasket. It looked like it was waiting for the bank bag to drop into it.

Looking up and down both streets, Rafferty moved his head from side to side. "There's nobody there."

"What did you expect?" Neal threw both hands into the air. "You think they'd have it all lit up with a circus clown making animals out of balloons and confetti falling from the sky?"

Rafferty faked a sad look. "No, but I was sure they'd have an organ grinder with a monkey doing tricks."

Neal pointed out the windshield. "Is that the organ grinder without his monkey?"

Rafferty and Freddy turned serious and looked out the window. Wearing a long tan trench coat, two sizes too big for his bony body, a tall man with granny glasses and a bowed back, tottered up to the wastebasket. Almost falling over, but catching his balance at the last instant, he reached in and pulled out a crumpled newspaper.

From the back seat, Freddy whispered, "Is that the guy that's supposed to pick up the bank bag?"

"Can't you remember from one minute to the next?" Neal said with irritation. "Our guy will be wearing a straw hat."

Rafferty jerked his head to the left. "Like that guy over there?"

Next to the newsstand, a skinny man, with a friendly smile, leaned on a streetlight post and lit a cigarette. He reached around his back, pulled out a straw hat, and placed it on his head.

Freddy gasp. "That's him."

"Even if it is him," Neal said, "With that old coot digging garbage out of the basket, we can't drop the bag in it."

Neal pulled away from the curb and steered the Ford around the corner. Driving past the man with the straw hat, he waved. The man didn't wave back, but he held his hand to his side and jerked his thumb upward.

"He gave us a sign," Neal said. "He must have the money in the third 'New York Times'."

"Yeah," Rafferty said. "All we have to do is wait for that old geezer to get the hell away from that basket."

"No problem," Freddy said. "He'll be moving in a second."

In one motion the man with the straw hat swished his hand down, picked an iron paperweight off a stack of newspapers, and flung it at the bent-over bum. Twang! It hit the sidewalk and ricocheted into the side of the basket. The old man jerked. As he stood, angry and wobbly, a questioning look formed on his unshaven face. The man in the straw hat placed his hand under his arm and stared at him. The bum jammed a torn newspaper under his arm, and straightened up. After an indifferent shrug, he teetered away.

"The coast is clear," Rafferty said. "Go around the block, drop the bank bag off, and we'll pick up our delivery fee."

Neal wheeled around the block, drove down the street against traffic, and pulled next to the basket. With the bank bag clutched in his hand, he held his arm above the basket, but he didn't drop it. He cut the wheel to the right, and with the tires squealing, he cut right in front of a yellow taxicab and sped away.

Freddy's dream of collecting the money and going home vanished. He leaned over the front seat and yelled in Neal's ear, "What are you doing? We agreed to give them the bag and collect the money."

Neal kept one hand on the steering wheel and waved his other hand in front of his ear. "I know, I know. It seemed just the thing to do at the time, but I just couldn't do it." He held up one finger. "And besides, we forgot to wrap it in newspaper like Blondie said."

Freddy jerked his thumb over his shoulder. "Well, then turn around. We'll get a paper at the newsstand."

"I think it's too late," Neal declared. "And anyway, do we really know if there's actually money under the third 'New York Times'?"

Leaning forward, Freddy said in a begging tone, "Let's just get the money form the 'Times' and drop off the key."

Neal and Freddy exchanged glances.

"We just can't let grass grow under out feet," Neal said. "We only got so much time before our internal innards start to rot with age."

"What are you talking about?" Rafferty asked.

Freddy leaned over the front seat and patted the bank bag. "I think he just wants to see what's in this bag."

Neal turned to Freddy and broke into triumphant laughter. "You got it."

171

CHAPTER 18

In almost hypnotic fascination, Blondie peeked between a stack of magazines and watched Neal's hand and the bank bag being pulled back into the window of the Ford. He stepped from behind the newsstand and watched the fleeing Ford. Racing away from a yellow taxicab, its sergeant-striped taillights vanished down the street. As the exhaust died into the night, it looked like what Doughnut and the evil side of life couldn't accomplish with force or slaughter, these kids were accomplishing through sheer luck.

Blondie had not slept in three days, and the past few days were enough to tax a rested man's strength. Tendrils of exhaustion invaded his mind and interrupted his reasoning. He wanted to get a room, take a healthy slug of scotch, and go to sleep for a week. But the stakes were too high. Slowing down his thinking would be a mistake. The last thing he needed to do was let Freddy and his friends get away. If he did, he would have to stay in Buffalo and take his chances in the Arm. But the people of the Arm had it in their heads that as their power and money increased they'd become superpowers.

Blondie had wondered why the great illegal and successful gambling casino, called the Jungle Inn, had come to an end. It had been a perfect set up. Racketeers had legally incorporated a little village and called it Hall's Corners. What began as a little house of prostitution grew into a sprawling money maker, but it was located near Youngstown, Ohio, where crime figures had planted and set off at least seventy-five bombs in ten years. The bombs were aimed at notorious racketeers, prominent citizens, and officials in the Youngstown area who wouldn't obey the rules. The bombings became so common that Youngstown became known as 'Bomb Town.'

The brothers, who owned part of the Jungle Inn, ordered a man, who worked at the casino as a garbage man, to fill the office of Mayor. When the man was asked why he never met with anyone as a governing body, he'd said, "Because there was no business to conduct."

When the sheriff in neighboring Trumbull County was questioned about the legality of the place, he exploded in anger and said he would look into it. But a temper tantrum was often a defense mechanism used by corrupt officials to dodge the truth. The village of Hall's Corners had no law enforcement agency of its own, but the racketeers who ran the casino, enforced the law according to the doctrines of the Mafia. When the racketeers tried to expand into Youngstown, State Liquor Control agents came in and shut the place down.

After these types of people had killed his friend, Freddy, Blondie came to realize that the Arm couldn't be trusted, and expanding their violence would eventually bring everyone in the Arm crashing down. Getting the bag was his one last chance to grab freedom. He wasn't as energetic as he should be, but when Freddy and his friends had rushed out of the burning building, their steps weren't exactly lively either. And he had a gun and they didn't.

When he walked away from the newsstand and around the corner it was nearly midnight. But no matter how many times what was in front of him had given him a good feeling, he was still pleasantly surprised. Waiting at the curb was his 1957 Oldsmobile coupe. Looking like something out of California car show, its soft magenta paint sparkled under the lights of the street. The huge chrome bumpers flashed brighter than buffed mirrors. Sparkling like diamond dust, spinner hubcaps added more glitz to the white-walled tires. Inside, the interior had been rolled and pleated with white leather. Under the hood, a V-8 engine that had been pulled from a police car and rebuilt from top to bottom provided more than enough power for the heavy-duty transmission. With an overdrive gear system, the car's high gear was well over one hundred and twenty miles an hour. This Oldsmobile was fast.

If the Olds wasn't enough to make men stop and stare, the woman sitting behind the wheel was. Even though she had been rushed to leave on a moment's notice and wore no makeup, her prominent cheekbones accented her silky black hair. Although a little disheveled, it fell to her shoulders and flowed over the man's white dress-shirt she had hastily thrown over her bra-less body. She reminded Blondie of a movie star. Looking vulnerable in a way he loved, she flashed Blondie an engaging smile.

"Did you get the bank bag?" Carolyn asked.

Blondie walked around to the passenger side, opened the door, and slid into the seat. Carolyn leaned over to kiss him, but he pulled back, and growled.

174

"Too many people want to take our future,' he said. "Don't broadcast that we've been here to the whole world."

"Why?" She smiled a coy smile. "Are you ashamed of me?"

Blondie's voice softened. "You know I could never be ashamed of you."

Two couples, who looked like they were on their way to a bar and needed something to talk about, stared at the car. Carolyn stared back at them.

"Don't look at those people," Blondie said and kept his head turned away from the gawking couples. "We can't attract attention."

She pillowed her head on his shoulder. "Well, then, let's go somewhere where we won't attract attention."

Blondie gave the couples a sideways look. With their arms around each other's waists, they peered inside the car. Blondie turned his face away from them and nodded. Carolyn slid behind the wheel and pulled away from the curb. After she passed the newsstand, she steered toward the intersection. "I assume there were too many people around for those kids to drop the bag. Where to next, big boy?"

Blondie leaned back. As exhaustion and disappointment ran though his body, he withered into the comfort of the seat.

"Just turn right and drive."

CHAPTER 19

Behind the steering wheel, Neal watched as streets ran off the side of the road and funneled into endless destinations. As his eyes lit up, he pointed to a road that led to the right.

"I wonder where that goes," he said. "Wouldn't you like to go down there just to see what's at the end of it?"

At another time, Freddy might have shared Neal's excitement of going down an unknown road, but right now all he wanted to do was go home. He stared out the windshield. The side streets grew fewer, and the end of the wide road yawned before him.

Without looking at him, he asked Neal, "You sure you don't want to go back, drop off the bank bag, and go home?"

Neal leaned back and danced his hand on the steering wheel. "Ah, ahem, ah, yes. Of course, I want to drop that bag off and go home. But we don't know what's in it." He held up one finger. "We lost the bet to be back at the Burp in twelve hours. What will the gang say when we pull into town empty-handed?"

At this point Freddy didn't care what was in the bag, or what the kids at the Burp would say. He was about to tell Neal just that, but Rafferty spoke first.

"Maybe they put poison in that bag."

"So what?" Neal said. "We'll get some rubber gloves, put a handkerchief over mouths, and open it."

Freddy saw his chance to convince Neal to go back. "If we take the bag back, we could double that money in that envelope and wave it in front of the kids' faces at the Burp. Why open the bag and take a chance on getting blown up, poisoned, or shot at?"

Neal cast Rafferty and Freddy a sideways glance. "They can't shoot what they can't catch." He tromped the accelerator, and broke into his little tune. "Dit-a, dit-a, plonk-oh!"

Freddy should have been used to Neal's never ending surprises, but he leaned back and froze in pure astonishment. Staring in the rearview mirror, he watched the glimmering lights of the city of Buffalo. Winking into the night they shrank to a single shimmering light, and vanished. For a few miles Neal didn't say a word. Finally he turned to Rafferty and flashed a shifty grin.

"Just think what we can do with what's in that bag." He pointed to his own eye. "I watched a lot of people who were afraid to take a chance on anything. You know what happened to them? They got stuck in the go-to-work-every-day routine."

"Yeah, they did," Freddy said, "but some of those people have nice easy desk jobs."

A tremor of concern passed over Neal's face. "Those people that ride desks like to make work out of nothing. I don't know about you, but I don't need phone calls from halfwits asking where something is when it's right in front of them." He leaned into a turn. Under the strain of the high speed, the tires howled for mercy. Pulling out of the turn, he exhaled. "Money cuts right through the entire world's bullshit."

Rafferty turned to Freddy. "Do you want to open that bag?"

177

Expectantly looking at Freddy, Neal said, "Yeah! Freddy." He broke into an ear-to-ear tooth-flashing smile. "You wanna?"

Just to take his mind off of what could happen if they opened the bag, Freddy nervously placed his hand on the gun he had tucked in his belt. "I don't think I have a choice."

"Sure you have a choice." Neal waved his hand around. "You can help us open it, or you can sit back, relax, make yourself comfortable, and watch us open it."

Suppressing a laugh, Rafferty turned toward Freddy and flashed him a big ear-to-ear smile.

Freddy was defeated, but he tried anyway. "What if we open it and Doughnut or Blondie show up?"

Neal patted himself on the side of the chest. "No problem. You got the gun."

Freddy wasn't sure he could shoot another human being. "I don't know," he muttered.

Keeping one hand on the steering wheel, Neal turned to the side and reached over the seat. He held out his hand. "If you're afraid, give me the gun."

Freddy wanted to say, 'That's all we need, Neal with a gun.' But he didn't. Instead he said, "I would," and patted the gun. "But I've kinda grown fond of it."

"It's your call." Neal flopped his arm back over the seat. "But I got to know what's in that bag. We're pulling over at the next good-lighted place."

Around the next bend, below a line of flapping orange and white triangular flags, a single light bulb hung over a round white sign with big orange letters that read 'GULF'. To lure customers into the station,

178

the sides of the flat roof had been festooned with attention-getting orange and blue banners, but the sign on the glass door read, 'CLOSED.'

Neal downshifted. The Ford rumbled onto the blacktop. After parking next to a gas pump, he reached under the seat, pulled out the bank bag, and yanked on the zippered lock.

"This thing's pretty strong,' he said. "But I still got the master key in the trunk."

Freddy leaned over the front seat. "You mean that tire iron?"

A look of delight beamed from Neal's face. "It fits any lock."

Rafferty opened the passenger door. The dome light was burned out, but the single light bulb hanging over the sign beamed enough light for Freddy to watch Rafferty placed one foot on the blacktop, stand up, and turn to Neal.

"Are we gonna talk about it," he said, "Or are we finally gonna see what's in that bag?"

Freddy eased out of the back seat and left the passenger side door opened. Neal jumped out of the Ford, let the driver's side door hang open, walked to the trunk, and opened it. He grabbed the bag, placed it on the bumper, and lifted the tire iron. As he got ready to slam down on the lock, Freddy looked up. From out of the black night, headlights funneled through the trees. They bounced and dipped and threw long shadows. Then they rushed right at them, getting brighter and brighter. Neal threw the bag and the tire iron into the darkness of the trunk, slammed it shut. With his face locked in revulsion, he turned to the oncoming threat.

Frozen with fear, Freddy could not grasp the heartlessness of such an act. "Ah, man," he said under his breath. "He's not going to stop."

Neal's face unlocked and his lips spread into a smile. With the headlights fifty feet away, he held up his arms. As if he were guiding an airplane into its hanger, he clinched his fists, held his thumbs out, and motioned for the oncoming car to come forward.

Rafferty grabbed him by the shoulder. "He's not stopping. Get out of the way."

Neal shrugged off Rafferty's hand. "If it's Doughnut and his friends, they won't hit us. We still know where the bag is and they don't. Help me wave him in, and make him feel welcome, smile."

Forcing a smile, Rafferty got into the act, but stood off to the side and waved his arm in a come-here gesture. The car lights beamed bright, and the car skidded to a stop. The purple glow from the dash lights revealed a silken-haired female driver. She propped her elbow on the door and killed the headlights, but she kept the parking lights on. And there it was: shining as if it had just been painted, a 1957 Oldsmobile graced the night.

Ruining the elegance of the moment, Blondie stuck his head out the passenger side window and waved a gun. Using Rafferty's shadow as a shield, Freddy jumped into the front seat of the Ford, dropped to his knees, and watched from the narrow opening between the front seats.

Neal held his hands in the air. "Don't shoot."

Rafferty edged toward the Ford.

Blondie jerked the gun at Rafferty. "If you want to keep breathing, just stand there."

Looking toward the Ford, Rafferty watched Freddy. Making sure Blondie couldn't see the gesture, Freddy held up his hand and pointed his finger as if it were a gun. He hoped Rafferty understood what he was going to do. He took the gun from his belt, but still wasn't sure he could shoot anyone; and he didn't know what would happen if he actually fired the gun. Taking a deep breath, he pulled back the hammer, and waited.

Standing in the bright headlights of the Oldsmobile, Neal flashed Blondie a big welcoming grin. "Can we help you?"

"Don't get cute," Blondie snapped and held out his hand. "Give me that bag."

"Ah, ahem, ah, yes." Neal scratched the side of his head. "Of course, we would do just that. But we don't have it."

"I know you got that bag." With the pitch of his voice rising, he ordered Neal to, "Just get it, and shut up."

With his hands in the air, Neal walked backwards to the Ford. When he got to the driver's side door, he pointed inside.

"It's under the seat," he said. "I'll have to crawl under and get it."

"Go ahead," Blondie said and jerked the barrel of the gun. "But don't get smart, or I'll put a hole in your buddy big enough for an elephant to walk through."

Bending over the seat, Neal looked up at Freddy. Freddy waved the gun and nodded. Neal reached under the seat. As he rummaged around, for a reason unknown to Freddy, he laughed.

After he pulled the money-filled manila envelope out, he looked to Freddy, and whispered, "When Blondie takes his eyes off Rafferty, start shooting."

Holding the envelope in his hand, and with both hands raised over his head, he walked to the Oldsmobile.

"We don't have the bag," he said and held out the envelope. "But here's your money back."

When Neal was ten feet from the car, Blondie jerked the gun at him.

Neal stopped.

"I'm not telling you again," Blondie said. "Go back and get the bag."

"Ah, ahem, ah, yes." Neal shook the envelope. "But like I keep telling you, we don't have it."

Blondie smiled, but there was contempt in his voice. "Don't feed me that shit. I saw the bag in your hand when you didn't drop it in the basket."

Neal looked like a rat with his tail caught in a trap trying to claim he wasn't anywhere near the cheese bait. His guilty look changed. He gave Rafferty a look that said to bolt at the first opportunity. A random gust of wind kicked up. The triangular orange and white flags below the Gulf sign flapped. The split second Blondie swiveled his eyes to the side to see what it was, Neal flung the manila envelope at him. It sailed through the night air and whapped him on the side of the forehead, bounced off, and skidded onto the ground. When Blondie jerked his head, Rafferty ran for the car. Neal was in such haste that he passed Rafferty. Like a baseball player sliding headfirst for home plate, he dove into the Ford. Inside, he franticly pulled down the ignition wires, and jammed them together. Rafferty dove into the front seat so fast that he tumbled over Freddy and ended up in the middle of the seat. Freddy slammed the door shut.

The engine started, but Neal was still lying on the floor. He pressed on the accelerator. The exhaust bellowed back at Blondie. Blondie aimed his gun. The Oldsmobile's headlights beamed blinding-bright.

Blondie's voice rang out. "Stop! Or I'll shoot."

With the white light blasting the back of the Ford, Freddy reached out the window, held the gun over the back of the roof of the Ford and pulled the trigger. The gun fired. A single flash of bright light brightened the dark night. The jerk of the gun and the flash caused Freddy to lose his grip on the gun. He re-gripped and pulled his hand into the window. Blondie jerked his hand and the gun inside the Oldsmobile. In one smooth motion, he pulled the girl's head below the dash, and ducked down.

Like a Jack-in-the-box, Neal popped up behind the steering wheel, hooked first gear, and jammed the accelerator down. With the engine roaring, he let the clutch fly up. The Ford's tires squawked on the blacktop of the gas station and raced toward the road. With the engine screaming, the tires bit into the little strip of gravel at the side of the road and blasted a shower of stones onto the Oldsmobile's shiny surface.

Watching out the back window, Freddy, squinted through the bright white of the Oldsmobile's headlights. Blondie jumped out of the car, glanced at the dinged finish, scooped up the envelope, and ran to the driver's side. He threw open the door, pushed the girl to the passenger side, and jumped behind the wheel. With both back tires howling into the night and blue smoke rolling up under the fenders, the Olds canted to one side then shot away from the gas station. The chase was on.

Rafferty looked to Neal. "Why did you throw the money away?"

"We can't spend it if we're dead," Neal snapped back, depressed the clutch, and shifted gears.

Craning his neck to look out the back window, Freddy said, "That Oldsmobile's got a big engine in it. It'll probably catch us pretty quick."

Neal rolled his eyes. "Not with those thousand-pound bumpers and that heavy body."

"I don't know," Freddy mused. "Those big cars get up the speed on the straightaway."

"Maybe with a regular car." Neal affectionately patted the dashboard. "But this baby's not a regular car. She might not go real fast on the straightaway, but she can handle tighter in the turns."

Neal hit high gear. Under the '40 Ford's hood the Cadillac Ambulance V-8 engine howled and the rpms rose.

Freddy stared out the back window. In the distance, the bright headlights of the Oldsmobile faded to dull silver. Neal steered the Ford around a bend in the road, and the Oldsmobile's threatening headlights blinked black.

CHAPTER 20

With the muscles in his neck and arms cramping, Blondie steered the Oldsmobile into a curve. Trying to catch the fleeing Ford and get the bank bag, he mashed the gas to the floor. With the tires howling for mercy the car's heavy body leaned to one side. When he steered out of the bend, an S curve snaked through a maze of oak trees. He had no choice. He slowed down.

For miles, every time he gained speed, the road would turn, hook to the right or left, or twist off at sharp angles; and he would have to ease off the gas. When the road finally straightened out, the big Olds gained speed. Blondie settled back into the seat. As the nervous tension subsided, he tossed the envelope, Neal had thrown at him, into Carolyn's lap.

"Here, count it."

She didn't open it. "Is this stolen money?"

"Sure, but the people we took it off of stole it first."

Carolyn placed her hand on his chest. "You mean there are that many guns out there?"

"They don't need guns." Blondie lowered his voice. "They stole it with crooked accountants, typewriters, and ballpoint pens."

"But aren't there laws to make them give it back?"

"Laws are useless when crooked lawyers and crooked judges are on the take."

Carolyn held the envelope in front of face and shook it. "Do you still want me to open this?"

Blondie studied the envelope for a moment. "That doesn't look right. Yes, open it."

Carolyn looked inside. A worried crease appeared on her face. "Those kids got your money."

"What?" Blondie jerked his head toward the sharp turn in the road ahead.

Carolyn held the bag open. "There's nothing in here but an old pair of work gloves."

Blondie steered out of the turn. In the past, moments like this would have affected his judgment. If he were to get completely free of the Arm's influence and live a normal life, he couldn't continue to be like Doughnut and the others. He couldn't let his anger swell into a fury. He suppressed it, smiled, and shook his head.

"I'll have to hand it to those little bastards," he said. "They never miss a trick."

He slowed down and motored around a corner. On the straightaway, he pressed the accelerator to the floor. The speedometer climbed to ninety-five. The high beams of the headlights cut the blackness far ahead, but no telltale red sergeant stripes of the Ford's taillights glowed in the night. He made a fist and pounded on the steering wheel. "Damn. Where did they go?"

Holding the envelope, Carolyn stared out at the open road ahead. "Was there a lot of money in this thing?"

Blondie gritted his teeth. "There was enough to make those kids nibble at an idea of being rich, but that bank bag has the mother lode in it."

"Couldn't you go to Harlem and make money instead?"

Blondie couldn't believe how naive she was. Although New York City was the most important Mafia base, and big enough to accommodate five families, if a person did any business there he had to hand over a sizable chunk to them. When you did business in Mafioso territory you earned a lot of money, and you had to pay your taxes on it. If you asked why, they said that it was because they let you do it, and that they were the real government. Sure, millions were being made in Harlem, but it was in the heroin trade. The dealers would get a pure kilo and cut it to three percent. Then, to keep the girls who packaged it for street sales honest, they made them package it in the nude.

The New York police department was mostly on the take. When the heroin dealers paid them off, even if only one time, they would be afraid of their jobs and afraid of ending up being another bloated body in the sewer system. Then, the dealers had them forever. The Mafioso called it 'respect', but it was really fear that brought power.

Blondie and Freddy had thought they had found a way to controlled fear. They agreed that they should never go into any fight thinking about what the other guy was going to do to them. They always went in *knowing* what they were going to do to the other guy. That way, they'd never lose; and they'd never be afraid. But now his friend, Freddy, was dead.

He glanced over at Carolyn. Crossing her legs, she looked as if she were expecting a cup of tea and a slice of pound cake. He loved her long-legged big-busted body. And when she walked, she walked like a lady. When she sat, she tucked her skirt around her legs nicely. She had good posture. She sat next to him like she was proud of herself. She had class.

As she had suggested, Blondie could go to Harlem and make millions, but the heroin trade was making Harlem look like a third world country. He had lived there in a railroad flat. He didn't like it. Like most of the other buildings, it had had the stoop with dirty-black iron railings; and filthy garbage cans always sat out front near the curb. Inside had chipped plaster, peeling paint, and the big ugly radiator matched the cheap furniture. The smell in the room was so bad, even perfume couldn't hide the fact that the apartment was a dump. He could never take Carolyn to a place like that. He didn't want to live out his life there. It didn't have enough class. And besides, when he got that bank bag, he wouldn't have to even think about selling dope or watching behind his back.

Getting ready to increase speed, he reached for the overdrive handle. A deer's eyes glowed at the side of the road. He pulled his hand back and eased up on the gas.

Carolyn tugged at his shirtsleeve. "Why are you slowing down?"

"Look up ahead on your side of the road."

"Oh, honey, don't hit that big dog."

Blondie let out a little laugh. "It's not a dog. It's a deer. Where there's one there's more. At ninety-five, I wouldn't be able to stop in time to miss it."

After passing the deer, another one with a huge rack of horns ambled out from the berm and stood in the center of the road. Blondie yanked on the wheel. The Olds careened over the centerline. From

188

around the bend, a speeding car came at them with its headlights on high beam.

Blondie slammed on the brakes. The back wheels locked up and squealed on the pavement. Smoke and the smell of burnt rubber filled the car. The other car kept right on going. As it zipped past, for a fraction of a second, Blondie caught a glimpse of the oily-haired driver grinning a mouth full of rotten teeth. Then the Oldsmobile's back fender grazed the rear end of the deer. But as if it were an everyday occurrence, the deer jerked sideways, sprang off the road, and vaulted into the forest.

"Damn," Blondie said, and took his foot off the brake. "That thing was big enough to mess up the radiator." He squinted into the darkness; still, no red taillights. "We should have caught up to those kids by now." Gaining speed, he looked far ahead. "They're not invisible. They have to be somewhere."

Carolyn leaned toward him. "Is it really that important?"

Blondie's fist crashed against the dashboard. "They got it all." He jerked his head to the side. "I got it all to get back."

Carolyn backed away from him. He slowed and drove on in silence. A few miles down the road, a thin veil of dust hovered over the road. Carolyn rubbed her teary eyes and sat upright. "What is that?"

Neal lifted his foot from the accelerator. "If that's not fog, it could be dust from that Ford."

At the spot where the dust hovered, he pulled onto the gravel lot of a mom and pop gas station and grocery store. The station had been built of cement

189

blocks and whitewashed. One gas pump that had been brush-painted dark red, stood in front of the structure. Off to the left, a juniper-lined pond curled around a stand of trees and vanished into the darkness.

Blondie looked toward Carolyn. Four yellow bug lights hanging from slanted steel poles on the sides of the store reflected light onto the building's big glass window and cast a golden candle-like light through the side window of the Oldsmobile. The outline of Carolyn's lovely figure silhouetted through her thin white shirt.

Blondie never liked to apologize to anyone, but she looked so petite and frail that he was ashamed of his outburst. He put his hand on hers and looked in her face. Her black hair glowed warm against her skin and accentuated her lovely face.

He whispered, "I'm sorry I yelled at you." She gave him a slight nod and moved closer. Then he hit himself on the side of the head. "They had Pennsylvania plates." He smiled. "If that's where they're going, they haven't broken the code." Carolyn let out a sigh and laid her head against his shoulder. Blondie put his arm around her and gently squeezed. "They couldn't have gone far."

Carolyn pointed out the windshield. "Look! There's tire tracks in the gravel."

Blondie cut the wheel to the right. "Let's check around the back of this place."

CHAPTER 21

Sitting in the back seat with the smell of juniper coming through the Ford's opened window, Freddy looked up. The gravel shore of a newly built pond curled into a sharp bend and hid deep in the cover of trees. Neal figured that because the pond was new, the gravel would still be solid. He had taken a chance; and even though the rear tires had pawed at the mud and slung it into the air, he had driven across the shallow end of the pond and pulled up on shore.

Although trees and juniper bushes surrounded them and they were stopped at the far end of the pond's curl, they had a good view of the station.

Freddy looked across the pond's dark surface. Yellow bug lights hanging from slanted steel poles on the sides of the mom and pop gas station and grocery store cast a golden glow over the roof of Blondie's Oldsmobile, it slowly pulled away from the gas pump. Leaning toward Neal, Rafferty looked out the driver's side window. "You think he sees us?"

"So what if he does," Neal said, and shrugged. "He'll never go across that water."

The Oldsmobile started for the back of the station. Freddy suppressed a sudden fear. Then the Oldsmobile pulled to the edge of the pond and stopped. Its high beams shot across the water and the front tires lurched forward.

Rafferty grabbed Neal's shoulder. "He's coming across."

The front tires of the Oldsmobile hit the water and sunk down about an inch. The brake lights flashed bright red. The girl inside screamed. The car backed away from the water. Neal let out a low laugh.

"That Oldsmobile's a tank," he said. "If he comes after us, he'll sink."

Freddy wasn't sure it hadn't been just luck that they had made it across the pond the first time. And he didn't like the idea of hitchhiking all the way back home. He reached over the seat and shook Neal's shoulder. "We won't we sink on the way out, will we?"

"We're lighter and we're not going through slow," Neal said, with cocksureness. "We'll fly through it just like we did when we came across."

Rafferty said, "If Blondie had any brains, he might be able to make it if he went fast enough."

"As long as he doesn't catch us," Freddy said, keeping a wary eye on the Oldsmobile, "he can stay as dumb as he wants."

The Oldsmobile backed away from the shore and aimed its headlights behind the station. Towers of old tires leaned against the back of the station wall. Next to those, two fifty-five-gallon drums that looked to be full of used oil stood on rotted wooden pallets. Like thinning hair on a bald head, sickly stands of grass grew between rusted car parts that lay in haphazard rows.

Blondie cocked the Oldsmobile's front tires and pulled away from the station. As if he were in no hurry, he turned back to where he had come from, and cruised down the highway.

"How about that?" Rafferty said. "He must think we went another way."

Neal opened the door, half getting out, he said, "Now that Blondie's busy looking in the wrong place and we're back here where no one can bother us, let's see what's in that bank bag."

Rafferty opened the passenger door. "That's been botherin' the bejesus out of me." He stepped out of the Ford. "Let's go."

Neal got out. Using the long strides of Groucho Marx, he walked to the trunk and opened it. He pulled out the bag, set it on the bumper, and lifted the tire iron.

"Here goes." Thump! He hit the lock on the bag. It mashed and broke. Holding the bag toward Freddy and Rafferty, he asked, "Who wants the honors?"

Freddy was afraid the bag might blow up, but he was more afraid that nothing of value would be in the bag. He waved his hand down. "Not me."

Rafferty gave a twist of his head. "Just open it."

"Yeah," Freddy urged.

Neal took a deep breath, and let it out. "Here goes."

As if he were defusing an explosive device, Neal held the bag away from his body, leaned back, and squinted. With one hand holding the bag and the other unzipping the zipper, he opened the bag. No poison sprayed into the air, and no explosive bottle of the thick, pale-yellow, liquid nitroglycerin went off. Nothing happened.

"Whew!" Neal wiped his forehead.

Freddy and Rafferty crowded close.

"What's in it?" Rafferty asked.

Neal looked inside. "I don't see any money."

Rafferty twisted his palm down. "Dump it out."

Neal turned the bag over. An 'L' shaped piece of metal the color of gold, fell out and clunked onto the floor of the trunk. Neal turned the bag back over and reached inside. "There's something else in here." He pulled out a yellowed piece of paper that looked like an old bill or business form.

Rafferty picked up the piece of metal. "Is this gold?"

Neal held out his hand. "Let me see."

Rafferty dropped the metal into his palm.

Neal put the metal to this mouth and touched it to his tongue. "It's brass."

"Are you sure?" Freddy said.

Neal spit the taste from his mouth. "Here, taste it."

Freddy touched it to his tongue. "Damn, what's going on?"

Rafferty grabbed the bag, turned it upside down, and shook it. Nothing else came out.

Neal leaned back against the fender of the Ford. "Ah, ahem, ah, yes," he said, rubbing his chin. "Of course." Holding the paper, he crossed his arms. "Let me think."

"It's got to be worth something," Rafferty said, "or Blondie wouldn't have come after us."

Freddy rolled the brass in his hands. The flat metal was half an inch thick and seven inches long. The body of the L was three inches wider than its bottom that was only an inch high and stuck out two inches like a little foot. Four notches ran down one side, and the top of the L came to a dull point. In various places, other rectangular slots had been cut into the brass. He held it by its L-shaped end. "Maybe it's a key."

Rafferty smiled. "If it is, it unlocks a big lock."

Studying the paper, Neal stepped away from the Ford. "I can't read this. There's not enough light." Forgetting the dome light had burned out, he went to the front seat and turned the light switch. "There's no light here." He squinted at the paper. "This thing's weird."

"What do you mean weird?" Rafferty asked.

"It's so old some of the words look like they're faded."

Freddy held out this hand. "Let me try under the headlights."

Neal gave him the paper, bowed, and gestured to the front of the Ford. "Be my guest."

Freddy walked to the front of the Ford and looked at Neal. "Turn on the headlights."

Neal turned on the headlights, put his arm around Rafferty's shoulder, and they walked to the front of the car. Freddy put the paper on top of the brass and held it in front of the headlight. "It's some kind of a letter from a place called Zephyr Manufacturing Company."

Neal dropped his arm from Rafferty's shoulder. "What good is it?"

Rafferty bent over and studied the key. Hit by a sudden realization, he threw his hand into the air.

"Hey, my uncle always said he was in the OSS."

Neal cocked his head to one side. "What's the OSS?"

"That's the Office of Strategic Services. I don't know if he was actually in the Office of Strategic Services, but he showed me how they used keys to read secret messages."

Neal held out his hand toward Freddy. Freddy handed him the key. Neal held the key in his hands and stared at it. Shaking his head, he looked up. "How can you read a secret message with something that's supposed to open a lock?"

Rafferty let out a friendly laugh. "It's not the kind of a key that opens a lock. It's a decoder key."

Neal encouragingly waved the key around in a little circle. "And?"

"Did you guys ever watch a teacher grade tests after we filled in the answers by marking a little circle?"

"I remember that," Freddy said. "The teacher had a little piece of cardboard with a bunch of holes in it. It was like a stencil. When she placed it on the test, if the circle wasn't filled in, the answer was wrong." He looked to Neal. "Let me see that key again."

Neal handed him the key.

Freddy held the key in one hand. With his other hand he ran his finger over the slots. "If this is a decoder key, I wonder what kind of message we can see if we match up the slots with words on the letter."

Neal nudged him in the elbow. "Try it and find out."

Freddy placed the key on the paper and held it in front of the headlight. Where strong light from the headlight didn't penetrate the brass, a pattern seemed to form, but it didn't make sense. He tried a different position. "Wait." He repositioned the key. Where the notches of the key had not blocked light from going through the flimsy paper, a few

196

sentences formed a string of almost readable words. "I think I can read something in the slots."

Neal bent to the paper. "What's it say?"

Before Freddy could utter a word, a big, black dog came barreling out of the woods. Clutching the brass and the letter, Freddy jumped aside and dove into the Ford. Neal and Rafferty were right behind him. They slammed the doors shut. The dog jumped up at the passenger side door and snapped just inside the open window.

Rafferty leaned back and rolled up the window. "Why are we always getting chased by dogs?" He looked to Neal. "Do you carry steaks in your back pocket or what?"

Neal reached over the front seat. "Where's that gun, Freddy? I'll shoot a couple of rounds up in the air and scare him away."

Freddy reached for the gun, but before he could hand it to Neal, a voice yelled from the gas station. "Who's there?"

"The owner of the station must've seen our lights," Neal said.

"So, what's he gonna do?" Rafferty said. "Smack our hands with a ruler?"

Neal's face wreathed with a smile. "Now that's a comforting thought."

The voice boomed louder. "Get the hell out of there or I'll blow your goddamn heads off."

Neal wagged his finger at Rafferty. "If he's got a ruler, it must shoot bullets."

Rafferty opened his door and slammed it shut. The dog stopped barking and ran toward Neal's window."

The voice boomed again. "I'm not going to ask you again. Who's there?"

A devilish smile spread across Rafferty's face. He rolled down his window and yelled across the water. "It's the game commission!" he lied. "We're looking for poachers."

The dog barked six times at Neal's window, ran around to Rafferty's window, and barked five times. Rafferty giggled at the convenient lie and the dog. Then Neal opened his door and slammed it. The dog ran to Neal's window. Panting, the dog barked two feeble barks. Rafferty opened his door and slammed it. The dog quit barking and walked to Neal's window. With a big smile on his freckled face, Neal waved at the tired dog. Rafferty opened his door and slammed it. The dog turned from Neal's door and stopped. As if it were wise to their little game, it walked away.

Neal reached down and grabbed the ignition wires. The engine roared to life. He backed up. The headlights of the Ford beamed across the mirrored surface of the still water and revealed a man standing with a shotgun in his hands. A salt and pepper beard covered most of his face and hung down to his little potbelly. A red bandanna hung out of his patched overalls, making him look like a clown who had escaped from the circus. But he held the barrel of the shotgun turned down toward the ground. Feeling that he was going to sit in the back seat while Neal drove the Ford into the water and sink into the water like an idiot, Freddy looked Neal in the face. "What's the odds of getting back through that water?"

Giving Freddy a wink, Neal revved the engine. "The odds are always good when it's the only hand you got."

He hit the gas and let out the clutch. Gravel spit from under the tires. The Ford charged into the water's mirrored surface. With splashing waves of water fanning out the sides, the car crashed across the pond. Just before it got to shore, it started to sink; but the momentum kept it moving. The front tires rolled up on shore. Just before it was about to stop, the back tires gripped the bottom, dug in, and sprayed gravel-filled water across the surface of the pond, disturbing any frog's peaceful evening. Using both hands to hold the shotgun in front of his chest as if it were a shield, the clown-like man jumped back. Kicking up a great cloud of dust, the rumbling Ford zipped past. Bouncing and dipping as if they were coaxing the Ford to go faster, the headlights swung across the road. When the tires hit the pavement they screamed down the highway, peeling rubber into the night.

On down the road, Freddy rolled the piece of brass in his hands and looked at the paper. "Blondie really wants thing back. If there's a secret message, I wonder what it is."

Rafferty looked back over the seat. "Maybe it's a map to a gold mine."

"Could be," Neal said. "My uncle told me there were secret gold mines in Maryland and Virginia, and the veins stretched all the way up into Pennsylvania."

Rafferty pointed to the key. "Put that paper on it and see what those words say."

"I tried," Freddy said. "There's not enough light back here."

Rafferty held out his hand. "Let me see it. Maybe I can read it with the dash lights."

Freddy handed him the brass and the paper. Rafferty placed the brass key over the paper and looked up. "I think I can read it."

Neal leaned toward Rafferty. "What's it say?"

Rafferty squinted. "It says." He paused for effect. "If you're looking up to read this, you're peeing on your shoes."

Neal laughed and leaned back. "The next place where there's good light, we'll pull over."

"Okay," Rafferty said. "But this time, take those steaks out of your pockets and make sure the place doesn't have any dogs."

CHAPTER 22

Half an hour down the road, Freddy pointed through the Ford's windshield. Up ahead, lights struggled to cast their beams into the darkness. But when Neal drove closer, the lights intensified. Trying to shield his night vision from the brightness, Neal reached up and flipped the sun visor down. As he slowed, Rafferty covered his eyes with his hand and peeked through the small cracks between his fingers. "Hey, Neal, is that enough light for you?"

"It might be." Neal pulled into the all-night truck stop.

Flashing 'EAT' into the thick blackness of night, an orange neon sign hovered on top of the roof. At each end of the white building, perfectly pruned cedar bushes stood in rows like sentinels ready to march away at the slightest command. Off to the side, three green-and-white gas pumps stood in a row. Their hoses curled upward. At the ends of the hoses, nozzles rested in their holders, resembling generals sloppily returning a salute.

Neal stopped at the gas pump and looked at Rafferty. "Does anybody have any money?"

Rafferty turned to him in surprise. "What are you asking us for? You know we emptied our pockets back at the Burp, and you threw the envelope full of money at Blondie."

With a mischievous grin, Neal reached under the seat, pulled out the Canadian flag, and placed it on his lap. As if he were making an offering to a God, he unfolded the flag and held it with both hands. A banded stack of bills sat in the center of the flag.

"How's this for a souvenir?"

Freddy hunched over the seat and stared. "I thought you threw that money at Blondie."

"You think I'm crazy? Nobody throws money away."

Freddy cast an appraising eye on the money. "Wait a minute. An empty envelope couldn't have gone far enough to hit Blondie. What was in it?"

Smiling, Neal tilted his head to the side. "When Blondie had the gun pointed at us and you guys were crapping your pants, I dumped the money out and wrapped the flag around it. Then I jammed a pair of old gloves into the envelope."

Freddy didn't want to admit to being afraid. "We weren't crapping our pants. When you were reaching under the seat, I was wondering why you were laughing."

"Pretty good souvenir," Rafferty said. "But we never did get that cup of coffee."

A sleepy-eyed attendant, with a green and white paper garrison hat on his head, sauntered up to Neal's window, stopped, and mumbled through a yawn, "Fill 'er up?"

Neal peeled off a large bill. "Yeah, pack it in the tank. Is the food inside any good?"

Reaching for the nozzle with one hand and stretching with the other hand toward the night sky, the attendant said, "The truckers like it."

After the attendant filled the tank, checked the oil, and washed the windows, Neal paid him, got the change, pulled the Ford into a slanted parking slot in front of the truck stop, and killed the engine. With the realization that he was finally going to see what was on that paper, Freddy sat in stunned silence.

Neal turned sideways and winked at Rafferty. "Let's get in the light and see what's on that paper."

Freddy held back. "I don't think we should take the brass key in. It' so big, somebody might see it and think we're nuts."

Giggling, Rafferty held the key in his hand. "Everybody already knows that."

"He's got a point there," Neal said. "But there's no use attracting attention. If that key's worth something, somebody else might want it, too."

Freddy held out his hand to Rafferty. "Give me that key." He took it and laid it on the paper. Squinting in the dim light, he tried to align the slots of the key and reveal a message but nothing made sense. He held out the key to Rafferty. "Hide this thing in your pocket. There's not enough light out here. We'll have to take it inside."

A few patrons had spilled out onto the side of the truck stop building. Their voices sounded like the murmur of bees. Neal pulled on the screen door. It screeched on its worn hinges and yawned wide. Rafferty, Freddy, and Neal stepped in. A soft light, the aroma of good food, sporadic laughter, and enthusiastic trucker's talk greeted them. As they walked to a table draped with a red-and-white checked tablecloth, clinks of dishes and cooking utensils interrupted music that flowed from a juke box blinking blue and orange lights. They stopped and scanned the area. The air tingled with friendly energy. White-uniformed waitresses scurried from booth to booth taking orders and replenishing steamy mugs with dark coffee to keep bug-eyed truckers awake. The whole place breathed with life. Neal waved toward a booth with shiny-red leather seats.

"That one's open," he said. "We can sit with our backs protected and see the whole place."

A waitress with a short, tight skirt and a shorter white apron wiggled up to the booth and wobbled her breasts. Mesmerized, Freddy watched her place glasses of ice water onto the table. Usually Neal would make a big deal out of someone as sharp as this waitress, but he only gave her a once over and ordered three of the trucker's special: home fries, eggs, and all the coffee they could drink. Then he leaned over and nudged Freddy in the ribs. "Get that paper out."

After the waitress left to fill their order, Rafferty pulled the key from his pocket. Freddy pulled out the paper and laid it on the table in front of Rafferty.

Rafferty slid the key toward the paper.

But when Freddy and Neal horned close, Rafferty shrugged away from them. "Don't pack up on me. Everybody will look."

So what," Freddy said. "We're not going steady."

A dejected look formed on Neal's face. He wrapped both arms around Rafferty's shoulders and sobbed into his shoulder. "You mean you don't love me anymore?"

Rafferty shrugged Neal's arms off. "Come on, you guys. A truck stop isn't a good place to make somebody think we're a bunch of faggots." Freddy and Neal backed off, but stayed close enough to read the paper.

204

Holding the brass key next to the paper, Rafferty's head wrinkled. "This thing is a letter from Zephyr Manufacturing Company."

The letter read:

Zephyr Manufacturing Company
33rd and 15th Street, New York, New York
Telephone 7-714
November 9, 1931
Mr. Wayne Bulick
Bulick Sales Company
2000 N. SantaFe Street
ElPaso, Texas

Dear Mr. Wayne Bulick:

Your engrave is gone from Chicago. We have forwarded your order
of 2,000 pounds, butt watch out for breakage when it arrives by mail.
Mother Hubbard toys will also be on sale next month.
Just in time for the gift giving season, the owner's son has a new line
of porcelain. He has only a few items available, and he is working very hard.
He also has Alphonse's new gravey picture. If you would like to
take stock in this new promising item or any of the old
Jungle Inn products, please let us know by telegram. Any broken
items will be replaced with no questions asked.

We look forward to your second order. Our new factory will be completed just

as soon as we can buy enough brick to repair our brand new method of

increasing production. As of now our broken down exhaust stack is backing up

smoke that seems to be coming from the coal chute.

Thank you for your order. We look forward to a long lasting relationship.

Your friends at the Zephyr Manufacturing Company.

Ray and Al Zephyr.

"Okay, Rafferty," Neal said. "Show us how your uncle used that key."

Rafferty turned the key over so that it resembled the letter L. Then he placed the key on the paper in various places, but no message appeared in the slots. He broke into a hopeful smile and looked toward Freddy. "There has to be some guide to show us where to put this thing. You got any ideas?"

Freddy looked at the key and then looked at the letter. "One side of the key is straight," he said. "And one side has an end sticking out. He ran his finger along the left margin of the text of the letter. "This side is straight." He jumped his finger to the right side of the text. "This side is uneven and lines stick out."

"I got it," Neal said. "Put the straight side of the key on the straight side of the words with the bottom of the L on the right side and see what we get."

Rafferty placed the key on the paper and aligned one side with the edge of the text and slid the key down until the name Wayne Bulick appeared in the first slot.

"It still doesn't make any sense."

Neal wiggled his finger over the key. "Move it down further."

Rafferty slid the key three lines down the paper. "It still doesn't tell us anything."

"I know what," Freddy said. "Keep moving the key down until all the slots have words in them."

Rafferty slowly slid the key down the letter and stopped at each line, but words were missing from some of the slots. He took his hands off the key and leaned back, and moaned. "Now what?"

Running his finger down the straight side of the key, Freddy said, "I think this side goes on the left."

Rafferty placed his fingers on the key. "Maybe if..." He turned the key over so that the pointed end pointed to the bottom of the paper and the key resembled the letter F with the center line missing. He moved the key down line by line until he found a place where all the slots were filled with words. In the first slot the words 'grave is gone from Chicago' appeared. He tilted his head. "You think that's it?"

"It has to be," Freddy said. "It's the only place where the slots are filled with words."

Neal placed his hand on Rafferty's and shook it. "What's the whole message?"

The words inside the slots read: "Grave is gone from Chicago, 2,000 pounds, butt watch out, Mother Hubbard has Alphonse's new grave. Take

207

stock in Jungle Inn. Replace second brick down from coal chute."

Neal put his hand on the paper and dragged it across the table. "Is that all it says?"

Perplexed, Freddy looked to Neal. "You tell me. You're looking at it."

Neal ran his finger under the letterhead. "This Zephyr Manufacturing's address is 33rd and 15th Street."

Rafferty and Neal exchanged glances.

"So," Rafferty said. "Are we going to go there?"

"We can't," Neal said. "I was there once. There's no such street; 33rd Street only goes to 12th Street. Then it is stops at the water." He squinted and re-read the coded words. "'Grave is gone from Chicago, 2,000 pounds, butt watch out, Mother Hubbard has Alphonse's new grave'. Al's short for Alphonse. Al Capone was the big boss in Chicago, but he got sent to prison."

"Yeah," Freddy said, and shifted in his seat. "But they let him out after eight years, said he went buggy from syphilis."

Neal's face split into a wicked grin. "That might have been what you read in the newspapers. But when he was supposed to be in jail, my old man said a lot of people saw him in a bar called Peacock Alley."

"If they did," Rafferty held up two fingers, "he must have had a double in prison."

Freddy tilted his head and took a thoughtful look at the ceiling. "I think they said Capone died after World War II was over." He lowered his head. "Maybe in 1947."

"So, what would be so important about Al Capone's grave?" Rafferty asked.

"I don't know," Neal said. "But I'll bet Blondie knows."

Rafferty rolled his shoulders. "Well, why don't we just ask him?"

"Yeah, right," Freddy said and reached for the paper. "Hey, they spelled butt wrong. Let's see what else is wrong."

As Rafferty covered the key with his hands, Neal jerked the paper back and slipped it into his pocket. "We'll do that on the road."

Freddy looked up. The waitress stood there balancing all their orders on her hands and arms. Her face looked worn, pained, and her eyes looked like she hadn't had enough sleep.

"Well hello there, hot stuff," Neal said, with a pleasant tone to his voice.

The waitress smiled a weary smile.

Another waitress came up to her. "Becky, your mother just called again. She's worse and needs you."

With her bosom spilling out of the top of her uniform, and Neal's eyes following her every move, Becky bent over and hurriedly placed their orders on the table.

"You'll have to excuse me, gentleman," she said and frowned. "I have to go and check on my mother."

She turned and walked toward the door. Reaching into his pocket, Neal called after her. "Hey, hot stuff, get your tip before you leave."

But she kept on walking, pushed the door open, and was gone. With a dejected look on his face,

Neal slapped his hands to his sides. But when Roy Orbison's song 'Crying' surged from the jukebox, his eyes lit up. "That broken radio in the car got me starved for music."

He smiled, slid out of the booth, stood up, and surveyed the place. As if he couldn't stop himself, he slow-danced over to the jukebox and stopped. He stretched his arms wide, and embraced the brightly-lit blue and orange glass of the record playing machine. Then, with his eyes closed tight, and feeling every word of the song, he reached up with both hands, held his head, and sang along. Hauling back, he blew out a bawling breath, high and wide, almost screaming a perfect pitch into the air.

As if a curtain had been raised to present a long awaited show, the usual rhythm and the sounds of the truck stop ceased. All heads turned toward the sound of Neal singing. An old man with a bronze complexion sat on the edge of a wooden chair at his shoeshine stand. As he tapped his foot and nodded, a big smile spread across his face.

A waitress with a red apron and a white ribbon in her hair, who had been working in the kitchen, rushed out, stumbled over a chair, and stared at Neal. Sweat flashed in her face and her mouth was open. In the corner booth, a fat man stopped eating his giant hamburger. As if it were a mask to hide his feelings, he held it in front of his face and watched Neal. And his sad face looked as if he were about to cry. A big-busted waitress with blond pigtails set her tray down and clapped her hands above her head. With her hips swaying to the beat, her high-pitched voice squeaked out. "Sing it, man, sing it."

210

Neal let out a sad wail of, "Crying," and bent over until he touched his shoe tops with his outstretched fingertips. Sucking in a breath just in time for the next note, he straightened up and continued. After he crooned that line out, he hunched over and drew a breath for another blast of feeling. With his misty eyes closed, he leaned back and held a high note for a long time. Buried in the crowd, a teary-eyed truck driver wearing a worn leather vest pulled the visor of his baseball cap over his eyes. For once it wasn't just a usual night in a clapboard-sided truck stop. The little humid building with its greasy spoons and discolored plates and thick coffee mugs was anew with a crazy air, and all because of Neal. He was slumped almost onto the floor, caressing an invisible microphone, insanely singing with the feeling of the song playing on the jukebox.

A skinny unshaven man, with his front teeth missing, squared his shoulders. Then, as if he were the utmost authority on everything, he made a crazy sign by circling his hand around his ear and pointing to Neal. But nobody cared about that guy.

A look of great sorrow filled Neal's face, and tears formed in the corners of his eyes, but he kept them shut. His lips curled with feeling, and he sung every single note. He had worked his charismatic magic, and whether or not they wanted to do it, everyone in the place was being exposed to the harmony of the shared feelings of their suppressed sad side of a lonesome life that comes from a lost love. The waitress and people gathered around and wanted more, but Neal hit the last long high note, and the music stopped. The jukebox's mechanical

211

arm put the record back into the slot and Neal was done.

A spattering of applause filled the white building. People nodded with approval. Some sat blanked-faced in their booths or at their tables and took sips of coffee. Like a falling star that seemed to cry, a little tear fell from the fat man's eye. He wiped it off his cheek and continued eating his hamburger. And the usual rhythm of the truck stop sounds returned.

Freddy had never seen this compassionate side of Neal before. Now he knew why the girls loved him. Then, as if he had just come out of a trance Neal looked up. Red-faced and shaking his head, he walked back to the booth.

"Damn, Roy Orbison's good," he said in almost a whisper and sat down.

Freddy reached across the table. Loosely holding the chrome napkin holder, he stared into space. "If he's so good why don't you play it again?"

Neal's face clouded. "I would, but I just can't take it." He jerked his head. "Did you hear how he hits those high notes?"

Rafferty let out a languishing sigh. "A girl could hit those notes."

"Girls, smirls," Neal said, not biting on the jibe. As if it were an afterthought, he raised his arm and reared his foot up. In one motion he stomped down and swung down his arm with excitement. Leaning back with his face to the ceiling, he said, "I can't explain it. It's crazy. I can see Roy moaning, slumped over the microphone, never missing a beat. The man just keeps right on singing. Man, oh man, he doesn't only sing the song. It's the things, man, it's the things he feels. He lives every word. Damn...he's good."

Freddy shouldered his way next to Rafferty. "If he's not going to sing along with Roy again, I guess we'll have to listen to dit-a, dit-a, plonk-oh!"

Rafferty faked a grimace. "How could we pass up a generous offer like that?"

Neal shook his head and smiled.

After they ate and went outside, Neal held his hand toward Rafferty. "Give me that key."

"Here you go." Rafferty tossed him the key.

Neal opened the hood to the car. Freddy peered into the engine compartment. "We got engine troubles?"

"No." Neal bent over the engine. "We got key trouble." He took the top of the air cleaner off, placed the brass key inside, and put the top back on. "If Blondie finds us, the only thing that'll keep us alive is him not knowing where the key is."

They climbed back into the Ford and pulled away from the truck stop. As they sped through the darkness, Freddy stretched across the back seat and watched out the little triangular side window. Buildings that could have been farms and outlines of forest trees, flicked past. He closed his eyes. He was tired and with a full stomach he should have dropped off. But sleep didn't come. He kept thinking about that piece of brass hidden in the air cleaner and the note.

Grave gone from Chicago, two thousand pounds, butt watch out, Mother Hubbard has Alphonse new grave. Take stock in Jungle Inn. Replace second brick down from coal chute.

In the opposite lane a flatbed semi blew past. Its wind wave rocked the Ford on its suspension. Freddy jerked up off the seat. "Hey, wait a minute."

Neal jerked his head in Freddy's direction, took one hand off the steering wheel, and pointed at him. "Don't tell me you have to pee."

"No, not that," Freddy said. "That note said, 'Grave gone from Chicago, two thousand pounds, butt watch out, Mother Hubbard has Alphonse's new grave.'"

Neal waved his hand. "So?"

"That's right," Rafferty said, with enthusiasm. "If Al Capone's grave was gone why would they move it?"

"I don't think Al Capone would be buried in a grave like an everyday person," Freddy said. "He had real money. He'd be buried in a vault."

Neal placed his hand back on the steering wheel. "Ah, ahem…ah, yes." He hesitated. "Compared to where he'd be buried, a grave would be like a lemonade stand." Coming out of a sharp curve, he snapped his fingers. "That's it. Not a cemetery vault, a two thousand pound money vault." His voice rose. "Al Capone has a vault, and that piece of brass might be the key."

Rafferty slouched down in the seat. "I don't know. It sounds too easy."

"Blondie wants that key really bad," Freddy said. "It's got to be worth a lot of money."

Rafferty sat up. "So, what if it is a key to some great vault. We still don't know where the Jungle Inn is."

Neal slowed the Ford. "Blondie knows where the Jungle Inn is. Look for a good place to pull over and hide."

Befuddlement filled Rafferty's face, "What for?"

"You'll find out."

As they searched the sides of the road ahead, Rafferty leaned over and thrust his hand in front of Neal's face. "There's a place."

At a bend in the road, a narrow grass-covered road snaked into the cover of trees. Neal stopped the Ford, but didn't back onto the road. Rafferty leaned toward Neal. "Why don't you back in?"

"I don't feel like getting stuck in a muddy spot." He pulled across the road and positioned it to back up. Then he made a shooing motion with the back of his hand. "Okay, Rafferty, get out and walk ahead while I back up. If you don't sink, the road should be safe to drive on."

Rafferty stepped out and walked in back of the Ford. Neal threw his arm over the seat, twisted his body, and craned his neck to watch Rafferty. He backed the Ford into the cover of the dark trees and stopped. Rafferty jumped back into the Ford.

"You think Blondie will see the road, too?"

Neal leaned back and laced his hands behind his head. "With this road being on a bend and at the speed he's going, he'll zip right on past." He shut the motor down, and switched off the car's lights.

Staring into the darkness, Freddy asked, "Then what?"

"After he goes past, we'll follow *him* for a change."

CHAPTER 23

With the '57 Oldsmobile purring down the long road and Blondie behind the wheel, Carolyn snuggled close to him.

"You make pretty good money," she said. "Why can't you just keep on doing what you do?"

"The job's never permanent, and there're too many idiots in the system."

"What do you mean?"

"I spent my childhood around the Chicago Mob. Back there, a lot of tough wise guys claimed to be clip artists, but Old Sam, the boss, said he was lucky if he had a handful who knew how to kill, and many of them would faint at the sight of a drop of blood."

"They sound like a bunch of sissies."

"They're like most people who claim to be tough. All show and no go. Most of those guys wouldn't even carry out the job." He exhaled and looked at the road ahead.

Carolyn gasped. With her eyes open wide, she put her arm on his shoulder and pushed away from him. "How many men have you killed?"

Blondie lowered his head, and softly said, "Thank God, I've never killed anyone, and I don't want to start. That's why I can't keep on doing what I'm doing."

Carolyn slid close and rested her head on his shoulder. "But, honey, even if you're not going to kill anyone, you can't quit now. You just transferred to Canada."

"The only future there, is going to the slammer or having your dead body floating in the sewer system."

"But you never got caught before. You're too smart for that."

"The prisons are full of people who were too smart to get caught."

An oncoming car with its high beams boring into Blondie's eyes sped around a bend. The automatic high-low beam sensor on the Oldsmobile's dashboard clicked the headlights to low beam. The oncoming car raced past. "If I hang around those idiots in Canada, I *will* get caught." Horrible rumors from the California Corcoran prison in California flooded his brain. "And I don't need fish cops down on my ass."

Carolyn jerked her head up off his shoulder. "What do you mean, fish cops?"

"Prison guards that strangle inmates under water while the other guards yank their testicles."

She made a face. "That's awful."

Blondie waved his hand to shoo away the thought. "That's right, but something that will be worse than awful is if those kids figure out what that big brass key fits."

"Can't you do anything to stop them?"

"I hope I did." He rubbed his chin and smiled a self-assuring smile. "Before Doughnut gave the bank bag to Neal, I picked the lock on the bag, took out the brass key, and read the note. I got it memorized, but I didn't have time to replace the brass key with a different key. I still need that brass key."

"If that key is so important, how did those kids get it?"

"Simple, Doughnut and Swill were so drunk when I switched bags they didn't know the difference. And I never tipped off the cops that the kids were making a dope run, so they never picked them up." He hit himself on the forehead. "Damn, if Neal would've just dropped the bag in the basket like he was supposed to, everything would have worked out just fine. But he didn't drop it."

Carolyn cringed and looked up. "Oh, honey, you were so close."

Blondie arched his head back. "I hope we can catch them before they decode the note and get to the Jungle Inn."

Up ahead, little cedar bushes streamed alongside a white truck stop building with an orange neon light flashing 'EAT'. It looked inviting. Carolyn stroked Blondie's arm. "Could we pull in and get something to eat?"

"We can't." Blondie lifted his foot from the accelerator. "But we could use some gas. And those kids might be parked around the back of the building."

He pulled in front of the green and white gas pumps. After an attendant with gray hair and a stout stomach filled the tank, Blondie asked him if he had seen a '40 Ford.

"I haven't seen anything," the attendant said. "I just came on duty."

Blondie paid the man, and started to pull back onto the highway but stopped. "Maybe those kids went in to eat."

He pulled toward the truck stop, and parked underneath the shade of a bushy maple tree. Seeing nothing outside that even resembled a '40 Ford, he took Carolyn by the hand and they went inside. After ordering two trucker's specials and a cup of tea for Carolyn, he looked up at the waitress. "Excuse me, Miss."

The waitress held her pen on the ordering pad. "Did you want something else?"

Blondie turned his palms up, tilted his head toward her, and gave her his best sad-eyed dog expression.

"No, the order is just fine," her said. "But my cousins were driving ahead of us, and we were wondering if they happened to come in here a while ago."

"I don't know. What did they look like?"

"Oh, there were three of them," Carolyn butted in. "One was very attractive with nice black hair. Another one looked to be a weightlifter, and you couldn't miss that skinny carrot-topped kid with the freckled face."

"I don't know," the waitress said, "but while I was out someone put on a little show."

Blondie put his hand on Carolyn's and looked at the waitress. "Was anyone driving a 1940 Ford?"

"I don't know the years of cars. The only customers I've waited on were truck drivers."

Blondie stood up and pulled a roll of money out of his pocket. He flicked off a few bills. Placing them on the table, he looked at Carolyn.

"None of those kids have any talent to put on a show. We already wasted time looking back where we came from. If they didn't stop, they're getting ahead of us." He jerked his head toward the exit. "Let's go."

The waitress held up her finger. "Maybe Becky waited on your cousins. But she went home to check on her sick mother. If you can wait, she'll be back in a few minutes."

Carolyn didn't get up. "We didn't pass them," she said. "If they pulled off the road and hid, we might be ahead of them. And if they stop, we'll be here."

Blondie figured the little '40 Ford was too slow to cover as much distance as fast his big Oldsmobile had done.

"We should have caught them by now. They must have pulled off." He sat down. "Okay, we'll stay long enough to eat and talk to Becky. But if by some slight chance they were here, I'm going to run that big Oldsmobile right up their tailpipe."

Twenty minutes later, Becky came back. She told an impatient Blondie that the '40 Ford with his cousins had left just before she went to her mother's house. Blondie jumped up and threw more than enough money on the table to cover the tab. Then he grabbed Carolyn's hand. As she rose to her feet, he looked at Becky. "Thanks, honey, you've been a great help."

He grabbed Carolyn's hand and pulled her out the door. They dashed to the Oldsmobile and jumped in. Catching his breath, Blondie turned the key. The car's powerful engine roared. As he raced out of the parking lot the back tires spun with awesome power. He glanced in the rearview mirror. The back wheels sent a spray of gravel into the night air. Once on the paved road, he gripped the wheel with both hands and hung on. Careening sideways with the tires screeching, the Oldsmobile roared onto the pavement. The smoking, howling tires and the fishtailing rear end sprayed a blast of blue smoke behind them.

Barreling down the highway, Blondie reached down and pulled the chrome overdrive handle. The engine groaned for a moment then smoothed to a pleasing purr. The speedometer effortlessly climbed. When the needle hit the one hundred twenty miles an hour mark, it jammed against the stop pin and didn't waver. Carolyn didn't blink, but with a worried look on her pretty face, she stared at the needle.

As the Oldsmobile careened around a bend, the headlights flashed off to the left of the road. When the headlights beamed back onto the road and shone directly in front of them, three of the biggest deer Blondie had ever seen in his life stood staring back at him. There was no way around them. Blinded by the Oldsmobile's headlights, the three deer weren't moving. Blondie jerked the steering wheel in a panic of disbelief.

"No!" he gasped.

The color rushed from Carolyn's face. Trying to stop the car with a non-existent brake on the passenger side, she tromped her foot on the floor and held it there. Blondie jumped on the real brake with both feet. As if it were on ice, the car went faster. He downshifted into second gear and let out the clutch. But the engine was running too fast for the clutch to catch. Beneath the floorboard the pressure plate spun and the clutch slipped at great speed. As if it were in pain, the transmission cried

221

out in a dull whine. Smoke from the burning clutch blasted up the floor and rushed out from under the dashboard. The Olds sped toward the edge of the road. For the briefest moment, time stood still. The speeding car's bright headlights flashed into the forest.

In a small clearing in the forest, as if it were thanking Blondie for not hitting its mother, a small deer stood on top of a gray boulder and blinked its yellow glowing eyes. If this was the last thing he would see before he died, Blondie thought it was a beautiful thing. But then he got back to the task at hand: steering the car and trying to stay alive.

He cut the steering wheel to the left. It had no effect. The Oldsmobile had sling-shotted off the road. Its front wheels spun in midair. Blondie glanced out the side window. Looking from a great height, he watched a small stream zip beneath the car. With Carolyn's legs straight out, frozen with fear, the car sailed over the tops of a stand of blue spruce trees. Blondie stiffened and held both hands on the steering wheel. With his elbows locked straight out, he waited for the worst. At the top of the car's arc, he felt a tingling sensation in his stomach. Then, as if it were in a slow motion movie, the car came crashing down through a thicket of thorns, elderberry bushes, and blue spruce trees.

When it landed, as if a great weight had been dropped onto his body, Blondie's head and shoulders slammed down. Underneath his buttocks, he felt the springs of the heavy upholstered seat sag and then spring down until they ripped off their pins. On the passenger side, the back of Carolyn's seat thudded and broke backwards, causing her stiff

222

body to slam back flat against the seat. She cried out in agony. When the dust and flying pine needles settled, Blondie turned to her.

She wasn't moving.

"Are you all right?"

He watched her eyes glaze. It was as if he were seeing a replay of Nose's death. Pain and disbelief filled his heart. As her chest rose and fell for what seemed to be the last time, he reached down and checked her pulse.

CHAPTER 24

Hiding in the darkness Neal, Freddy, and Rafferty watched Blondie to drive past. Neal motored back on the main road and followed. After a few minutes, Freddy looked to his left. A ways off the road, in a dark stand of trees, a dim light revealed a little cloud of steam streaming into the night air. With his belly full and the comforting thought of going home Freddy wanted to drift off to sleep. But the steam clouds bothered him. Focusing to stay awake, he reached over the seat and shook Neal's shoulder. "Hey, look over there."

Neal turned his head to look, but the Ford had already passed the odd sight.

With his head cocked, Freddy begged, "Come on, go back. It looks like a car wreck."

Neal made a brusque gesture with his hand. "We don't have time for other people's problems. Blondie's ahead of us. We got to find out where he's going."

Freddy worried that someone could die if they didn't go back. He didn't think it was possible, but he figured he could trick Neal into going back.

"What if Blondie wrecked?"

Neal shook his head. "No way!" He paused and snapped his fingers. "Wait a minute. It could be Blondie, but better yet that waitress at the truck stop was in a hurry to go see her sick mother. Maybe she fell asleep and flew off the road."

"Yeah," Rafferty said. "If you go back, maybe she'll give you her phone number."

Neal nodded weakly. Then in a flash, his whole manner changed. "I don't think it's Blondie, but she is a hottie. It's worth a try."

He did a U-turn and sped back down the highway. Now that Neal had done what he asked him to do, Freddy had second thoughts. "What if the cops come?"

Neal slowed the car a bit. "You got a point. They'll find our money and take it."

Rafferty, who had scrunched down against the door, turned to Neal. "I haven't seen a cop for miles. At this time of night, they're probably all sleeping."

"The cops might already be there." Freddy looked at Neal. "Do you still want to go back?"

Neal increased his speed. "Ah, ahem, ah, yes, of course. What else are we gonna do with our time?" He flashed Freddy a crooked smile. "Yawn and worry our lives away?"

When they approached the scene, in the shadows, the steam emanated a faint jaundiced glow. Neal positioned the Ford off the road at an angle and stopped. The headlights radiated light into the forest. When he hit the high beams, part of the back fender of a '57 magenta Oldsmobile jutted out from a broken blue spruce tree.

Neal gave out a startled gasp. "It's not that girl. It's Blondie." He franticly shifted the transmission into low gear and revved the engine. "Let's get the hell out of here."

Rafferty held his hand in front of Neal's vision. "Wait a minute. Didn't you suggest asking Blondie where the Jungle Inn was?"

Neal stuttered and went into his usual routine. "Ah, ahem, ah, yes, of course not." He looked at

Rafferty. "I didn't, but you did. All I said was that we should follow him." As if he were holding a gun, he stuck out his pointer finger. "You must've forgotten Blondie's got a gun."

Freddy felt the gun in his belt. "We got one, too."

Rafferty opened the door and put one foot on the ground. "I don't know what you guys are afraid of. Blondie's probably dead, and I don't think his girlfriend will hurt us."

With newfound courage Neal jumped out of the Ford. "Let's go." He took five steps. With his feet at the top of a wall of huge square stones, he looked down. A steep drop of about twenty feet extended down to a dark stream.

Freddy looked to the right. A sloping path led away from the wall and to the stream below the wall. "This way," he said and started down the path.

At the bottom, the ankle-deep stream flowed around a rocky bend and continued to someplace into the dark where it bubbled eerily. Freddy stepped into the stream and stopped. Like a graveyard, the air carried the cold chill of the earth. He wasn't as afraid of Blondie shooting him as he was of going to the wreck and finding mangled dead bodies. Such a sight would give him nightmares for a long time, but if Blondie and his girlfriend were still alive, he couldn't let them die.

From out of blue spruce tree branches, Blondie's pain-filled voice rang out. "Hey, anybody, come over here. Help us."

Freddy breathed a sigh of relief. "He sounds all right," he said, and fear took the place of his concern for their safety. Searching for movement,

226

he stared into the darkness. From the broken radiator, like ubiquitous spooks, steam hissed and sent wisps of white into the night. He looked back at Neal. "Should we go in and get him?"

Neal shrugged. "You got the gun. It's your call."

Blondie called out again. "Somebody get us out of here and help us across that crick."

A mischievous grin formed on Rafferty's face. "You are across, you big dummy."

A disgusted moan came from the car.

Freddy shook his head in Rafferty's direction. "You shouldn't make fun of him. He might be hurt really bad."

"Yeah, I know," Rafferty said. "But before we go in I'd like to know if he's going to shoot us."

"I think we'll be all right," Freddy said, and sloshed across the stream.

Neal and Rafferty looked at each other, shrugged, and followed. Pulling broken spruce limbs away, Freddy stopped. The dash lights cast a soft light into the interior of the car. In the front seat, Blondie slumped over the steering wheel. Where he had held onto the outer rim, it was bent forward. A trail of blood ran down one side of his face, but the bleeding seemed to have stopped. With one hand on the gun in his belt, Freddy reached over and pulled on the door handle. It didn't move.

Rafferty stepped next to the car and looked at Freddy. "Why don't you try unlocking it?"

Embarrassed, Freddy reached over, lifted the lock, and pulled the door handle. The dented door creaked opened. Blondie leaned back in the seat and looked up in a daze.

Neal popped his head between Freddy and Rafferty and looked into Blondie's face. "You okay, man?"

Blondie pointed to the girl on his right. "I'm okay, but she's hurt real bad."

Freddy relaxed his grip on the gun. Tramping through brush alongside the car, Neal broke branches and crashed toward the other door. It was jammed. He called through the window at Blondie. "I'll go back to the truck stop and call an ambulance."

Blondie held up his hand. "You can't. The cops will come, too. I'm a wanted man."

Neal rested his elbows on the door frame. "What do you want us to do?"

"We're all in this together now," Blondie said, and took a deep breath. "You don't have an inspection sticker on that Ford. If the cops come they'll write you up." He turned and grimaced. "Hell, they'll probably search your car and find that money you took out of that envelope and replaced with those dirty gloves. Then, they'll say you robbed somebody."

Freddy knew he was right, but he couldn't let the girl die. "But we have to get her to a hospital."

Rafferty looked over his shoulder. "You want to carry her up that hill and put her in our car?"

Blondie looked toward the hill. "If she's not hurt too bad," he said. "It might work."

He reached over, put his arm under Carolyn's legs, and gently pulled. Grimacing in pain, Carolyn held up her hand in protest. "Please don't lift me." Tears formed in her eyes. "It hurts too much."

228

Blondie backed off. "Okay, honey." He looked to Freddy. "She needs professional help. If we move her, we'll only make it worse." Blondie attentively watched Carolyn. She looked up. Their eyes locked. With a tear rolling down his cheek, he asked, "You think you'll be okay here for a while?"

She reached up and placed her left hand on his hand. A loving glow radiated from her face. "I'll be fine." She wiped the tears from her eyes with the back of her right hand. "Please call the ambulance. They'll take me out on a stretcher."

"But I don't want to leave you here," Blondie said, almost crying.

Freddy looked at him. "No matter how we do it, it'll take the same amount of time."

Rafferty turned to go. "Let's get out of here and get to that truck stop."

"Ah, ahem, ah, yes," Neal said. "Of course we'll go back to the truck stop." He raised his hand. "I'll go in and make a phone call. When the cops and the ambulance get here they might think she was the driver."

"No they won't," Blondie said. "The way this steering wheel's bent and the broken seats, they'll know I was driving."

Neal shrugged. "So what do you want to do?"

"We go to the truck stop. It doesn't matter if they know I was driving. Like I said before, I'm wanted anyway."

Blondie leaned over and kissed Carolyn. "Hang in there, honey. When it's safe, I'll call. We'll still do everything just like we planned."

Blondie twisted in the seat and placed his feet on the ground, but when he tried to get up, he

229

moaned. He reached around and pressed his fist to his lower back to ease the pain. Freddy stepped next to him and put his arm around his back. Then Blondie hooked one arm around Freddy's waist, and they swayed to a standing position.

With pleading eyes, Carolyn looked up at Blondie. "These boys seem honest. Why don't you try to work with them?"

Blondie glanced back at Carolyn. "Don't worry about a thing. It'll all work out."

"That's right, baby," Neal said. "We'll take care of everything."

Rafferty peered into the window. "Stick with us, honey. After we find the Jungle Inn, you'll be wearing horse turds as big as diamonds." He looked at Neal. "Did I say that right?"

As if he had been hit with a great realization, Blondie's eyes bugged wide open. Freddy felt his body tense. Although he hadn't intended to do so, Rafferty's attempted humor had told Blondie that they had broken the code. Freddy hoped that after Neal called the ambulance, Blondie wouldn't try anything.

CHAPTER 25

Back at the truck stop, Freddy stood with his elbows resting on the door of the Ford. He peered over the roof and watched for Neal to come out of the restaurant. When he did, he flashed Freddy a thumbs up. That meant he had made the anonymous phone call. The ambulance and the police were on the way. Neal walked to the Ford, but before he jumped in, he slapped himself in the forehead. "I'm going back in and look for Becky."

"Come on, Neal," Freddy said. "We have to get out of here."

"Becky is a hot stuff waitress. It'll only take a minute to get her phone number."

Neal ran back into the restaurant and quickly looked around. But Becky was nowhere to be seen. He came back to the Ford and sat behind the wheel.

Shifting his eyes about uneasily, Blondie sat up from the back seat. "Are you sure the ambulance is coming?"

"It's on the way," Neal assured him. "She'll be fine."

Rafferty looked over his shoulder at Blondie. "She'll be fine, but what about us?"

"Yeah," Neal said. "What are you going to do? Take the key and leave us for dead?"

Blondie's face turned menacing. "Didn't I whack Nose up the side of the head for you guys?"

As if ashamed, Rafferty's eyes flicked downward. "Yeah, you did that."

"Okay." Blondie's face relaxed. "And you guys kept my ass out of jail and saved my girl. Maybe

231

we're even. But the way I see it, you got something I need, and I got something you need."

"We got the key," Neal said, shaking his head. "But what do you got that we need?"

Blondie smiled. "Nice try. But you don't know where the Jungle Inn is?"

"So what," Neal said. "I've been around. I can find out where anything is."

"Maybe you can, but other people know about it, and they might get there first."

"So what if they get there first," Rafferty said, his green eyes glimmering with mischief. "We still got the key."

Blondie stared at him for a long moment. "You don't know what that key is for, do you?"

"We figure it's to some kind of a vault."

"It's a vault all right," Blondie said. "Al Capone had trouble in Chicago and had to move it to a safe place."

Rafferty snickered. "So…do you know what's in it?"

Studying Rafferty's freckled face, Blondie said, "That, my friend, should be self-explanatory."

Rafferty broke into a hopeful smile. "You're saying it's a money vault?"

"People usually put something of value in vaults."

Neal threw up his hands. "There you go, gentleman. Even if it's not money, it's something worth a lot of money."

Blondie nodded. "Capone was afraid of another stock market crash and the devaluation of money. They said he started hoarding gold."

232

Rafferty hit his forehead with the palm of his hand. "I should've thought of that."

Neal triumphantly smiled a big ear-to-ear smile. "Now all we got to do is go to the Jungle Inn and replace the second brick down from coal chute with the key."

Freddy's heart thumped with anticipation. "There might be a big underground gold vault right under the Jungle Inn."

As if he were opening a lock, Neal twisted his wrist. "And we have the key to open it."

"Maybe you have the key," Blondie said. "But there's a big butt connected to it."

Perplexed, Freddy shook his head. "What's 'butt connected to it' supposed to mean?"

Rafferty rounded his hands in front of his stomach. "Maybe there's a guy with a big fat butt sittin' on the vault."

"There could be," Blondie said, and smiled. "I'll let you know *if*, and when, we get there."

Freddy didn't like what he was hearing. "What do you mean *if*?"

"When there's that much money to be had, you can be sure a lot of people will be in on it." For a moment his face scrunched up in thought. Then, as if a horrible thought had entered his mind, his jaw dropped. "Hell," he said, "they may have made a duplicate key. If we take our time getting there that vault might be empty." He looked toward the truck stop. The flashing red lights of a speeding ambulance reflected in the windows and vanished into the night.

Freddy put his hand on Blondie's shoulder. "She's on her way to the hospital. She'll be all

233

right." But like the fading lights of the ambulance, Freddy's dream of riches began to fade.

"Al Capone's been dead a long time," he said. "How do we know the vault's not already empty?"

Watching the lights of the ambulance disappear, Blondie exhaled. "The only way we'll know is to go to the Jungle Inn." He lowered his head. "If the vault's not there, then we're too late."

Neal started the Ford, hooked low gear, and pulled out of the truck stop. He hadn't traveled a mile when he mashed the accelerator down and flew down the highway. "That vault's awaitin', we gotta get there before the bad guys do."

As Neal steered into a tight turn, to keep balanced, everyone had to lean into it. Blondie reached over the seat and shook Neal's shoulder. "Slow down, man. We don't need the cops down on our ass."

Before Neal could slow, from out of a hidden drive, a police car whooped a siren and flashed its lights. Neal pulled over and waited for the officer to come to the window.

Wearing aviator-style sunglasses, the officer walked to the Ford and stopped next to Neal. "May I see your license, sir?"

Neal reached into his back pocket. "Ah, ahem, ah, yes." He paused. "Of course, officer." He pulled out his wallet and fished out his license. "Here you go, officer."

Even though it was dark, the officer kept his sunglasses on. He took the license and shone his flashlight on it. "I see you're from Pennsylvania. What's the big hurry?"

234

"I guess I couldn't help it, officer," Neal said, almost whimpering. "But I just didn't realize how fast I was going."

The officer adjusted his sunglasses and stood at attention. As if he were reading from a police manual, he said, "You are supposed to be in control of your vehicle at all times. What do you mean you couldn't help it?"

"Well, officer." Neal sobbed. "I was thinking about my friend and if I would get there in time."

The officer shone his flashlight on the lower corner of the windshield. "This car hasn't been inspected. Why would you risk your life," he looked inside the car, "and the lives of your passengers for a friend?"

"I have no excuse, officer, I should not have been driving so fast, but my friend has leukemia." He looked down and held his breath as if he were about to cry. Then he lifted his head. "This car had the baldest tires you ever seen. I had to borrow money to get used ones to make the trip. I didn't have the time or the money to get the car inspected, because I promised his mother I would see him before he died."

Freddy could see that the officer was young and was falling for Neal's bullshit story. A rotten feeling fell into his chest. Some things were sacred, and lying about someone dying just didn't sit right with him. Once again on this crazy trip that had harmlessly started out just to get a cup of coffee and a Canadian souvenir, the stakes had become too high. One thing about Neal: he'd always keep you guessing. When you thought things were going to smooth out and you could relax or take a break from

235

the craziness of it all, Neal would tilt the whole world. But that was why everybody liked him. There was never time to yawn with boredom or do commonplace things. And the stress and strain of situations that wore others down invigorated him.

The officer folded his ticket book and looked at Neal for a few seconds. Neal placed his hand over his eyes and pretended to hide tears of sorrow.

"Okay," the officer said. "I'll let you go with a warning. But take it easy. If you get killed in a high-speed crash, you'll get to where your friend is going before he does."

Neal solemnly nodded, and muttered, "Thank you, officer."

The officer went back to his cruiser, pulled around the Ford, and sped away. Neal hit himself in the thigh and broke into a hee-haw fit of laughter.

"That gullible bastard," he said and chuckled, "he'd probably believe it if I told him I had leukemia up my ass."

"That's not right," Freddy said. "You're a rotten bastard."

"Yeah, I am," Neal said. "But I didn't get a ticket."

Blondie shook his head. "Hey, man, try to not take chances like that. If we get an older cop, we'll lose the whole deal."

"Ah, ahem, ah, yes," Neal said. "Of course, I get your drift, but I wanted to do that for a long time." He chucked Rafferty under the chin. "Did you see the sunglasses?" He hit himself in the forehead. "Oh, the sunglasses, the sunglasses," he repeated, twinkling with self-satisfied humor. "I knew anybody that wore sunglasses at night would

236

be as gullible as somebody's pet Neanderthal. And did you see the look on his face?"

"I didn't see that look," Rafferty said. "But I felt that brass key falling through my fingers."

For a moment, a bit of embarrassment shone in Neal's face. But he sloughed it off. "Man, oh man, that look on that cop's face was worth the gamble."

Rafferty looked ahead, and said, "Yeah, it was a just little ray of sunshine."

And there was silence for a long while.

CHAPTER 26

The next day, traveling down Route 62, and passing through the town of Hubbard, Ohio, Neal followed Blondie's instructions. They crept up behind a truck. When they were close enough to see the cattle inside watching them through the slats, Rafferty made faces at them, but they didn't acknowledge his antics. Spewing clouds of diesel fumes and slowing at each incline, the lumbering truck agitated Neal. He laid on the horn. The truck slowed even more and crawled at a walking pace.

Neal flared up. "That's enough of that stuff."

He hit the accelerator. The Ford jerked with a burst of speed, lurched forward, and spun around a curve so tightly Rafferty was thrown against the door. As it increased speed, trees passed in a blur. Just before the Youngstown border, Neal slowed and turned left onto Applegate Road. A few old homes appeared between stretches of thick woods and fields that lined both sides of the road that bent into sharp curves. Neal leaned into a sharp right turn, straightened out the Ford and a left turn was right in front of him. He spun the steering wheel and made the left turn and was greeted with another right turn. He jerked his head to one side.

"Damn," he said with astonishment. "Every place you go there's a corner to steer around. No wonder everybody calls this place Hall's Corners."

The road straightened, and Blondie sat upright. "This isn't the place."

For a moment, Neal let loose of the steering wheel and spread both hands apart. "Which way do you want me to go?"

Blondie pointed through the windshield. A narrow driveway was just on the right. "Turn around there. The Jungle Inn's the other way."

Neal maneuvered into the tiny opening, and wrestled with the steering wheel. After three backups, they were heading back to where they had come from.

Freddy turned in the seat and faced Blondie. "Are you sure the Jungle Inn is the right place to look?"

Blondie nodded. "Hell, before they closed the place down in '49, it was so wide open mobsters from all over the country went there. Even the government said the place raked in a couple of million in two years." He ran his fingers through his blond hair. "Come to think of it, the Youngstown newspaper called it the capitol for thugs and racketeers."

Almost getting burned alive in Canada by thugs was still fresh in Freddy's mind. If thugs and racketeers ran the place, he didn't want to go into a place like the Jungle Inn. Wondering if Blondie was telling the truth, he cast a suspicious eye toward him. "With that many bad guys in one place weren't people afraid to go in?"

Blondie waved his hand down. "Nobody was afraid to go in. A bunch of Jewish mobsters out of Detroit, who called themselves the Purple Gang, owned a percentage of the casino. Those sons-a-bitches had no conscience at all. They'd kill people who crossed them without a second thought, but no customers were ever in danger." The Ford rounded another sharp bend. Blondie continued. "I'd bet Jack White, who'd been arrested on twenty-three

239

charges of robbery and murder, had a share in the place, and he never hurt a gambler." He shrugged. "People who gambled there weren't like the high-rolling well-dressed people you'd see in Los Vegas. A lot of people came to the Jungle Inn after work, dressed in work clothes. Even old ladies came dressed in their everyday dresses. If the people in charge wanted to keep the people coming and losing money, they had to keep all the tough stuff away from the gamblers. For the average Joe, it was a safe place to be.""

Back at the intersection of Route 62 and Applegate Road, Neal eased the Ford to a stop. Craning his neck, he looked back over the seat. "Now which way?"

"I haven't been here for a while." Blondie's forehead wrinkled. Then, his lips widened into a tight smile. "Just go straight. The Jungle Inn's right down the road on the left."

After a mud-covered dump truck with black smoke streaming out its chrome stacks roared past, Neal drove through the intersection and continued down Applegate Road. He turned left onto a gravel-covered parking lot and coasted to a stop. The unmistakable junkyard smell that came from years of parked cars dripping oil from cast iron motors filled the air.

And there it was: the old safe haven for a sprawling casino that had thrived and prospered in the protective cocoon of Hall's Corners. Metal gun turrets, where guards could have shot from slots with little danger of return fire hitting them, protruded from the walls of the building.

240

Cringing, as if about to be shot, Neal let the engine run and pointed to the gun turrets. "Is there somebody behind those things?"

Rafferty's face took on a look of amusement. "If you're worried about them, use an old Indian trick." He waved his hand toward the gun turrets. "Just pay no attention to them. After a while you won't even know they're there."

Blondie lifted a finger of rebuke and gaped at Rafferty in befuddlement. "No one's behind them now. But when the place was in full swing the owners claimed the turrets were only there to scare away robbers who would like to steal the money the place made."

Neal's eyes lit up. "How much money are you talking about?"

"I don't know everything about the place," Blondie said. "But they had bingo games that paid a thousand bucks every night for coverall. It was so popular that teenagers from Farrell and Sharon used to come over and try to win it." He felt his lips smile. "When they lost, they would drop a few coins in the slot machines then head over to Budd Street in Masury and get laid at the Clover Club."

Neal looked at the sprawling building. "That place is pretty big. What else did it have?"

"They had a bar and a restaurant, but that was mostly for decoration. The real draw was all the different games." He shook his head and sighed. "They had dice, poker, roulette, and chuck-a-luck. But the big money maker was the slot machines. They made over a thousand a day."

Freddy stared at the massive building. "Is that all they had?"

241

"They had horse races. Some people say they raked in two thousand five hundred a day, but on Saturdays they collected a cool three thousand five hundred."

"Sounds like a pretty good business," Neal said. "But gambling's illegal. How'd they get started?"

As if he had lost an old friend, Blondie stared at the closed casino. "Way back in the 30's this place started out as a whorehouse, but after a bunch of guys created their own village of Hall's Corners, they became the government and the law. Then, because the owners were the only law in town, the place was wide open. Three thousand people swarmed into the place every night. And those people believed the place was run on the up and up."

Freddy interrupted. "Was it?"

"There was no need to cheat people. The Jungle Inn made tons of money running honest games. If word got out that they were crooked, the people wouldn't come back."

Freddy pointed off to the right. Connected to the structure, a former two-story house with a peaked roof, stood taller than the rest of the building. "What was that?"

"That was the entrance to the restaurant. They could feed a couple hundred people in there."

Blondie stared at an addition in front of the restaurant entrance and tried to imagine how it was before liquor agents closed it down. In that section of the building awnings yawned over little windows, and the walls were covered with asphalt shingles that resembled stone-facing. In the very center of the building, the window of a white door reflected a

242

bright beam of sunlight. As if it were beckoning gamblers to an enticing emerald city of sin, it danced and blinked.

Blondie turned his head to the left. The single-story gambling section's wooden addition sprawled along, and up high and off to the left, the main entrance had another gun turret. Further on, other entrances looked to be delivery doors or drop off points.

"That's a big place," Freddy said. "What's in there now?"

"Would you believe it?" Blondie said to the air. "It's a window warehouse."

Rafferty pointed to the gun turrets. "With those things up there, they must be pretty expensive windows."

Freddy leaned forward and stared out the windshield. "If there's no gangsters inside, why are the gun turrets still there?"

Rafferty smiled brightly. "Maybe they're guarding the vault."

"Don't worry," Blondie said. "No one's manned those things in years."

Neal killed the engine and looked at Freddy. "You got the key?"

Freddy gave Neal a questioning look. "You think it's okay to get it?"

Neal looked at Rafferty.

"It's your call," Rafferty said and shrugged. "You know where to get it."

Neal cast a suspicious eye toward Blondie. "You better be on the up and up. But stay here while I get it."

243

Neal jumped out of the car and went around to the front. Then he lifted the hood. While Blondie and the others waited, he did something. After he closed the hood, he held up the big brass key. "Let's unlock that vault."

Freddy, Rafferty and Blondie joined Neal and walked behind the restaurant section of the building. Here, the former parking lot was cracked and weed-choked except for a small area below the coal chute which was dirty-black with bits of old coal and dust.

A barrel-chested man with cropped blond hair came around the corner and confronted Blondie. "What the hell are you doing back here with these kids?"

Blondie shrugged. "My son and I," he put his hand on Rafferty's shoulder and looked toward Freddy and Neal, "we just came back to see what they were doing."

"My friend got sick," Neal lied, and patted Freddy on the back. "He didn't want to throw up in front of the building."

The man jerked his thumb toward the front of the building. "I got a lot of windows in that building. Too many kids make me nervous. Get the hell out of here."

Blondie didn't think of Freddy and his friends as kids. They were ignorant in the ways of the world, but they didn't need to be treated like kids. If he said something to make them feel important and grown up they would trust him, maybe even make them feel he was on their side. He was about to tell the man they were young men, but Neal spoke first.

"Ah, ahem, ah, yes. Of course," he said. "We can do that, sir."

They all took a few steps toward the Ford. Blondie figured that if he went along with the man's assumption that they were kids, it would give him time to check out the coal chute. He waved his hand in a shooing motion.

"Come on, you goddamn kids," he said with authority. "Get the hell away from here. This man's got a respectable business to run."

They slowly shuffled toward the Ford until the man went back into the building.

"Okay, he's back in." Rafferty said and removed his hand from the car door handle. "Let's try again."

Blondie gestured at Rafferty. "Go in and keep him busy."

Rafferty looked confused. "What should I tell him?"

"He thinks I'm your father. Tell him your old man is chasing those kids away, but he wants to buy some windows for your bedroom."

Rafferty turned to go. "He'll ask me why you're not with me."

"So what?" Blondie lifted his hands in a questioning gesture. "Act like a spoiled brat. Tell him your father buys you anything you want. Tell that guy you want to see if he has anything you like. If you think we need more time, hold your butt cheeks together and tell him you have to go to the bathroom and that I'll be there in a few minutes."

"What if he doesn't believe me?"

Impatience crept into Blondie's his voice. "Tell him anything. Just get us some time." He motioned to the others. "While you stall him, we'll go around

245

to the coal chute and see if there's a slot for that key."

Holding the back of his pants and walking as if in pain, Rafferty went into the building. Blondie held up his finger. "Remember, the note says, 'Butt watch out,' whatever you do, don't use that key until we check out where it fits."

At the coal chute, Neal stopped. He looked away from the building and across the field of tall grass and weeds. Suddenly, as if he were glad to see someone, he began waving his hands in the air

"We were waiting on you," he said. "Why, just yesterday, my buddy, Freddy here," he looked at Freddy, "was saying that we should ask you what is so damn important about a hunk of brass."

Blondie looked to where Neal was looking. As the figures drew close, he recognized them. Nose and Swill were walking through the tall weeds and grass. When they were a few feet from the building, they stopped. Nose's hooded eyes tracked Neal's every action. Swill stuck out his opened hand in front of Freddy and held it there. "Give it to me."

Blondie knew Swill's psychopathic personality didn't include compassion for anyone, and that he believed people were to be used and tossed aside. The only thing on his mind was to have what he demanded and 'right now'.

Blondie nodded to Freddy. "Give him the key."

Freddy gave Swill the key.

"Thanks, asshole."

Swill bent over in front of the coal chute. He pulled out the second brick down and inserted the key. Something clunked twice. Then a brick that was right even with Swill's head fell out. The squeal of metal skidding on hard brick pierced the air. Neal jumped back.

"What's that?"

Breaking through a mass of spider webs, the end of a silencer-equipped shotgun barrel mechanically slid out the brick space. Swill jerked away. Before he could clear the barrel, the shotgun went off with a muffled boom. Swill's chest looked like raw hamburger. He jerked the key from the brick space, but it fell from his hand and landed on the coal-black ground. Gasping for breath, he crumpled to the ground. His brown eyes dulled, and his face turned pale. He tried to speak, but blood sprayed from his mouth. With his hand clawing in bits of old coal, he reached toward the brass key. Before he could grasp it, his body went limp.

Except for his whisky-blossomed nose, color drained from Nose's face. Without the slightest hesitation, and with no hint of reverence for the dead, he placed his foot on Swill's shoulder and pushed. Swill's body rolled away from the coal chute.

As the blood pooled around Swill's body, Blondie shook his head from side to side and wondered when all the killing would stop. Rafferty's face paled and he stood with his eyes wide open. Neal clenched his fists and braced for the worst. Looking nauseated, and looking as if he were wondering what Nose would do next, Freddy stood helpless.

Looking for another booby-trap, Nose reached into the secret compartment and pulled out the shotgun. He held his breath and waited. Cautiously he bent over and looked into the brick hole. "It's empty," he said, took two steps back, and looked up.

Blondie was starring him right in the face.

Nose glared back with icy disdain. "What the hell do you want?"

"The owner of this building heard that shot. He's calling the cops right now."

With a panic-stricken face, Nose said, "I gotta get outta here, but Swill's car's not here."

Neal nodded. "Nice deduction, man." He looked at the only car in the parking lot. "Where's Swill's car, Nose?"

Nose jerked his finger toward the trees. "I parked it in a thicket down the road." He glanced at Swill's body. "By time I get back there, the cops are gonna be here."

As if he weren't worried about the cops coming, Neal stepped next to him. "So what do you want us to do about it?"

Holding the shotgun in one hand, Nose used his other hand and jerked his military issue Colt 45 from his shoulder holster. He waved it in the air. "We got a dead body layin' here. Quit screwin' around." He pointed the barrel of the Colt toward to the Ford. "Let's get in that goddamn car and get the hell out of here."

Blondie reached for the shotgun in Nose's hand. "Give me that."

"Yeah," Neal extended his hand. "Then, we'll take you anywhere you want to go."

Nose pointed his Colt at Neal. "I'm not Swill. You're not going to tell me to go fuck myself." He placed the barrel of the Colt next to Neal's temple.

"Maybe I'll give the police another body to clean up."

Blondie stepped between them. "Come on, Nose, put the gun away. He was only joking. Don't forget, I saved your ass from that burning building. You owe me."

A trace of compassion crossed Nose's face. He lowered the Colt. Then he breathed deep, relaxed the grip on the Colt, and holstered it. But he kept the shotgun glued to his chest.

Rafferty came running out of the building headed for the Ford.

Neal motioned toward Nose. "Hey, man, what are you getting excited for?" He pointed to the empty brick hole. "If that's Capone's vault, there'll be enough for all of us."

"Don't be ignorant." Blondie pulled Neal away from the coal chute. "The vault isn't here. The note said: 'Take Stock in Jungle Inn'. There's a map or a clue in the stock of that gun."

Nose stood and stared at Neal.

Neal gave Nose a questioning look and shrugged. "It's you call."

Nose lowered the shotgun from his chest.

Blondie grabbed him by the shoulder and gently tugged. "Come on, Nose. We got the stock. Let's go."

With the shotgun still in his hand, Nose nodded.

They all ran for the Ford and jumped in. Neal started the engine and pounded his fists on the steering wheel. With his arm raised like a hero in a movie leading a Calvary charge, he shouted, "Al Capone's vault's just down the road! Follow me."

He revved the engine, let out the clutch, and left a spray of gravel behind them. Down the road, he slowed the Ford and hit the brakes. Blondie and Nose jumped out before the tires stopped turning, jumped into Swill's car, and followed.

CHAPTER 27

Five miles down the highway, Neal turned on to at a high-tension tower maintenance road. As the Ford buffeted along the uneven ground, Freddy bounced and swayed, and jerked around in the car. He was uncomfortable.

But Rafferty wasn't. Grinning with his legs pumping and his arms sawing back and forth to the uneven rhythm, he looked like he was enjoying a carnival ride.

With Blondie following close behind, Neal drove down the weed-choked road. Here and there, small trees plowed under the front bumper and scraped along the undercarriage. When the cars couldn't be seen from the highway, they stopped.

They all piled out of the cars. Like streams flowing together, they walked to the trunk of the Ford. Neal opened it. Nose set the shotgun on the trunk floor. Blondie rummaged through a toolbox until he fished out a screwdriver. Then he removed the screws in the shotgun's butt plate and took it off.

"I'll be damn," Neal said with astonishment. "That's what '*butt*, watch out' meant."

"Now you're thinking," Blondie said and looked at the butt of the walnut stock. The end of a rolled up piece of paper stuck out from a deep hole. He slid it out and unrolled it. A peacock feather fell out and gently rocked to the ground. The only word on the paper was 'Petroleum'.

Freddy bent over and picked up the feather. "What's this for?"

Blondie slumped over and sat on the bumper. "Damn, if I know." He jerked his head toward Nose. "How about you?"

Nose shook his head.

Neal stepped forward. "Ah, ahem, ah, yes." He wagged his finger. "Of course, we might be able to tell you guys what that feather means, but what's in it for us?"

Blondie squinted one eye and turned toward Neal. "Look." He moved his hand in an encouraging gesture. "You guys came this far. Do you want to quit now?"

Neal looked at Rafferty. "Whadda ya say?"

As if the weight of the decision was too much for him, Rafferty limply sagged. Then his eyes narrowed. "I don't know if we can trust these guys."

"Yeah," Neal fired at Blondie, "how do we know you won't just shoot us after we help you find what you're looking for?"

Blondie didn't answer right away. He watched Freddy twist the peacock feather, and then glanced at Neal. "You don't."

Freddy wanted to trust Blondie. "But he saved us from the fire."

"That's right," Blondie said. "If I wanted you guys dead, you'd be roast beef now."

Rafferty butted in. "Would we have been medium rare or well done?"

Neal chuckled and slapped the sides of his thighs. "You got a point there." He gave Nose a suspicious glare. "But what about your buddy here?"

252

"That's right," Rafferty said. "Maybe the next time, you'll make one of us look down the barrel of a shotgun."

Blondie shot Neal an inquiring glance. "So, what are you saying? That you want to quit?"

Like a traffic cop, Neal held up his hand. "No way, man. There should be enough money in that vault for all of us." He tilted his head toward Blondie. "You ready to go to Petroleum?"

Blondie slammed the trunk of the Ford. "What makes you think you know where it is?"

"I don't think," Neal said and tucked his thumbs in the sides of his pockets. "I *know* where it is."

Nose made a face that enhanced his ugly split nose. "You're just a young snot. How could you know anything?"

"My old man ran the bug number for years, but betting on a daily number was illegal. To draw attention away from himself, he hauled my young ass around to just about every bar east and west of the Ohio/Pennsylvania state line. I can't remember the Jungle Inn. Maybe they didn't allow my old man to put his number in there, but believe me, I know where Petroleum is."

Walking to Swill's car, Blondie waved his hand. "Lead the way."

Like a mad man running away from the nut house to freedom, Neal ran to the Ford and jumped in. With his arm out the window waving for Freddy and Rafferty to come on, he blew the horn. Freddy and Rafferty rushed to the car and jumped in. Neal hooked first gear. They took off, rumbled down the tower road, and pulled out onto the highway. Only

253

this time, Blondie wasn't chasing them. He was following them.

CHAPTER 28

Blondie didn't like to be seen in such a family type car, but he sat behind the steering wheel of Swill's 1952 puke-green Dodge station wagon. The car was a sad tribute to Swill's excessive gambling and boozing, and it showed the world that the owner didn't care what anyone thought about him. It was one more reason Blondie needed to get out of the Arm.

Even though Nose drank excessively and he always managed to keep a straight head when doing business, Blondie didn't know if he could trust him. Between keeping his eyes on the back of the '40 Ford, he made furtive glances toward him and looked for nervous signs of betrayal. Nose's face was expressionless, but that split-open nose broadcasted meanness.

Nose took a half empty bottle of clear liquid from under the seat and swilled it down. He held the bottle up until the last drop was gone and threw it out the window. Exhaling, he held his hand over the dashboard. As if he had a nervous twitch, his hand shook.

"Well, Blondie." He grinned. "What did you do with that bitch?"

Blondie had never told him about Carolyn, and he didn't want to tell him anything that would let him get his grimy hands near her, but Nose continued. "You know, that bitch that drove your Oldsmobile in Buffalo."

Blondie hoped Nose was guessing. "What are you talking about?"

255

"Don't play dumb, ole buddy. Me and Swill watched you and her take out after Freddy and his pals."

"Why didn't you chase after them and get the key?"

"We didn't know they had it with them. But we figured you'd find it and show up at the Jungle Inn. We waited in the bushes for hours. What took you so long?"

For a moment Blondie relived crashing into the pine trees. "I had a little accident."

Nose grunted. "Accident?" he asked, and let out a huge horselaugh. "What did you do, shit yourself?"

Blondie ignored his jab. "Just as bad. I flew off the road doing a hundred and twenty."

"What about the bitch?"

Blondie didn't want him checking hospitals and pumping her for information. "That's one cunt that won't be taking my money anymore."

"What did you do, shoot her?"

"Didn't have to," Blondie lied. "When we hit the ground, her neck snapped. She never knew what hit her."

Nose wrinkled his split nose. "Damn, I would've like to have had a piece of that."

"What for? You never went with a girl more than once in your whole life."

"You know me. Master of the four F's: find 'em, feel 'em, fuck 'em, and forget 'em."

Blondie couldn't understand why anyone would be so callous toward a woman. He shuddered at the thought.

Nose lethargically bobbed his head with sadistic laughter and repositioned his body. "So, how'd you manage to get Freddy and his half-assed buddies to drive you to the Jungle Inn?"

Blondie clapped his hands and let out a fake laugh. "After I wrecked, the dumb asses stopped to see if anyone was hurt."

"So, why didn't they call the police or an ambulance?"

"Freddy's wanted by the police," Blondie lied again. "If he stuck around they'd take him in for sure. And anyway, they didn't know where the Jungle Inn was."

"So, you said you'd share the take with them for the key and a little taxi service?"

"Had to, they had the key."

"We should've blown them away after we got the shotgun."

Blondie wondered if Nose's brain was so far gone that he was beginning to forget things.

"Don't you remember where we're going?"

Nose let out a rasping snort and hit himself in the forehead. "That's right. We don't know where Petroleum is."

As if he were a psychiatrist studying a patient, Blondie stared at Nose. "I don't know what you and Swill were drinking, but I'm glad I didn't have any."

"Oh, hell," Nose said, and a stream of slobber ran down the side of his mouth. "I'll be okay in a few days. My mind always comes back." He looked up, and then jerked his head down. "Is Freddy going to take care of those kids after we find the vault?"

Blondie was glad Nose still didn't know the real Freddy was dead, and he hoped this young Freddy would come in handy, but he didn't want to kill him. If he did, he would end up like Nose: imitating humanity, but having nothing whatsoever in common with the human species. As long as Nose believed he was the one in control and that Blondie was only along for the ride, things should work out fine.

"The way I see it," Blondie said, "a vault is no good when it's empty. So, after we use them to help us carry out the loot, we'll lock them inside."

"Yeah, maybe we should knock one of them off. It'll make the other ones work faster."

"Let's keep it clean and neat. We'll just lock them in. Then there's no mess to clean up and the cops won't be nosin' around."

Blondie had intended to keep his word and split the vault contents with Freddy and his friends, but now that he was with Nose, he was having his doubts. If he shared the wealth, he would have Nose to contend with. And the way Nose's mind was wandering, he might shoot him anyway. But if he locked Freddy and his friends in the vault, and the Chicago gang found it, and Freddy told them Blondie had been there and had saved them from burning up in the Canadian fire, Blondie would never live long enough to spend anything the vault brought. If he killed Freddy, it would be like killing his lifelong friend. Now, if they found the vault, he wasn't sure what he would do.

"I'm getting thirsty," Nose said. "How long's it gonna take to clean the vault out?"

"Hey, Nose, relax. We got to find it first."

Blondie stared forward through the windshield at the empty road ahead.

With a blank look on his face, Nose stared straight ahead, too

Blondie wondered if what they were doing was registering in Swill's mind.

259

CHAPTER 29

A few miles down the road in the outskirts of Masury, Ohio, Neal pulled the Ford off the road. Freddy looked out the window and across a small stretch of land.

"We're here, Neal said."

A dirty-white street sign with black letters stood in the middle of a bunch of tall weeds. It read, 'Petroleum'.

Freddy hunched his shoulders and looked to Neal. "You got to be kidding me."

Petroleum wasn't actually a town. It was a small triangular strip of land that separated two roads. No one would know it was Petroleum except for that little metal street-like sign that everyone drove past but never really noticed. Blondie pulled the Dodge station wagon up behind the Ford and stopped. Everybody got out and stood looking at the lone sign.

Neal shrugged. "We're in Petroleum. Now what?"

Blondie took the peacock feather in his hand and held it up. Its sheen reflected the days light and the colors danced on its surface.

"Well, gentleman,' he said, "here's the other half of the clue. What's it mean?"

Freddy scanned the tall weeds of the strip of land. "Peacocks scratch around on the ground. Maybe the vault's under the ground here."

"I don't think so." Neal looked right then left. "I never saw this place dug up."

Blondie stepped into the tall grass. "Let's check around anyway. There might be another clue."

260

After an hour of swishing through tall weeds and examining what could have been holes in the ground leading to a vault, they walked to the Ford and leaned on it.

"The Jungle Inn was a gambling casino," Freddy said. "Is there a bar or something around here with peacocks?"

Neal leaned forward and placed his hands on his knees. "I came here a lot, and I never heard of one."

Freddy placed his hand on the pole of the Petroleum sign and leaned against it. Being loose in its base, it rotated from his hand. He took his hand off.

"People raise turkeys and chickens on farms," he said. "Did you ever see a peacock farm around here?"

"Farms with fields?" Blondie mused. "I don't even know where there's a garden?"

Straightening up, Neal rubbed the sides of his head. "Man, oh man. That's *it*." He hopped on one foot, switched feet, and hopped on that one.

Rafferty looked up at the sky. "When you get done jumping around like an Indian doing a rain dance, let us know what *it* is."

Neal stood still. Excitement showed in his face. "Okay." He took in a breath. "Peacock Alley is just down the road."

"Rafferty shook his head. "The only thing that's down there is Melody Lane."

With a huge smile spreading across his face, Neal's eyes bulged with astonishment. "That's right!" He snapped his fingers and jerked his finger at Rafferty. "Back in the 30's Melody Lane used to be Peacock Alley."

Staring at the Petroleum sign, Freddy sighed. "I'll be damn."

CHAPTER 30

While the others waited in the cars, Blondie and Neal walked inside the Melody Lane bar. Sitting at the center of the bar, a man with a gruff voice in a black and red-checkered flannel shirt grunted to the bartender. "Give me a boiler-maker."

The bartender drew a mug of beer and set it in front of the man. Then he filled a shot glass of whiskey and held it over the mug. He dropped it. Glass and all plopped into the beer. Foaming up, the beer looked as if it were going to boil over the side of the mug. Before it could, the man picked it up. In one smooth motion he threw it down his throat. He slammed the mug down on the bar. The thick shot glass clinked against the side of the empty mug. With a satisfied look on his face, the man wiped his lips on the back of his hand and waved to the bartender. "Catch you tomorrow, Biff." And he sauntered out the door.

Blondie sat down on the round bar stool and wanted to strike up a conversation. But before he could utter a word, Neal spoke up. "Hi, Biff, give us two drafts."

Blondie looked around the bar. "Nice place you got here. Didn't it used to be called Peacock Alley?"

Drawing the beer, Biff looked up. "Not this place." He jerked his head toward the door. "Right at the end of the parking lot, that's where Peacock Alley used to be."

"What happened to it?"

Biff set the glass of beer in front of Blondie and drew another. "It burnt down. If you scrape some of the gravel away, you can still see the cement block foundation."

Blondie's heart sank. If the place burnt down, all the clues, or worse, all the money could have been burnt up, too.

Biff stared at Blondie. "You look like you seen a ghost. Is something wrong?"

"Well…just a little," Blondie lied. "Years ago, my father wrote his name in the wet cement at a place called Peacock Alley. It's not important to anyone else, but he died last month." As if he were holding back tears, he paused. "I thought I might be able to see his name."

"Peacock Alley would've been a nice place to visit," Biff said, and set the beer in front of Neal. "After prohibition not too many places could afford the thousand dollars for a liquor license. Peacock Alley used to be a streetcar stop that sold illegal booze."

Blondie placed his elbows on the bar and leaned in. "A lot of people sold booze back then."

"Sure they did," Biff said, rolling up the sleeves on his white shirt. "This area was a haven for a lot of people."

"What kind of people?"

Biff's eyes lit up. "To name a few: John Dillinger and Machine-gun Kelly. Back then it was illegal to chase bank robbers over the state lines. So, they came from Chicago, Buffalo, and Ohio."

"Why didn't the cops arrest them?"

"Everyone around here kept their mouths shut. It was an unwritten law. Everyone knew not to tell the cops a damn thing."

Blondie took a sip of his beer. "What would they do if you did talk?"

"If the cops weren't on the take, they'd probably blow your head off." Biff gestured to a wooden booth along the wall. "Hell, it was so safe, some people say Al Capone used to come here and sit right in that booth. After prohibition he gave the owners of Peacock Alley enough money to get the license and go legal."

Blondie could feel excitement rushing through his veins. The vault could be right outside buried in the old foundation, but he couldn't seem too anxious. He hungered for more information about Capone. He took another sip of his beer and stared at the mirror behind the bar.

Neal leaned his head back and studied his surroundings. "I don't think Capone was ever here. The owners probably said that just to keep people coming back."

Biff lifted the bar rag and waved it once. "I don't know about that. I was just a kid then. But I remember one night a big black car stopped right outside. "He pointed toward the door. "A bunch of guys in dark suits got out. The way they looked around, I figured they were bodyguards. Then, one of them opened the back door and said, 'It's okay, Snorky.' Then a husky guy in a three-piece suit and an expensive white hat got out of the car. After they came in, they wouldn't let anyone leave the place while he was in here."

"What did they do," Neal said and cocked his with suspicion, "tie everybody up?"

"Oh, hell, no," Biff said, and waved his hand in the air. "Those bodyguards were all over the place.

Some were even down by the crick with machine guns."

"Why would they go by a crick?"

"I guess they didn't want anybody sneaking through the old tunnel that runs under the road. The old timers said that it was part of the Underground Railroad for the colored people."

Blondie took a sip of his beer. "Did you actually see Al Capone?"

"Damned if I know," Biff said, as if he were getting agitated. "I wouldn't know Al Capone if he came in here and sat down right next to you."

"So you're not sure it was him?" Blondie asked with disbelief.

As if he had been slapped, biff snapped back, "Nobody can be sure about anything." He reflected for a moment. Then, he raised one finger. "But later on, I did find out that Snorky means classy or high class."

With an ambivalent attitude, Neal rolled his hand. "So what's that got to do with Capone?"

Biff whirled around and faced Neal. "What's that got to do with it? Capone believed he was a classy, stand-up guy, one of his nicknames was Snorky." He shook his finger in front of Neal's eyes. "That's what it's got to do with it."

"Don't get excited." Neal raised his hand in a stopping motion. "You may have something there."

As if in deep thought or letting his hear slow, Biff paused. "You know, after he left, they made everybody stay in the bar for an hour. If it wasn't Al Capone, it was somebody really important."

Blondie took out a twenty dollar bill and placed it on the bar. "Mind if we go and look around?"

Biff picked up the twenty. "Go ahead. I'll get your change."

Blondie gestured for Neal to leave.

Neal tilted the glass to his lips, threw the beer down, and started toward the door.

Waving the change for the twenty in his hand, Biff yelled at Blondie, "You forgot your change."

At the door, Blondie turned to Biff. "That's okay, Biff. Keep it."

Biff smiled big. "Thanks, it seems like old times."

Outside, Nose, Freddy, and Rafferty sat in the Ford, waiting. Neal and Blondie walked up to the Ford and stopped. Neal stuck his head into the window. "Peacock Alley burnt down."

A hangdog look filled Freddy's face. "You mean we went through all this trouble and the place is gone?"

"Ah, ahem, ah, yes," Neal said. Then he lifted one finger. "It may be gone, but the bartender said we could look around."

"The way I see it," Blondie said, "if the vault was gone, the Chicago mob wouldn't still be looking for it." He waved his hand in a come-on motion. "Let's check out the old foundation." He walked to the end of the parking lot.

After everyone go out of the Ford, Rafferty's scanned the empty lot. "What foundation?"

"The bartender says the cement block foundation is still under the gravel," Neal said. "For all we know there might be a place to put that key."

"If there is," Rafferty said, "I'm not getting my head blown off."

With the zeal of sudden inspiration, Freddy lifted his hand. "I'll do it."

With a look of puzzlement, Rafferty turned toward Freddy "Why so eager?"

"If the place burnt down any gun shells would have exploded in the heat of the fire."

Rafferty let out a mirthless chuckle. "That could be true. But that fire might have burnt the money, too."

In alarm, Neal whipped himself around and faced Rafferty. "What did you have to say that for?"

"Because, it's true."

For a moment, Neal's face clouded. Then he looked down at the gravel. "It doesn't matter." His voice resounded with enthusiasm. "It could be right under our feet."

At the end of the parking lot, they pawed at the gravel with the toes of their shoes. Neal bent down and scooped away the gravel with his hands until the top of a broken cement block appeared. "Here it is!"

The others joined in and scraped gravel away with their hands and feet. A line of worn cement blocks was gradually uncovered.

Freddy looked up. "That key fit three bricks down at the Jungle Inn. If there's a keyway here, it's probably a few blocks down. We're going to need shovels and picks."

From the door of the bar, Biff yelled, "Hey! Stop digging up my parking lot. I said you could look around, not rip the place up."

Everyone stopped scraping and looked up.

"Ah, ahem, ah, yes," Neal said, and nodded to Biff. "Of course, we understand."

Nose reached into his suit coat and placed his hand on his Colt 45. "I got two shovels and flashlights in the station wagon. If I go up and blow his goddamn head off, we can dig all day and all night."

Blondie stared at him. "You do, the cops will be here. Then, we'll never get this thing dug up."

"And not only that," Freddy added. "The newspapers will be here taking pictures. How are we going to explain why we were digging up an old foundation?"

"That's right," Blondie said. "If this digging thing hits the newspapers; the Chicago Mob will be right down here looking for the vault."

Nose relaxed his grip on his Colt. "So, what are we gonna do?"

"Nothing," Neal said, and looked toward Biff. "Hey, man we're sorry!" he yelled back. Then he took his foot and pulled gravel back over the foundation. "We'll put it back the way it was."

Blondie took the hint and pushed gravel onto the foundation. "Yeah, we're sorry, Biff."

"What are you covering it back up for?" Nose asked.

"We'll come back at night," Blondie whispered. "We want the blocks to still be here. If we leave them uncovered someone might find the vault."

"The way I see it," Neal said, "Biff did us a favor."

After the gravel was back the way it had been, Neal went to Biff and apologized until he was about to fall over.

Biff nodded and waved his hand in a dismissing gesture. "No problem."

They jumped in the cars, sped away, and waited for night.

CHAPTER 31

After the bars closed at three-thirty AM, the two-vehicle convoy skirted the edge of the city of Hubbard, Ohio and drove down Route 62. Eventually, they left the main highway and passed though streets lined with sleeping houses. Then they ascended around sharp bends that led to a slight series of switchbacks that straightened out. With the Dodge behind, Neal pulled the Ford off the road and parked next to the foundation of Peacock Alley. Blondie pulled the station wagon next to the Ford and took out the shovels. As moths swooped around the dim light of a lone light bulb at the entrance to the bar, to make it look like it had a flat tire, Neal jacked one side of the station wagon up. He had also parked the Ford on a slant to block the views of occasional cars that might happen past.

As if he were preparing to do some serious digging, Nose got out of the car, took off his suit coat, placed his Colt and shoulder holster on the front seat, and rolled up his sleeves. But instead of getting to work, he leaned on the fender of the Ford and watched. Freddy knew that when there was work to be done, Neal didn't like people setting themselves up as being better than others. He wasn't going to like what Nose was doing.

Freddy and Rafferty scraped loose gravel away from the foundation with their feet while Neal and Blondie lifted shovelfuls of dirt from around the side of the cement blocks. After digging for fifteen minutes, Neal slapped at a mosquito on his sweating forehead and walked over to Nose. He was still leaning on the car fender and holding the key.

Neal held out his hand. "Come on, Nose, make yourself useful." He jerked his hand. "The mosquitoes are eating me up. Give me that key. I think it might fit over here."

Nose clinched his fists and glared at Neal.

Blondie knew money had a knack for creating monsters. In Nose's case, one of these monsters could be lurking beneath the surface, ready to jump out. They were too close to finding the vault to have a fight start now. To defuse a developing confrontation, Blondie stepped between Nose and Neal.

"Come on, you guys," he said. "Let's work together. There's enough money for us all."

Nose growled low, but handed Neal the key. Neal plodded to the foundation and bent over. His movements were slow and mechanical. Looking too exhausted to carry on, he tried to fit the key into a slot, but it was too small.

"It doesn't fit," he said and straightened up. "Let's check some more?"

Nose held out his hand. "Give me back that key."

Neal jerked the key toward Nose. "If you think you can make it fit, here, try it."

Nose took the key and placed it in his pocket. "Maybe it'll fit someplace else."

Blondie scanned the exposed foundation. "We've checked every place on this thing. If there was another slot, it was bulldozed away after the fire."

With his eyes staring into nothingness and as if he were in deep thought, Rafferty dragged his foot and pushed some gravel into the hole next to the foundation. "Gentleman, I think we hit a dead end."

"Yeah, man," Neal said, and began shoveling gravel to cover the foundation.

"Wait a minute," Rafferty said, and placed his foot over the slot. "Maybe the block's not cemented in place."

He bent over and pushed on the block. It moved, but the dirt next to it stopped it from tipping over. Blondie grabbed the shovel and stabbed it next to the block. "Let me dig that dirt out."

Rafferty stepped back and Blondie removed the dirt. Neal put the toe of his shoe on the block and pushed. The block tipped back. Underneath was a small chamber a little bit wider than the shovel blade. Inside, a black box with a padlock on its side waited to be opened. Neal reached down to pull the box out, but Blondie yanked on his shoulder and pulled him away.

"Not so fast," he said. "Remember what happened to Swill?"

Letting out a loud horselaugh, Nose nudged Blondie in the ribs. "Let the dummy open it. When the dynamite goes off, we'll watch him fly."

Neal looked up at Nose. "Very funny."

Rafferty moved in closer. Blondie squinted one eye in Rafferty's direction. "Aren't you going to move back?"

"No, I'm just going to stand here like an idiot and get blown up." He stood back.

Holding up his hands in surrender, Blondie looked at Neal and Nose. "What do you guys want to do, find the vault or stand here and argue all night?"

"I would do both," Neal said, and looked at Nose. "But I never argue with anybody that's mentally unarmed."

Nose didn't understand Neal's cut, and Blondie didn't give him time to figure it out. He held the end of the long handle of the shovel and placed the blade on the lock of the box.

"If you don't want a quick trip to the pearly gates," he said and waved his hand in a shooing motion, "stand back!"

With the threat of being blown into the sky, Nose and Neal quit arguing, stepped back, and watched. Blondie jiggled the shovel. The box moved. He let out a slow breath and waited. Still nothing. He looked to the others. "Cover your faces."

With one arm protecting his face, he hauled back and rammed the shovel blade against the corroded lock. It snapped open. Shielding his face with his arms, Neal bent over for a closer look. "I think it's safe." He bent over, and lifted the black box from the chamber. A copper wire attached to the bottom fell off. He dropped the box and jumped back.

Relieved, Blondie whooshed out a breath of relief. "Whatever that wire was connected to must've burned up in the fire."

Neal ran his hand across his sweat-soaked forehead. "That's okay by me."

Rafferty placed his hand on the box. "Let's open this thing."

Bowing at the waist, Neal gestured toward the Ford. "Be my guest."

274

Rafferty picked up the box, walked to the Ford, and placed it on the front fender. Standing back, he opened the box. Everyone horned in close and looked inside. Another key, similar to the one they already had, glared back at them.

"Oh, just great," Neal said. "We already have a key that we can't find what it fits, and now we have another one."

Blondie picked up the key. "Maybe there's a note under this thing." They huddled close and looked into the box. It was empty. Blondie ran his fingers over the new key and looked to Nose. "Let me see that other key."

With surprise irritation, Nose held his hand on the key in his pocket. "You can't have it."

Blondie shook his head. "Now what's the matter?"

Nose held out his hand. "Nothing, I'll check them both."

Blondie didn't want to hand another key over to Nose. At one time he may have been helpful, and Blondie thought he still could be. But now he realized that Nose's drinking had caused his intellectual capacity to be reduced. He could easily be confused. If Nose tried to keep the keys there was only one of him and four of them. They could surely get the keys back. He decided to humor the man. He shrugged and handed him the key. "It's in your hands."

Nose laid the keys side by side on the fender. "Look here," he said, with excitement in his voice. "The new key has two holes and the notches are different."

"So what?" Neal said.

Nose put the new key into his pocket. As if he had just made the greatest discovery on earth, he tilted his head back, smiled, and patted the key. Holding the other key he shook it.

"This key's a two-holer," he said. "That's a shithouse with two holes." As if he were in shock from using his brain for the first time in his life, his eyes on the sides of his ugly nose became glassy. "The vault's in the bottom of a shithouse."

Freddy faced away so Nose would not see him grinning. To keep himself from laughing, Blondie cleared his throat.

But Neal laughed out loud. "That's the dumbest thing I ever heard of."

Displaying a mocking grin, Rafferty chimed in, "The vault's not at the bottom of an outhouse, but maybe that's where your brain is."

Freddy turned to Nose to see how he would react. Turning to Rafferty, Nose balled up his fist. His smile turned to an exaggerated frown. "You want me to kick your ass right here and now?"

"You might as well," Neal said, with a grin. "It'll be the most work you've done all night." He held out his hand. "Give me those keys, and get your lazy ass on the end of a shovel and help us fill in that foundation, cunt-nose!"

Blondie cringed. "Don't call him that."

But it was too late. Nose had heard it. The muscles in his shoulders tensed and swelled up like stacks of hardwood.

With his usual smile erased from his face, Rafferty looked at Nose. As if he were sorry he had made the outhouse remark, he tried not to laugh. But, "Ha, Ha," burst out. He tried to stop, but it was too late. He backed away from Nose and groaned. "Oh, man."

Nose grumbled something unintelligible and lashed out at Rafferty.

Rafferty ducked under his swishing hand and ran around the car. Neal ran around the other side of the Dodge, grabbed a shovel, and stopped at the edge of the cement blocks. Waiting for Nose to be chasing Rafferty so he could blind side him with the shovel, Neal looked back. Rafferty was on the ground. Nose was clutching his throat in an iron grip.

Neal bent over and shouted in Nose's ear, "Hey, cunt-nose."

Nose jerked his head in Neal's direction.

Neal stepped to the front of the Dodge and leaned the shovel against the bumper. Then he placed his thumbs in his ears and wiggled his fingers. "Na, na, na, cunt-nose."

Nose let loose of Rafferty's throat, jumped up, and rushed to the front of the Dodge.

But Neal wasn't there.

As if the sudden rush was too much for his out-of-shape body, Nose stopped, leaned on the hood, and took deep labored gasps.

Leaning on the shovel handle, Neal stood next to the foundation.

Nose stepped away from the Dodge, lumbered along, and stopped in front of Neal. Breathing heavily, a cold smile formed on his lips. "What did you call me?"

Neal could have apologized. He could have said he had said something else, but he didn't. He arrogantly leaned on one foot and held out the shovel. "Don't try to think about what I said, cunt-nose. You'll only get a headache." He jerked the shovel handle toward him. "Here, cunt-nose, grab this shovel. Forget about your shithouse theory, and give me those goddamn keys."

Nose's words came out measured and threatening. "Nobody calls me cunt-nose."

Neal jerked his opened hand toward Nose and shouted, "Cunt-nose! Cunt-nose! Cunt-nose!"

Red rage blew the cold smile from Nose's lips. "You little son-of-a-bitch." He lunged for Neal.

Neal sidestepped.

Nose stumbled past.

Neal slammed the heel of his hand into Nose's back. As he threw out his hands and hit the gravel, one of the keys fell from his pocket. Immediately, he jumped up and started for Neal. Neal looked back at Nose, skipped past the Dodge, and sprinted across the road. Nose stopped, reached into his pocket, and took out the other brass key. As if it were a gun, he aimed it at Neal. With his trigger finger, he pulled on a notch in the key. Realizing his stupidity of thinking he had his gun in his hand, he reared back and flung the key at Neal. The key flew into the air and zinged right past Neal's ear.

Running down an embankment at the edge of the road, Neal playfully yelled back in a cartoon voice, "Ha, ha, cunt-nose, you didn't get me."

The roar of a car's racing motor grew loud. From around the bend, headlights beamed onto the puke-green of the Dodge station wagon. Nose flung open the door of the Dodge, reached in, and grabbed his shoulder holster. In the bright beam of the headlights, he rushed onto the road. A frozen image of him jerking on the gun's handle, and trying to free the weapon from its holster was cut short. The speeding car slammed into him. He flew into the darkness. The car didn't stop. Nose landed with a hushed thump in the tall weeds at the side of the road. As he lay face down, the red taillights raced down the road and faded into the night.

Laughing, Neal came up out of the weeds of the embankment. "What the hell was that?"

Freddy pointed to Nose. "Nose just got hit by a car."

Neal ran to Nose. "Hey, old buddy, I was only kidding." He reached into his pocket, took out the key, and offered it to Nose's face-down body. "You can have it back."

Blondie walked over to Nose and pulled on his shoulder. Nose didn't respond. Blondie crouched down, reached over and lifted Nose's wrist.

Freddy crouched down next to Blondie. "Is there a pulse?"

Blondie held the wrist and waited for a pulse. "Nothing, he's dead."

Neal held the key in front of Freddy. "Here, hold this. He's fakin' it."

Freddy took the key, held it close to his chest, and looked down at Blondie. "Are you sure he's dead?"

Blondie nodded and dropped Nose's wrist.

Neal rolled Nose over. His nose no longer looked like a vagina. It had been mashed into a bloody mass that clung to his smashed-flat skull. Neal reared back, placed his hands on his knees, gagged, and retched onto the side of the road.

Freddy managed to say, "We got to call the police. That's hit and run."

Still hunched over, Neal closed his eyes. "If I was driving and hit a man with a gun, I don't think I would've stopped either."

As if he were fighting back the smell of death, Blondie closed his eyes and leaned on the shovel handle.

"It doesn't matter why the car didn't stop, if we call the police, we'll all go to jail." He looked at Freddy. "And you'll go for abetting a lawbreaker in a criminal act."

Holding his hand over his mouth as if he were about to throw up, Rafferty stood back and held the other key. He swallowed and managed to blurt out, "And we'll never find that vault."

Freddy shot him a glare. "Thanks for that comforting information."

Neal wiped his mouth with the back of his arm, and stood erect. "What should we do?"

Blondie glanced at the key in Rafferty's hand. "We'll just have to think on it a while."

Freddy looked to where Nose lay. Trying to block the grotesque image out of his mind, he turned and faced the parking lot. "We got to fill this foundation back in and get out of here."

Just as sun was spilling its first rays into a new morning, the old cement block foundation of the former Peacock Alley bar was back the way it had been; except after all these years, it had given up its secret key. Brushing has hands together, Neal looked at Blondie. "Are you going to drive the Dodge?"

Blondie shook his head. "We don't need any wise ass cops snooping around. If we leave it here the police will think Nose was fixing a flat when he got hit."

Neal threw the shovels into the trunk of the Ford and ran to the jacked up tire on the Dodge and bent over. Blondie placed his hand on the door handle of the Ford, and looked to Neal. "What are you doing?"

Neal reached into his pocket pulled out his knife. "It'll look suspicious if the cops check this tire and it isn't flat."

Holding the back of the knife against the base of his palm to keep it from slipping up and cutting his hand, he jabbed the blade into the side of the tire. A gush of air blew around his hand. The tire went flat. Neal jumped behind the steering wheel, and everyone, except Nose, headed down the road.

CHAPTER 32

After driving over the Pennsylvania state line, Neal stopped at the Dinner Bell restaurant in the town of Sharon. Freddy, Neal, Rafferty, and Blondie walked under the moving neon outline of a blue bell and stepped inside. At a booth in the back, Blondie sat so he could watch the door. As Freddy sat down, an undertone of conversation and the clink of crockery greeted him.

Near the cash register a thin man sipped his coffee from a thick mug with a blue stripe around the top. Another customer, a big man with broad shoulders, on his way out of the restaurant jogged the man's elbow. The thin man spilled the coffee down the front of his clean white shirt. He jumped up and yelled at the big man, but the man walked out of the restaurant and kept going. The thin man cussed, sat back down, and ordered another coffee.

Even though there were many things going on, Freddy couldn't get Nose's death out of his mind. If he could go home and take a nap, he would feel better. But he couldn't trust Blondie, and the last thing he or the others wanted him to know was where they lived. The waitress stood behind the counter with a pot of coffee in her hand. A baseball-hatted man with a big nose and a scar down his cheek sat at the counter and turned to the thin man with the fresh coffee stain down the front of his shirt.

"If John Dillinger was in here," he said, "that big galoot wouldn't have knocked over your coffee and ran."

The thin man held his cup in front of his mouth. "What makes you say that?"

"I was in here when John Dillinger used to come in." The man tipped his baseball hat to the waitress. "Yeah, I was sitting right here in this same stool. Dillinger told the waitress to give everybody what they wanted and left." He winked at the waitress and laughed a deep belly laugh. "I'll tell you, honey, I got a big steak that day."

The waitress smiled and refreshed the man's coffee. "Did he come back and pay?"

"Oh, sure, he came back. He paid for *everybody's* meal. The damage came to around eighty-nine dollars. A lot of money back then. But Dillinger was a great man." He looked down at the man's stained shirt. "No matter how big that guy was, John Dillinger wouldn't have let that happen. He was always helping out the little guy."

The thin man suddenly spoke up. "Wasn't Dillinger shot in Chicago?"

The baseball-hatted man lifted his cup, and nodded. "Yep, some lady named Anna wore a red dress as a signal to the FBI. She set him up in front of the Biograph Theater."

The waitress finished with the coffee and carried a round tin tray with four glasses of ice water over to the booth where Freddy and the others sat. She placed the glasses of ice water on the table, tucked the red tray under her arm, and stood with pencil and pad ready. As Neal eyed her up and down she took their orders.

After Freddy finished his eggs and toast, he leaned back in the booth. Neal pulled out the new key and examined it under the table. Then he looked at Blondie. "I wonder why this thing has two holes in it."

Rafferty's freckled face glowed with merriment. "Like Nose said, maybe it's for a two-holer outhouse."

Shaking his head, Neal looked at Rafferty. "Always a wise guy."

Rafferty formed an exaggerated smile. "I try."

Blondie's forehead wrinkled. "It might fit something next to an outhouse, but I don't think it's a key to one."

"Maybe it isn't," Freddy said and looked toward the door. "But it's the only clue we got."

Neal placed the key in his pocket. "Maybe Nose knew something we don't."

Rafferty held up one finger toward Neal. "You know where there's any good outhouses?"

Neal tapped the key in his pocket. "We could check the old Applegate-Sodom Road that runs past the old Jungle Inn."

Rubbing his forehead, Blondie scrunched his face. "Okay, but we'll have to do it while it's light. Moonshiners used to stash their booze there. They didn't like people snooping around. They claim that's the place where a lot of people were murdered."

"So what?" Neal said. "Are you afraid of moonshiners?"

"I don't think we have to worry about that," Blondie said, and took a sip of his ice water. "They had a big standoff with the liquor agents at the Jungle Inn and closed it down in August of '49."

"What's that got to do with anything?" Rafferty asked.

"If they shot someone, they're probably buried along Applegate-Sodom Road."

Rafferty persisted. "So what?"

"I don't want to be digging up old bodies in the dark." Blondie shrugged. "But I guess there's nothing to worry about unless you're afraid of ghosts."

Rafferty's body shook as if he were shivering. "What's the chance of us finding a body after all these years?"

"You figure it out," Blondie said. "Every night, three thousand people used to gamble at the Jungle Inn. Now that the casino's gone, moonshiners and murderers have no reason to be at Applegate-Sodom Road. And anyway, they said a guy named Mike paid off people to keep the Jungle Inn open. But they called in the state liquor agents anyway. After that, he said that legitimate business was too crooked for him. So, he sold the Jungle Inn to the window place that's there now."

As if he already knew the answer, Rafferty flashed Blondie a big-toothed grin. "Why do they call it Applegate-Sodom Road?"

"Because it ran right in front of a whore house."

Blondie reached into his pocket, pulled out a large bill, laid it on the table, and they left.

CHAPTER 33

When Neal drove down Applegate-Sodom Road, the light of the sun revealed the only thing that could possibly be a hiding place for a vault. Off to the right, in a grove of gnarly black trees, stripped leafless by some unknown disease, stood an old broken-down building. Leaning to one side, the building seemed to present itself as an outhouse. Neal pulled off to the side of the road. With the right side tires hugging the lip of a drainage ditch, they all got out. Neal navigated through the tall grass and ducked under the low branches of scarecrow-like trees. Freddy and the others followed.

Beyond the trees and the small building, dry thorny weeds and spots of brush encircled a cement block building's ragged ruins. The remaining cement floor was strewn with broken glass and one dusty, old tire. With Freddy looking over his shoulder, Neal opened the door to the small building. As if the slightest touch would knock it over, the top of a rectangular wooden box slanted to the side. It was high enough to sit on; and the two side-by-side holes that had been cut through its surface, were big enough for a person's butt. Spider webs laced the holes, and dirt half an inch thick coated the ancient wood. It was an old two-holer outhouse. Except for a few ragged boards that clung to the sides of the walls, the floor had rotted away.

Rafferty smiled at Neal. "Maybe there's no treasure. Maybe it's some kind of joke, and that brass key really is a key to an outhouse."

Neal backed away from the outhouse. A black snake crawled out the opened door. "There isn't

286

anything our key will fit in there." He turned toward the cement block ruins. "Maybe there's a place in this cement."

After they searched the area, Rafferty pawed the ground with the edge of his foot. "Do we have to dig up this whole place?"

"No way," Blondie said. "I don't even know why we came here. Nose's great theory is only crap. Capone had too much class to put his treasure next to an outhouse."

Freddy looked across the land and back toward the Ford. As if touched by the hands of murdered gangsters seeking revenge, the wind tussled the grass around the spooky-black trees. As if from a cold hand, a chill ran up his back. "This place gives me the creeps."

Rafferty stared at the moving grass. "This place feels cold. Let's get out of here."

A canny smile curled Neal's lips. "What are you afraid of? It's only a little wind."

"I'm not afraid of anything," Freddy lied. "We almost gave up at the Peacock Alley's foundation, but at the last minute we found that two-hole key. Maybe we should check Petroleum again."

A glimmer of hope radiated from Blondie's face. "You may have something there."

"I don't know about you guys," Neal said, and yawned. "But I think better after I've had some sleep."

Suppressing a yawn, Rafferty nodded. "I could use a few Z's myself."

They took one last look around, hopped back into the Ford, and took off. Freddy and his treasure-seeking friends managed to get a few hours of

287

restless sleep under the cover of tall weeds and trees that lined the high-tension tower road. Then they were back on the road again. Several miles later, Neal swung south and they were on their way back to Petroleum.

Right before the afternoon rush hour, Neal drove the Ford onto the road that led to Petroleum. On Standard Avenue, in front of the General American Transportation Corporation railroad car plant, traffic was heavy. Various makes, colors, and models of cars lined the sides of the road. Behind the steering wheels, women sat waiting for their husbands or boyfriends to come out of the plant.

"It must be payday." Neal rubbed his fingers as if her were counting money. "Sometimes that's the only time wives and girlfriends show up."

"Yeah," Rafferty said. "It's called 'payday love'."

Up ahead, two cars were stopped in the middle of the road.

"There must have been an accident," Neal said, and slowed the Ford.

Two women got out of their cars and examined the front and back bumpers of their cars. Then, they smiled, got back behind the wheels, and pulled off to the side.

In front of the railroad plant, a carnival-like atmosphere filled the air. Acting as if they had great expectations and were afraid they would miss something entertaining, but were happy that it was about to happen, a stream of thirsty men ran to the parking lot in a hurry to get into their dust-covered jalopies and drive to the nearest bar: Libby's. Here they would relive their day's work. After they had quenched their thirsts with huge mugs of beer that had heads as thick as whipped cream they would talk about the day's work of years past.

Just before one horde of workers thinned, another stream of workers rushed from the main gate and passed in front of the field next to a high-voltage transformer pen. Stopping from time to time, they flexed their muscles; and in a noisy display of power, they shouted wise remarks at fellow workers as they raced toward waiting wives and girlfriends who would drive them home or to a bar.

Out next to the road, a freshly showered worker waved a '48 Plymouth down. The girl behind the wheel opened the passenger door. The smiling worker slicked his wet hair back with the side of his hand, jumped in, and zipped away.

Neal moaned as if he were in pain. "We find that vault," he said. "Then we'll never have to sweat and grub for money in a hot factory like those guys do."

"We'll be rich," Rafferty said. "But if we look for the vault with all this traffic going past, someone will want to know what we're doing?"

Freddy liked the money he made when he worked with Neal on the garbage truck, but he didn't like the smell; and he sure as hell didn't want to do something like that for the rest of his life.

"If someone sees us open the treasure," he said, "they'll want some for themselves."

Neal waved his hands next to his ear. "And they'll tell their friends, and their friends will tell their friends. Before it's done, the taxmen will be here for their share. If we don't keep this thing secret, we'll be lucky if we get enough for a cup of coffee."

Rafferty leaned over the front seat. "Don't tell me we're going to Canada again to get one."

"I would," Neal said, "but we need to figure out a way to check out Petroleum without anyone watching."

With total calmness Blondie slumped forward. "If you don't want anyone to know about something, the best time to do it is just before sunrise."

"What's so great about sunrise?" Rafferty wanted to know.

"No one wants to give up that last few minutes of sleep and will ignore just about any noise."

Rafferty leaned back and folded his arms across his chest. "Well, let's just wait for sunrise."

"Good Idea," Blondie said and patted his trim stomach. "I could use some time to think this thing through."

Neal turned the Ford off the Route 62 highway and onto a road that twisted and turned like a sharp S. The crooked road ran for several miles through cultivated fields of corn and a few lone houses. The Ford rounded a bend. Looking majestically perched on the crest of a hill, the top of the first in a line of high-tension towers could be seen. Neal pulled into the tall grass and drove back to the tower line maintenance road and stopped. Next to the passenger side door, a lineman's hardhat lay in the tall grass. Rafferty opened the door, picked up the white hat, and put it on his head. "Look, I'm a lineman."

Neal looked thoughtful. "I know we were going to wait until it got dark to check out Petroleum, but after all that plant traffic thins out, we could go check out the place in the daylight."

Freddy leaned forward. "No way. If someone sees us find that vault, they'll want a share."

Neal pointed at Blondie. "If he wears that hat, people will think he's the boss, and we're the lowly labors."

Rafferty offered the hat to Blondie. Blondie placed the white hat on his head and puffed out his chest. "Do I look like a boss?"

Rafferty giggled. "You don't look dumb enough." He smiled. "But don't worry about it. Those white hats have machines in them. When you put the hat on your head, the machine sucks your brains out."

Neal looked at Rafferty. "Sometimes you act like you've been wearing one of those hats all your life."

Rafferty shrugged. "You'll be okay, Blondie. No one will be able to see how stupid you look from the road."

Blondie tilted his head. "Thanks for the advice."

Neal pulled off the tower line road, downshifted, and put the car into a tight turn.

"Hold on to your ass," he said, over the squeal of spinning tires. "We're going back to the great glimmering metropolis of Petroleum."

Back at Petroleum, Blondie placed the white hardhat on his head, and they all got out of the car. From around the bend, a faded-blue car slowed. Behind the wheel, a curious man with thick lips gawked out the window. As if he were a foreman of a work crew, Blondie directed the others to certain

291

places; and they fanned out across the tall grass. The driver nodded, looked straight ahead, and drove on. Blondie joined the others and searched the little piece of ground for something the keys could fit. An hour later, Blondie bent over and swept some tall grass away from a hunk of old cement. Then, he stood up and waved to Neal. "Bring that key over here."

Neal and the others ran to the hunk of concrete. On the side of the cement was a hole that looked like a slot for a key. Neal handed Blondie the key. Blondie bent over, placed the key into the slot, and tried to turn it. Nothing moved.

Neal bent over and waved his hands excitedly in front of the key. "Come on, man. It must be rusted. Put some torque on that thing."

Blondie gritted his teeth and turned harder.

Neal dropped to his knees. "Let me try that thing."

Blondie leaned back. "Knock yourself out."

Neal tried to turn the key. Searching for a possible way to make it work, he moved the key in and out. Still, no movement. He took the key out, gave it to Blondie, and held out his hand. "Give me the other key."

Blondie gave him the other key. Freddy reached down and grabbed a corner of the concrete. "Let me try this."

Neal backed away. Freddy bent his legs, straightened his strong back, and pulled up on the concrete. As he straightened his muscular legs, the huge hunk of cement lifted from the earth and then broke free. He rolled it over. On the underside, there were no cables, wires, levers, or anything that would be connected to a vault. He brushed the dirt from his hands. "I guess this ain't it."

They all went back to the Ford and sat on the back bumper.

Dejected, Rafferty looked at Freddy. "There's nothing here. Got anymore bright ideas?"

As twilight drew near, Freddy kept looking at the ground around the Petroleum sign. It looked like some sort of scar on the earth, and he wondered why the sign seemed to have been kept up when everything else around it was let to weather and decay. He walked over to the sign and looked down. The sign's post had an unusual metal base. Although the dirt was moist everywhere else they had looked, a five foot round area below the sign was dry dirt with only a few scraggly plants trying to grow.

Rafferty got off the car bumper, and walked over to Freddy. "What did you find?"

"I'm not sure." Freddy pointed to the base of the sign. "I wonder why the ground is so dry here, and there's a round ring of black grease at the bottom of the pole." With the edge of his shoe, he pawed some of the dirt and grease away from the base of the signpost. The grease clung to his shoe.

Holding his nose, Rafferty stepped away from him. "What did you do? Step on a Tootsie Roll a dog made for you?"

Freddy flashed Rafferty a sly grin. "You wish."

As Freddy continued pawing the dirt away from the base of the signpost, Rafferty placed his hands on his knees, bent over, and watched. As if his shoe were a toy bulldozer blade, Freddy pushed the dry dirt away from the base of the post and revealed a round metal base.

Rafferty pointed at it. "Why did they make a base like that?"

Freddy examined the grease around the bottom of the post. "I don't know, but this grease is covering something." He took a few steps away from the sign and ripped out a handful of dry grass from the field. Then he went back to the signpost, bent over, and wiped most of the grease away. At the bottom of the signpost, black grease filled a jagged slot. He stood up. "I'll be damned. I think that key will fit in there."

Neal sprang off the bumper of the Ford. "What?"

He rushed over. Blondie followed and watched, too. Freddy placed the key in the slot and twisted it. Rafferty put one hand on the signpost and leaned on it. It tipped to a forty-five degree angle and stopped solid.

Neal jerked his head sideways and stared at the slanted signpost. "Now what?"

Freddy bent over to examine the area and found another slot. He held up his hand. "Give me that other key."

Neal handed it to him. Freddy put it in the new slot and started to push the pole back to an upright position. The ground moved beneath his feet. He jumped back. A frightful gasp escaped from Rafferty's throat. Looking at the ground he said, "What was that?"

"I didn't see anything," Neal said. "It's your imagination."

Blondie placed his hand on the pole. "If this thing stays crooked, it'll attract attention. Let's push it back the way it was."

He pushed the sign back to its upright position. Something deep in the earth groaned. Like an awakened giant opening his sleepy mouth, a dirt and weed-covered metal plate slid across the ground. As it opened, a four-foot-long lip of cement scraped a thin layer of the dirt and weeds into a dark hole. Freddy let out a whistle and looked down. A damp chill oozed out of a dark opening about the size of a man's shoulders.

Blondie stared at the opening and shook his head. "Remember what happened to Swill. Watch out for a trap."

"I don't like it," Rafferty said. "It might be just an old well they dumped bodies into."

Peering into the darkness and sniffing, Neal said, "I don't smell anything dead."

Blondie flashed a flashlight into the hole. A short set of stairs led down to a room about the size of a walk-in closet. He held the light on the small room and looked up. "Who wants to go in first?"

Neal gave Blondie a faint look of pleasure. "There's only room for about two people."

Blondie pointed to the hardhat he was still wearing. "In case somebody comes snooping around, I'll stay here and play boss."

Neal looked at Freddy. "You got us into this. Let's go."

Neal grabbed the flashlight from Blondie and ducked into the hole. As he made his way down the dirt and weed-sprinkled steps, Freddy was close behind. Keeping in mind what had happened to

295

Swill, Freddy felt like he was descending the steps to the gallows. But the promise of treasure quenched his fears.

At the bottom of the steps, a shadowy mass loomed in the dark. The flashlight beam illuminated the exterior of a metal door. Corroded hinges and a rusty padlock looked as if they hadn't been used for years. With great anticipation welling in his chest, Freddy stared at the door and whistled low.

Blondie hollered down the stairs, "What is it?"

Freddy looked up. "Hold onto your asses, and get ready to fly. It's getting interesting."

Neal called up the stairs. "Get me that master key out of the trunk."

Perplexed, Blondie looked to Rafferty. "What's he talking about?"

Rafferty smiled, went to the Ford, fished out the tire iron, and handed it down the stairs.

Neal inserted the bar under the padlock hasp and pulled. The lock twanged open. Neal reached over to open the door, but Freddy placed his hand on it and held it closed.

"What's the big deal?" Neal asked.

"Swill *was* the deal. Let's just be careful."

Neal stepped back.

Holding the beam of the flashlight on the door and being wary of an explosion, Freddy backed up the steps. Standing off to the side, Neal placed the end of the tire iron into the edge of the door and pried. The door opened about an inch. Neal listened and waited for something to happen. No surprise shotgun blast greeted him in the face, and no bomb went off. He wiped the sweat from his brow, put the tire iron at the edge of the door, and pulled. The door opened with a mournful creak. Musty air came out like the stale air of an old refrigerator. Freddy shone the flashlight into the opening.

It was about four feet high and had a hard rock ceiling held up by walls that had pick and shovel marks gouged into the sides. Next to a rusty kerosene lantern, two narrow gauge railroad tracks reflected dull silver, and ran into a mine tunnel of claustrophobic height.

Blondie yelled down the stairs, "It's getting dark up here. What's it like down there?"

Neal looked up. "It's an old coal mine."

"What a great place to hide something," Blondie said. "An old abandoned coal mine that nobody would think had anything valuable in it."

Freddy shone the light back into the darkness of the mine. Twenty feet in front of him, sitting on a granite platform was a box as big as a coffin. Stretching to seven feet and rising to a height of three feet, the box seemed to be brass coated by a thick green patina. He looked at Neal. Neal was looking at the box with similar astonishment, and occasionally glancing around the confined mine.

Neal nudged Freddy on the back of the shoulder. "Let's crawl in there and see what's in that thing."

Freddy hunched over, and took one step. He tried not to show the fear racing through his body, but the strain in his voice betrayed him. "It looks like a coffin. Maybe there's a dead body in it."

"It's not a coffin," Neal said. "Coffins have handles and fancy carving on the sides and top."

"I hope you're right." Freddy took another step, and stopped.

"Now what?"

"It looks too easy. Look for a trap." He shined the flashlight toward the ceiling of the mine. Almost hidden from view, a brass lever was tucked into a chiseled-out indentation of stone. He looked back over his shoulder at Neal. "I wonder what this thing's for."

"Whatever it is, any moving parts would have rusted solid by now."

"You sure?"

Neal smiled a mischievous smile. "Pull it and find out."

Holding his breath, Freddy, wrapped his fingers around the lever. "Okay. Here goes."

Before he could exert any real force, the lever fell down. Dust trickled down through gaps in the ceiling. For a moment, there was a grating noise. Freddy's stomach clenched.

As the railroad tracks creaked, noises that sounded like an arrangement of weights and pulleys moving gave out an eerie sound. As if they were on hinges, the tracks swept to the side. With an echoing crunch of stone and a flurry of dust, the floor of the mine in front of the green box slid open. A weak odor of dry, dusty clothes filled the mine. Freddy aimed the weakening beam of the flashlight into a square pit.

Lit spookily from the flashlight's fading orange light, hollow eye sockets of a skull peered back at them. Attached to the skull, a skeleton dressed in an oversized, raggedy, pin-striped suit with a big dirty-white gangster hat on his head, sat poised for action. The hand had one skeletal finger wrapped around the trigger of a rusty pistol.

298

Freddy stiffened and stared at the skull. All the horrors and stories of ghosts he had ever experienced flooded into his mind. He wanted to scramble up the stairs, but he froze with fear. With his heart pounding, he pulled on Neal's shoulder. "Is that Al Capone?"

"It looks like him."

"Let's get out of here."

Neal subsided into momentary silence. Then, as if he were throwing the horrible scene out of his mind, he jerked his head.

"What are you afraid of?" He smiled. "If that's Al Capone, he can't hurt you now."

Freddy had just been rattled out of his wits, but he didn't want to let Neal know it. He sagged against the wall of the mine. "This seems sacrilegious."

"Those crooks have been killing each other for years," Neal said. "If we don't open that box," he pointed to the skull, "the ghost of that guy will probably haunt us for being ignorant."

Freddy's mood changed. He drew strength from Neal and managed a slight smile. "Okay, we'll open the box, but what should we tell the guys up top?"

"That box looks heavy. If they get scared, they might not help drag it out. We won't tell them anything."

Neal reached up and placed his hand on the lever, but didn't push it back into place. "That dead guy probably stood in front of the box and somebody pulled this lever, but he shot them before he hit the pit."

"If he did, why isn't another body here?"

299

"'Cause somebody had to get out and close the trap door up top." He pointed to the skeleton. "He probably only wounded the other guy."

"Yeah, the guy probably got away, but died later or that box would have been gone."

Freddy looked back at the skeleton. "That thing still gives me the creeps. I wonder if that lever closes the trap door."

Neal stared at the dull silver railroad tracks. "The gears, or whatever makes this thing work, should have been rusted solid."

"They would have been," Freddy said. "But those tracks are stainless steel. They'll never rust."

"Do you think the gears are stainless, too?"

Freddy shrugged. "Push the lever and find out."

Neal pushed the lever back into its original position. The railroad tracks swept sideways and the floor grated shut. For some reason, the stench of old, dry, dusty clothes was sucked from the air. Freddy crooked his forefinger and thumb and signaled Neal an okay.

"Now that we know that works," he said, and exhaled, "let's see what's in that box."

With Neal close behind, Freddy dropped to his hands and knees and cautiously crawled toward the box. When he got to it, he rose to a kneeling position and put his hand on the lid.

"Open it," Neal said, waving his hand with encouragement. "But make sure there's no wires attached to it."

Freddy shone the flashlight over the box and felt around it.

Neal pulled at Freddy's pants legs. "Come on, open it."

Freddy looked back at Neal and then turned toward the box. Shielding his face with his arm, he pulled on the lid.

A grating noise filled the tunnel.

"Get out!" Neal shouted.

On all fours Neal scrambled for the stairs. Freddy was right behind him, but he wasn't fast enough. Shale and dirt showered down on him. He kept crawling. He was almost to the first step of the stairs when the dirt seemed to fall out of the sky in one big clump and land on his back.

He could no longer move, but he was thankful for the hard life that had caused his body to become strong. Anyone else would have been crushed under the enormous weight. With the beam of the flashlight pointing to the escape route, he watched the dust fill the air and Neal's supple body slither through the ground level opening. Then, the only escape portal was swallowed up in blackness. In the confusion that followed, he heard Neal's excited voice. "We found the vault, but the mine caved in. Freddy's down there."

Rafferty's voice seemed muffled. "Is he okay?"

"I don't know," Neal said. "But if we're going to find out. We got some digging to do."

Then, someone probed the cave-in with a flashlight and swept some of the dirt away. Behind the powerful beam there was just enough glow for Freddy to make out Neal's face.

Neal turned to the others, flashed his famous Neal McCord smile at them, and shone the light right into Freddy's eyes. "Look."

Waving his hand in front of his face and choking in the dust cloud that enveloped his head,

301

Freddy craned his head and peered upward. "Get that thing outta my eyes and tell those guys to get the shovels out of the car and c'mon down."

The light vanished. In the darkness Freddy's eyes filled with aureoles of color from the flashlight that had been like the unexpected dazzle from a camera flash.

"Let me get down there," Blondie said.

"Be my guest," Neal said. "I'll get the shovels."

Blondie descend the steps. "We might need more than a couple of shovels."

Neal came down the steps with a shovel and maneuvered Blondie out of the way. "What are you waiting on?" He took the edge of the shovel and plowed a big hunk of dirt away from Freddy's back. He reached for Freddy's hands. "Okay, let us pull you out."

Blondie and Neal grabbed Freddy's wrists and pulled. Freddy felt his face crease with pain.

"Wait," he pleaded. "My feet are stuck. You'll pull me apart. Dig some more."

"We don't have much room down here," Blondie said. "We need something to carry the dirt up to the top."

Freddy hadn't noticed it before, but he was having difficulty breathing. The pressure of fallen earth was squeezing around his chest.

"Tell those guys up top to scout around," he said, in between gasping for air. "When I was looking for this place I saw an old five-gallon bucket lying in the weeds."

Rafferty snapped his fingers. "I got it." He disappeared from the opening.

After an audible clunk and a few choice cuss words, Rafferty was back with the bucket he had tripped over. Neal held the bucket by the bottom and scooped dirt and shale into it. Then he handed it back to Blondie who handed it up to Rafferty who dumped it on the ground.

After twenty buckets full, Neal pulled on Freddy's arms. He came out huffing for air, but squeezed past Blondie and Neal and forced his tired body to scramble up the stairs. Neal and Blondie followed him out of the hole.

Up top, holding onto the post of the Petroleum sign, Freddy's knees sagged with exhaustion. Not wanting to show his weakness, he bent over. With one hand, he slapped the dirt off his clothes.

Neal passed a weary hand over his face and looked at him. "You going back down?"

Although the others were riding the adrenaline rush from the promise of riches, Freddy had used up all his surviving the cave-in. Just like that skeleton in the pinstriped suit, he could have been buried alive. Just the thought of it gave him a prodding feeling to quit the whole thing, to turn and walk away. But no matter what happened, it would be better than going back home penniless and suffering through a life of picking up other people's garbage. He shuddered, and tapped the post. "I'll think about it after you guys clear out that cave-in."

Rafferty's lips widened into a tight smile. "What if there's another trap?"

Blondie let out a triumphant laugh. "I think that cave-in set off any traps that may have been left. And besides, if we don't want anybody to come snooping around, we got to dig while it's dark."

"Who's worried about a little trap," Neal said with unbridled excitement. "There's a huge box full of treasure down there. All we got to do is dig it out."

CHAPTER 34

Below the Petroleum sign, hours passed into the night. Although only one man at a time could dig in the narrow mine, and another cave-in was a constant threat, Blondie and Freddy's friends took turns feverishly filling the bucket with shale and dirt. When Neal finally scraped the last bucket of dirt away from the big brass vault, the morning sun was just about to peek over the horizon. Neal popped up out of the hole and looked around. All around the Petroleum sign, little piles of dirt that had been bucketed out of the cave-in stood like miniature monuments to a long night's work.

Smiling a satisfied smile, Neal asked, "Who wants to go down and get that box?"

Freddy backed away. "I would, but it's not my turn."

"What's the matter?" Neal said. "Are you afraid of a little cave-in?"

"Not really." Freddy shrugged. "But I already had my cave-in. I wouldn't want to cheat somebody out of having one, too."

Neal glanced at the Ford. "Is that rope still in the trunk?"

"I can read your mind," Freddy said, lifted trunk, and took out the rope.

Neal patted him on the back. "That's a big box and we didn't dig out enough to open it. You're the only one strong enough to move it and get the rope under it. We'll both go down, and I'll watch for another cave-in."

Freddy furrowed his brow. "I just had a close call. I don't know if I should chance it."

305

Neal placed his hand on Freddy's shoulder. "You'll be okay. You should be full of energy. You didn't do anything all night."

Freddy felt a pang of guilt. "I guess you're right."

He descended into the hole. At the bottom he dropped to all fours, but the tunnel was too low. He lay on his stomach. With the end of the rope in one hand and the flashlight in the other, he wormed through the narrow tunnel until he came to the box. It wasn't as green as it had been before the cave-in, but he figured the shale and dirt had sandblasted the oxidization off and revealed streaks of bright brass.

"Tie it on really good," Neal said, from the bottom of the steps.

Freddy looped the rope around the box and crossed it as if he were wrapping a Christmas present, but he couldn't get the rope under the box. He backed out of the tunnel, stopped at the steps, and looked up.

Looking down at him, Neal asked, "Did you get it tied on?"

"I couldn't get under the bottom. That thing's too heavy to lift."

Neal descended the steps and pushed the shovel at him. "Use this as a lever and lift it."

Freddy crawled back into the tunnel. When he got to the box, he wrangled the shovel around in the limited space, put the back of the blade onto the hard granite base, and jammed it under the bottom of the box. Pulling down on the end of the long handle, he lifted the end of the box just enough to kick a stone under it. Right after the stone was under the box, under the tremendous weight of the

306

box, the shovel handle snapped. Thinking it was another cave-in, Freddy's heart jumped into his throat.

Neal hollered behind him, "Are you all right?"

Freddy breathed a sigh of relief. "So far. The shovel broke." He took the flashlight and shone it under the box. A big deep gouge was under one end, but he didn't see anything to trigger another cave-in. He slipped the rope around the box and tied it secure. Praying he wouldn't get caught in another cave-in, he pulled himself backwards with his toes, pushed with his elbows, and slowly backed out of the tunnel until he was at the steps. Neal grabbed the end of the rope.

"You ready?"

Freddy grabbed the rope, but then let it go. "If this thing caves in again we may not be so lucky this time."

"How good do you have that box tied on?"

"That rope will break before those knots give out."

Neal nodded. "You want to take a chance and pull it out from up top?"

"Good idea. With everybody pulling, even if it caves in again we should be able to pull the box out."

Neal shot the flashlight beam into the tunnel. The box sat as if it were streaked with gold just waiting to be taken.

"Okay," he said. "Let's go up and do it."

At the top of the steps, Freddy poked his head out of the hole.

Rafferty looked him directly in the face. "You guys ready to pull it out?"

Holding the rope in his hand, Freddy came out of the hole. "I hope so,. but this time we're all going to pull it out."

Neal stepped out of the hole. "All right, gentleman grab a hold of the rope, and whatever you do, don't stop pulling."

"That's right," Freddy said. "If it caves in again, we'll be digging all day."

Rafferty picked up the end of the rope and glanced at the Ford. "Why don't we hook the rope on the bumper?"

Dumbfounded, Neal slouched down. "Why didn't I think of that?" He jumped into the Ford, started it, and backed the bumper next to the hole.

Freddy tied the rope on and gestured to Neal. "Let her rip."

"Cross your fingers," Neal said, and hit the gas.

The rope went taut. Then it traveled across the little mounds of dirt like a racing snake.

Rafferty excitedly pointed down the hole. "The box's coming up the steps."

Before the words could register in Freddy's brain, dirt and shale avalanched down on the box. "It's caving in again." He motioned to Neal. "Keep pulling."

With dirt chasing the box, *Twang*! The rope broke off the bumper.

In great haste, Freddy reached down and grabbed the end of the broken rope. "Come on, you guys, pull."

They all rushed to the end of the broken rope, grabbed on, and pulled. When the box was just at the top of the hole, the rope broke again. About a foot of dirt and shale covered the box.

Waving the dust from the cave-in away from his face, Freddy let out an exhausted breath. "At least it's closer to the top."

Neal jumped out of the Ford and grabbed a shovel. "Let's see what's in that thing."

Digging feverishly, Neal uncovered the box in record time. Pulling the box through the dirt and shale had cleansed more of the green oxidation off. The box gleamed like gold.

Blondie reached down and pulled on it. "Hey, this thing weighs a ton." He looked at Neal. "Give me a hand."

Neal knelt down and grabbed the end of the box and pulled. "Come on, you guys, help."

Blondie held up his hand. "Wait. The lid's clear. Let's just open it here."

Rafferty banged the edge of the box with the shovel. "Let's check it." He stepped back. "There might be a bomb in it."

Blondie felt around the edges of the lid. "I don't feel anything that would set one off."

"If something goes off, it'll go straight up," Neal said. "The dirt around the hole will protect us."

Rafferty held the shovel out to Neal. "If you're so sure about that, open it." He stepped to the Ford and took cover behind the front fender. "I'll watch from here."

Neal scraped at the lid with the edge of the shovel. "Okay, everybody else, step back."

Somewhere nearby, a bird chirruped signaling that the sun was about wink into a new day. With the others watching from a safe distance, Neal inserted the blade of the shovel into the bottom of the lid and pried. The lid grated and flew open. He grunted with surprise. As the first rays of the sun beamed into the box, an awkward hush fell over the land.

CHAPTER 35

With a panorama of golden light flooding the eastern sky, Blondie rushed to the opened box and looked in. Rays of morning sunshine danced into the box and illuminated a yellowed page from a notebook and a folded piece of brown paper with one edge sewn shut with string that resembled the stitches on top of a bag of dog food. There was no gold and no money. Blondie's heart and his dreams for a better future sunk.

Neal tilted toward the open box, his eyes locked in an unseeing stare. "Now what?"

Blondie bent over to pick up the yellowed paper. Where a layer of brass had peeled away and a thin layer of cement had broken, a glint of gold flashed. A sudden surge of realization entered his mind: The treasure wasn't in the vault. The vault was the treasure. A layer of brass and a thin layer on concrete concealed at least two thousand pounds of solid gold. His sunken dreams for a better future took on a new life and swam to the surface. He pretended to lose his balance and caught himself with his hand in the yellow dirt. Then, he placed his dirty hand on the exposed gold and rubbed. The glinting gold dulled to the color of brass. He suppressed a sigh of relief and hoped his excitement hadn't shown in his face. He picked up the paper. With Neal looking over his shoulder he read it aloud.

"'Al, IOU five hundred thousand dollars, Ralph.'"

Neal held Blondie's note-holding-hand up and reread the note. "What? No money?"

Blondie faked a look of despair. "Not unless you can bring Dillinger back to life."

Freddy wrinkled his brow. "What does John Dillinger have to do with this?"

"Not many people know it," Blondie said, "but Ralph Alsman is the name Dillinger took after the FBI faked his death."

"Wait a second," Neal said and held up his hand. "Are you telling me that Dillinger wasn't set up by that babe in the red dress and shot?"

"That's right. The five hundred thousand must have been some kind of payoff."

Amazed, Neal stared at Blondie. "You mean Dillinger took all the money?"

Blondie wanted to reach down and hug the huge gold box that was going to end all his problems, but he fought the urge. He bent over and reached into it.

"He must've," he said. "The only thing left is this thing." He lifted the folded piece of brown paper that looked like a big bulldog instant win gambling ticket.

"Open it," Freddy said, with hope. "Maybe there's another clue in it."

Out on the road, a string of cars with workers on their way to the General American Tank Car manufacturing plant slowed. Behind steering wheels, sleepy-eyed men gawked out the car's windows and pointed. Blondie adjusted the white hat on his head, placed his hands on his hips, spread his legs, and stood watching the others

After the cars passed, Rafferty pointed to Blondie's exaggerated stance. "Where did you learn how to stand like that, foreman obedience school?"

Blondie relaxed his stance. "It doesn't matter where I learned it. It works." He held the piece of folded brown paper. After getting the correct end of the sewn string, he pulled it. It unraveled just like the sewn string on the top of a dog food bag. Then he unfolded the brown paper and another piece of yellowed paper appeared.

Neal hunkered in close. "Maybe it's some kind of valuable stock?"

Blondie unfolded the paper.

Neal rolled his hand with encouragement. "What's it say?"

Blondie broke into a disgusted smile. "It's a note."

Neal poked his head right in front of Blondie's face. "Does it say where the money is?"

"Here, read it." Blondie handed the note to Neal.

Neal grabbed the note and read aloud.

"Dear Double,

"If you're reading this you have found the other half of the million. Thanks for getting plastic surgery and gaining fifty pounds. The deal with Ralph was enough to get them to change your fingerprints to match mine. When we get you an early release based on insanity, it will be a nice touch for you to sit at my swimming pool in Florida with a fishing pole. It will keep them thinking that I have syphilis and brain damage."

Neal let his hand drop to his side. "I would've never believed it. Al Capone never went to jail. He paid some guy to go for him."

Freddy's eyes widened. "It looks like that fat guy at the bottom of the trap door might be Al Capone."

Blondie looked toward the vault. "What fat guy are you talking about?"

Freddy pointed to the cave-in. "There's a skeleton of a fat guy with a gun in his hand down there."

Rafferty raised his eyebrow. "I don't mean to be stupid, but how do you know a skeleton was fat a fat guy?"

Neal flashed him his famous full-tooth smile and spread his arms. "Easy, his suit coat was about twenty sizes too big for the skeleton."

"I think you guys are trying to pull something off," Rafferty scoffed. "When I was digging down there, I didn't see any skeleton."

Neal let out a breath of air. "That's because it's at the bottom of a trap door. We didn't tell you guys because we figured you'd get scared and wouldn't help us dig."

"You're right about that." Rafferty shuddered. "I hate dead things."

Blondie kept his attention on the vault. "Was that skeleton wearing a big white hat?"

"Yeah," Freddy said, "but it wasn't so white."

Blondie nodded. "Capone always wore a big white hat. It was sort of a trademark."

Tilting his head to one side, Rafferty held up one finger. "What would a skeleton of Al Capone be doing down there?"

A confused look appeared on Blondie's face, and he subsided into silence.

Neal threw both hands into the air. "He probably came to put the money in the vault, but someone shot him and pulled the lever and trapped him inside."

"If that's true," Rafferty said, "then why didn't the person that shot him take the money?"

"I don't know," Neal said. "That skeleton still has a gun in its hand. If it is Al Capone, he probably wounded the guy. Then the guy pulled the lever, and trapped him. If the guy was wounded bad, he probably went to get medical treatment."

"That makes sense," Blondie said. "The guy probably figured he would come back for the money after he got patched up, so he pulled the Petroleum sign and closed the stairway. But he must have died before he could get back."

Freddy stepped into the conversation. "And Dillinger came back, but he didn't know about the secret lever. He probably walked right over to the vault, and took the money. But he never knew Al Capone's was right under his feet."

While what they had discovered sunk into their brains, silence filled the crisp morning air.

"Ah, ahem, ah, yes," Neal said, breaking the silence. He reached for the note in Blondie's hand. "What else does it say?"

Blondie gestured to the empty box. "The same thing that's in there: nothing."

"Well, ahem, yes." Neal studied the box. "We could take it back to the Burp. It could be our souvenir."

Blondie wasn't sure what to do next. The box was solid gold, but he couldn't let Freddy and his friends know he wanted it. If he could convince them that the box was useless, then the box would be his.

"I'll tell you what," he said. "I'll keep the letters and you guys can have the box."

"That old brass box isn't going to be worth anything, but what the junk man will give us for scrap," Freddy said. "The only thing that might be worth anything is those letters."

Neal held out the IOU from John Dillinger. "We'll let you have the box for the IOU."

Blondie still couldn't let on that he wanted the box. "That box's worthless," he said. "How about we each take a note or the IOU?"

"Which one?" Neal said.

Blondie reached into his pocket and pulled out a half dollar. "We'll flip for it."

Neal cast a suspicious eye at Blondie. "Now, wait a minute. If it wasn't for us you never would have found the box."

Blondie shrugged. "Take the box and a note, too. I don't care. It's just not anything to fight over." He gestured at the box. "And besides, the damn thing's too heavy."

Neal looked at the box. "That thing's solid brass. The junk man will give us a few bucks for it."

Blondie shook his head. "I can't see a junk man giving you anything for that thing."

"Why not?" Neal pushed on the box with his foot. "It's heavy."

Being careful not to disturb the concrete layer beneath, Blondie bent over and peeled back a layer of brass on the corner of the box.

"This thing's only covered with this thin brass. Look!" He pointed to where he had peeled the brass

316

back. "It's worthless cement. But if you want it, knock yourself out. Haul it away."

Neal examined the peeled back section of the box. "This cement's so heavy, it'll break the springs in the Ford."

Rafferty bent over, pulled the brass back a little more, and stood up. Blondie hoped Rafferty hadn't peeled back enough brass to crack the thin layer of cement and expose the gold. He held his breath and placed his hand over his eyes to cover his apprehension. Rafferty's voice took on and earnest tone.

"Let's just leave it in the hole," he said. "If we want to come back and get it latter, it'll still be here."

Blondie held out the note and the IOU. "Which one do you guys want?"

"Since Dillinger dealt cards around here at the Green Parrot," Freddy said, "I'm kind of partial to his IOU."

Blondie held a half dollar in his forefinger ready to flip it with his thumb. "I like the IOU, too. Call it."

"Just in case it's a double-headed half," Neal said. "We'll take heads."

Blondie flipped the coin, caught it in midair, and smacked it down on the back of his wrist. "Want to change it?"

Neal made a dismissive gesture. "Keep it heads."

Blondie lifted his hand. The coin was heads. To keep up the ruse, he groaned. "You just got yourselves a John Dillinger IOU."

Neal let his hands fall to his sides. "We can't make any money around here." He looked at Blondie. "We're going home. You want us to drop you off somewhere?"

"Take me back up to the old Peacock Alley."

"You mean Melody Lane?" Freddy asked.

"Yeah, Melody Lane. Biff, the bartender, seems like a pretty nice guy. I'll call my girlfriend from there."

With the IOU from John Dillinger in Neal's hand, they padded out to the Ford, stepped in, and drove off into the gold-tinged mists of a newborn day.

CHAPTER 36

The latter part of afternoon of the following day, Freddy and his friends stood under the clown-faced clock of the peak of the burger stand called the Burp. They were back where their quest to win the silly bet to speed across the Canadian border, get a cup of coffee, grab souvenir, and be back in twelve hours had started. Freddy meticulously straightened the suit coat the cop in the apartment had given him. The suit coat Blondie had given Rafferty before the thugs had pulled the Italian rope trick on him was cut of the finest material. Without a suit coat, but wearing his familiar black T-shirt, Neal faced the crowd of kids. With much animation, he relived the trip to Canada, only he added many things that just didn't happen and couldn't have happened.

The kid with a broken tooth and thick glasses waved his hand down. "I don't believe a word you're saying."

Neal held the IOU from John Dillinger out at arm's length. "Look, read it for yourselves." He pointed to the first line of the IOU and read it aloud. "Al, IOU five hundred thousand dollars. Ralph."

The kid with the cast on his arm took the IOU. "Anybody could've written this." As he stared at Freddy and Rafferty, his lips curled. "Just because you're wearing expensive suit coats, it doesn't prove there was five hundred thousand dollars in a hole."

The pony-tailed girl turned her cute little head toward the kid with jet-black hair styled like Elvis. "Come on, Markey. You don't believe this tall tale, do you?"

Markey exhaled a stream of air out the side of his mouth and reached into his pocket. "Here's five bucks says there wasn't a mine cave-in, and there isn't even a box."

Neal held up a stack of crisp ten dollar bills and fanned them out. "Anybody want to put their money where their mouths are?"

A skinny kid with a polo shirt and yellowed teeth stepped away from the curb he had been standing on. "You told us about everything except where the box is. Are you going to take us to this place where this box is?"

"Ah, ahem, ah," Neal said. "Not really, but I will go and get the box and bring it back here."

Bull, the stocky kid with huge arms shook his head. "You could get a box anywhere. If we can't see the box at the cave-in, then all bets are off. And we're not forking over any money."

Neal reached up and rubbed his chin. "You know, I'm taking a chance. Somebody could have come by and picked up the box and sold it for scrap."

"Maybe," Bull said, eying him steadily. "But, like you said, it was only lined with thin brass. No junk man would take a cement box."

Freddy knew the box was too heavy for anyone to move without a tow truck, and he also knew Neal had embellished the trip to make the kids doubt what he was saying. He waited for Neal to put on a show to get them to bet against a sure thing.

"I don't know if I should bet," Neal whined. "There's only a fifty-fifty chance that the box will still be there."

Bull held out a wad of money. "And there's a fifty-fifty chance that it isn't there."

"Yeah," Neal agreed. "But someone might not have known it was cement." He threw his hands into the air. "It could be gone."

Watching Bull, Neal waited with a glimmer of private delight. Bull ran his thumb over the end of the wad of money he had won from the bet Neal had lost in his quest to drive to Canada and be back in twelve hours. "Are you afraid to bet?"

Neal changed his whining tone and held his wad of money out. "I'm not afraid of anything."

A huge grin formed on Bull's face. "Okay, double or nothing."

Pulling his wad of money back, Neal let out a painful groan. "I don't know."

Bull jerked his wad of money toward Neal. "You're afraid?"

"Try me," Neal said, took the money, counted it, doubled it from some of the money from the envelope, and handed it back to Bull.

More bets were made. After Bull tucked the money into his pockets, everyone at the Burp hopped into their cars and zoomed toward to Petroleum. In a convoy of cars, they headed down the highway. At Petroleum they all pulled over and got out. Neal led the way to the cave-in and waved his hands excitedly. "Come on, it's over here."

The followers rushed to Neal and stopped. Wide-eyed, Freddy stared down into an empty hole. Too late he realized that when he had wrapped the rope around the box he had seen a deep gouge in the bottom. When he had been looking for a trap, he had shone the flashlight onto it. There was no

321

cement under a thin covering of cheap brass on the bottom. The box was solid brass. He let out a low moan of emotional agony and turned to Neal.

"Hey, wait a minute. If that box was only brass-covered cement, somebody wouldn't have gone through the trouble of hauling it away." Neal's energetic face withered to concern. "I hadn't thought it was important before," Freddy continued. "But there was a gouge about three inches long in the bottom of the box. And there wasn't one bit of cement showing through."

Rafferty's eyes snapped wide open. "You saying the box was solid brass?"

Freddy nodded. "Y' know we've been had."

Neal hit himself in the head. "Brass my ass." As his arms went limp, he let out a moan. "If I had my bongo board I'd flip it up and make it hit me right in my brainless head."

Confused, Freddy looked at him. "What are you talking about?"

"In any good party, the cream of the crop always stays until the end. Blondie stayed with the box to the end. He knew the box was solid gold."

Freddy went numb with disbelief. The possibility of a treasure and the resulting enchantment suddenly renewed.

The kid with the horn-rimmed glasses peered at Neal through his owlish brown eyes. "If there was such a box, how much did this great box weigh?"

"We couldn't lift it," Rafferty said. "It had to weigh over two thousand pounds."

Neal held his finger and punched the air as if he were using an adding machine. "With gold being thirty-five dollars an ounce and sixteen ounces in a pound" — he paused — "two thousand times sixteen is thirty-two thousand. Take thirty-two thousand times thirty-five dollars and we have a grand total of..." He whistled low. "That box is worth one million one hundred twenty thousand dollars."

The kid with the horn-rimmed glasses wrinkled his brow. "That's if you're using avoirdupois weights that the grocery stores use. Precious metals like gold are measured in troy ounces."

Neal ran his fingertips over the side of his head. "What are you talking about?"

Polishing one lens of his thick glasses, the kid said, "If you want to convert regular avoirdupois ounces to troy ounces you have to multiply the regular ounces by twelve. So, twelve troy ounces times two thousand is twenty-four thousand dollars. Take that times the price on today's gold market which is thirty-five dollars an ounce and we get eight hundred forty thousand dollars."

"Ah, ahem, ah, yes," Neal said, with his face turning red. "Of course, you're right. That's just what I was going to say."

Rafferty looked at Neal. "No matter how you figure it, we still lost almost a million dollars. Now what?"

Bull stepped next to Neal and fanned the bet money in his face. "Now that we can see there's no box and you guys are full of crap, I pay off the bets. That's what."

Neal held up his hand. "Not so fast, Bull. I didn't say the box would be here at this exact moment. The bet was that box would be in the cave-in." He pointed to the hole. "I could go and get that box and put it right here."

A look of helplessness came from Rafferty's eyes. "How are we going to do that?"

"Simple," Neal said. "We go to Melody Lane and see where Blondie went. The box has got to be with him."

"Nice try," Bull said and waved the bet money around in the air. "You're not going to run us around the county on a wild goose chase. I'm paying off the bets now."

Neal held up both hands. "Give us a half hour to bring the box back."

"Bull glanced at his watch. "We'll wait here a half hour, then I'm payin' all bets."

Neal jumped in the Ford and Rafferty and Freddy piled in behind him. When the car was at the bend before Melody Lane, it was as if Neal suddenly realized what had happened, and he wanted to get even with the first person he saw. He stomped on the brakes, slid in the gravel of the parking lot, and brought the Ford to rumbling halt.

"I'm tired of being a nice guy." He clenched his fist. "I'm gonna go in that bar. If that bartender doesn't tell me what I want to know, I'm gonna wring his neck."

Freddy grabbed him by the shoulder. "Slow down, Neal."

Neal glared back at Freddy. "What for?"

"If you go in there and get the guy mad, he won't tell us anything."

Rafferty joined in. "That's a lot of money to lose. Let's be nice."

Neal's expression changed. "Ah, ahem, ah, yes." He exhaled. "You got a point there."

Drumming his fingers on the steering wheel, Neal sat in the front seat a few seconds, then opened the door. With Freddy and Rafferty right behind him, Neal stormed through the bar door. Biff stood behind the bar wiping the cash register off with a red rag. He turned, and before he could utter a word, Neal held his hand in the air. "How ya doin', Biff?"

Biff placed both hands on the bar, and leaned forward. "Just fine. Some blond guy said you'd show up." He turned to the side and held his hand toward the whisky bottles on the shelf. "Waddaya have?"

"Just some information."

"If I got it, you'll get it."

"Do you know where that blond guy went?"

"I don't know where he went," Biff said. "But he was one funny guy."

"What do you mean funny?"

"Oh, I don't mean funny in the fun sort of way, you know...funny." Neal wrinkled his brow and waited for Biff to continue. "I never seen anything like it. Right after you guys left, this blond guy calls a tow truck. It comes and he gets in. A half hour later he's back, and there's a big brass box hanging from the hook on the back of the truck."

Freddy's heart raced. "Did he drop it off here?"

"No, that's the funny part. He claimed the box was worthless, but because it was his father's, he wanted it for a souvenir." Biff pointed toward the door. "He did another funny thing though. He might've said it was worthless, but he stood by the door and watched the guy in the tow truck. That box

325

hung from that tow truck until a beautiful girl came in an old, green, beat-up Chevy pick-up."

Freddy figured that the girl could have been Carolyn from the accident. He held up his hand to check Biff's speech. "Did she have black hair?"

A gleam came into Biff's eyes. "When she stepped out of that truck, she had a figure like a movie star." He shook his hand as if it was trying to cool it off. "Wow, she was a hot number. Her hair was silky, black, and long."

Freddy exhaled and lowered his head. "So, that's what Blondie meant when he told her, 'When it's safe, I'll call. We'll still do everything just like we planned.'"

"That's right," Neal said and nodded. "Blondie planned the whole thing." He looked to Biff. "What did the girl do next?"

"She seemed to be in a big hurry. Before the blond guy could get out to the truck, she pulled the bed of that beat up Chevy right under the hanging box. Then the guy in the tow truck lowered the box into the truck. That old bed sunk down almost to the fenders." He shook his head. "The tires were so bald I thought they were going to blow apart."

With the realization of just how much money the gold vault was worth, Freddy said, "Wow! That thing must have been really heavy."

While Neal closed his eyes and moaned, Rafferty placed his hand on his forehead. "I don't feel so good."

Freddy hunched over and leaned on the bar. "I know the feeling."

Neal looked toward the ceiling. "Amen."

Biff placed his elbow on the beer-and-cigarette-smoke-seasoned wooden bar and rested his chin on his hand.

"And then another funny thing happened," he said. "The blond guy was in such a hurry that he never came back in to get his expensive suit coat." Biff pointed toward the coat rack. "It's still hanging by the door. That blond guy just jumped in that raggedy pick-up with the girl, and they hauled the box away.

"Is that all?" Neal asked.

"Not really." Biff reached under the bar, picked up a 'New York Times' tied shut with a string, laid it on the bar in front of Neal, and tapped the paper with his finger. "That blond guy gave me twenty dollars to make sure you got this."

"What's in it?"

Biff's face took on a look of caution. "I don't know. The blond guy said if I knew what was good for me, I wouldn't open it." He held up his hands. "I don't want no trouble."

Rafferty stared at the newspaper. "I wonder if our names are in it or something."

"We should be on the front page for being ignorant." Neal picked up the newspaper. Flanked by Freddy and Rafferty crowding close, he untied the string and unfolded the newspaper. An overstuffed envelope fell to the floor. Rafferty slid off the bar stool, picked up the envelope, opened it and looked down. A stack of money three inches thick stared back at him.

He snapped his head up and his eyes flew wide open. "It's the other half of the money for dropping off the key."

327

Neal smiled with a great flash of teeth. "I can get another bongo board and fix the radio in the car."

Rafferty flashed Neal a crooked smile. "But we already have enough for a stupid bongo board."

Neal made a thumbs-up fist and pointed to his chest. "I want a gold one."

"Now wait a minute, young fellows," Biff said and shook his head. "I hate to put a damper on your plans. But it is illegal to own gold."

Neal jerked back. "What are you talking about?"

"I don't know all the details, but in 1933 President Franklin Roosevelt put a ban on United States citizens buying, selling, or owning gold."

"Why would he do something stupid like that?"

"As far as I can understand, the ban stopped gold hoarders from making a sixty-five percent profit."

A puzzled look came over Neal's face. "That's better profit than any bank could give. Why did they do that?"

"Congress changed the gold value of the dollar. It went from about twenty dollars to thirty-five dollars an ounce. Then, the people who didn't turn in their gold couldn't make the sixty-five percent profit because it was illegal to own gold."

Neal went on the defensive. "So what? A person should still be able to sell his own gold."

"Only if you don't get caught." Biff felt under the bar. "I had the newspaper story here somewhere." He looked under the bar, and then straightened up. "I can't find it, but a while ago, federal agents seized gold coins from a museum."

328

Freddy and Neal exchanged glances. They couldn't say anything in front of Biff, but they knew they were thinking the same thing: Blondie tricked them out of the gold vault, but it was illegal to have it. He would have a difficult time trying to sell it.

Freddy stared at the money in the envelope. "There's a note inside."

Neal took out the note, and unfolded it. With Freddy and Rafferty leaning over Neal's shoulder, they all read it aloud.

"Neal, I didn't want you to feel out of place. The suit coat we owe you is hanging on the wall. Freddy, you said you never welshed on a deal yet. Neither have I. Thanks for the key and the Sunrise Souvenir.

THE END

THE END

www.ingramcontent.com/pod-product-compliance
Lightning Source LLC
Chambersburg PA
CBHW010822250626
47172CB00004B/968

* 9 7 8 1 7 8 6 9 5 3 7 3 5 *